The
Hollyhocks
Will Bloom Again

Maureen Chadsey

Maureen Chadsey

This book is dedicated to my family of past, present
and future courageous women

A grateful thank you to Amy, Betty, Charles,
Ginny, Joyce, Milly, Mona, Pamela and Sarah
for their invaluble advice.

Autumn

Coldly, sadly descends
The autumn evening. The Field
Strewn with its dank yellow drifts
Of wither'd leaves, and the elms,
Fade into dimness apace,
Silent.

— *Rugby Chapel*, MATTHEW ARNOLD

1

THE CRUNCH OF A FAST-MOVING GIG on the gravel road broke the lethargy of the prettiest Indian summer afternoon of 1775. The dust-raising wheels turned into the farmyard, scattering stones into the grass and sending children racing to be closer to the protection of their mothers.

Abruptly the occupant reined the horse to a halt before the lone oak tree where moments before the children had been scooping leaves into piles and jumping into the oak's golden treasure, laughing and reflecting the glow of the season on their faces.

Occupying the gig's entire seat was heavy-set Franklin Fremont. His booming "Halloo" coming from a tiny bow mouth set between fatty jowls stirred the people relaxing in front of the house. He lowered his large body with effort, looped the reins loosely over a tree branch, automatically gave a pat to his horse and strode toward the drowsy gathering.

Wariness and apprehension crossed the faces of the men as they rose to greet him.

"Please, please," the children shouted, surrounding him and begging for the candy treats he usually carried in his pockets.

"Hush, children," Alice Marsh, mistress of this farm, reprimanded their brash manners. "I have some apple pie and buttermilk handy, Franklin," she politely offered, reluctantly rising from her relaxed position on a quilt spread on the grass, vexed that her few treasured moments of rest in the week had been cut short, yet disturbed by his somber countenance.

"Not now, thank you. I need to talk to the men." His usual jovial face was forbidding and he marched past her, stepping over fat dog Porky lying on the stone step into the house. Refusing food! Why?

"It must be serious if Franklin is refusing food," Elizabeth Dowd commented as she watched the backs of the men dressed in their striped jackets, dark breeches and white flannel stockings disappear through the doorway behind him. Motioning her clinging seven-year-old daughter away from her side, she said, "Run and play, Abigail."

"It must be," Alice worriedly responded. "Why do they always leave us out of the conversation?" she grumbled, knowing they were not invited in to hear what was to be said. The idea that women were not capable of understanding situations in the world that affected them frustrated her. She sighed and shooed her children back to play.

"Affairs of the world are for men's handling," Aunt Dorcas countered. She pursed her lips in a tight line, adjusted herself rigidly upright in the black kitchen chair and swept her fan furiously from side to side, its breeze causing the orange plume on her straw leghorn hat to sway in rhythm. At a burst of childish laughter she gave a sniff and an obvious what-can-you-expect disapproving shrug of her sloping shoulders. Actually, she hardly seemed to have any shoulders at all under her plaid cape, which she insisted on wearing even in this heavy autumn heat. Strict with her own children, all girls, she felt Alice was far too lenient and permissive with her children. It annoyed her that Alice even let the children sit at the table to eat. "In my day children were expected to stand and be silent as they ate," she repeatedly reminded Alice. Now, here it was the Sabbath day and all children should be quiet, subdued and properly contemplating their sinful tendencies, particularly Alice's rambunctious brood of unruly children.

Alice glanced away from Aunt Dorcas. Though quite proper and keenly aware of Dorcas' defense of the old custom, she dared break this rule believing it was good for the young children to run and play. During the week there were far too many chores — food preserving, candle making, hauling hot water to the outside tub, scrubbing the dirty clothes and draping them over the bushes to bleach and dry, spinning yarn and on and on. The endless list demanded everyone's attention and allowed little time for play or for her to have the opportunity to watch them. Maybe, because she was so tired, she was secretly expressing her resentment of Aunt Dorcas and Uncle Ezra for being here. Even on this farm food was scarce but they had eaten extra helpings of the dinner food that she had planned to use for another meal during the week. As close relatives who had helped their nephew Josiah over the years, they assumed they were entitled to the best gleanings of the harvest for their own root cellar and had filled the back of their wagon this afternoon. Then Aunt Dorcas had condescendingly dumped a pillow case full of out-grown girls' clothes in Alice's lap for her to rework for her own daughters Penny and Susie. "I know they need the food as much as we do and Aunt Dorcas was just trying to be helpful," she chastised herself, feeling ashamed at her lack of charity and gratefulness.

Uncle Ezra's forceful voice interrupted the women. "Pompey, get the wagon ready," he hollered to his slave. "Immediately! Dorcas, get in the wagon!" he ordered. His wife gasped in astonishment. Within a matter of flurried minutes Aunt Dorcas and Uncle Ezra were out of the yard and on the way to their town, Pompey and the vegetables bouncing in the back, dust spewing into the air behind them.

"Can't be bothered with the time of day now, can he?" commented Paul Dowd wryly, motioning to the trailing cloud of wagon dust hanging in the heat. Paul, Elizabeth's husband, had strolled over from his farm across the road with his chattering five-year-old son Peter hop-skipping along beside him.

"Paul," Josiah Marsh spoke solemnly from the doorway. "Come in here," he ordered, motioning him into the house.

"Off and play, Peter," commanded Paul, giving his son an affectionate pat on the behind. Quizzically glancing at his wife he followed Josiah into the house.

"Whatever can be the trouble?" Alice questioned out loud as she automatically gathered glasses from chair sides and set them on a tray. Elizabeth was surely as much in the dark as she was about the afternoon's interruption.

"Oh, 'tis probably just another old political tempest in a teapot. You know how worked up these men get over the least little thing," Elizabeth replied, readjusting her heavily pregnant body on the tall kitchen stool while alternately fanning her perspiring face with her handkerchief and rubbing her forehead. She was trying to persuade herself it was not too serious. Ordinarily she was content with her small world and not too concerned over events or circumstances outside the sphere of her farm, church and immediate community.

The continual worry lines appearing lately on Alice's forehead deepened as she looked at her friend. "Are you feeling unwell?"

"'Tis just a headache. From the heat, I'm sure," she answered, trying to put forth a reassuring smile.

"Well, I wish I knew what was going on," Alice said as her worry increased. Absent-mindedly she arranged and rearranged the buttermilk glasses on the silver tray beside her. So engrossed was she in straining her ears to catch a word or two from the house, that she failed to pause and admire her chased tray. It had been an extravagant wedding gift from her family. They had taken many of their Spanish silver dollars to the local silversmith to have them converted into the tray she now held. Eleven years later it was still a prized and precious gift that filled her heart with pleasure whenever she used it to serve company. Seldom was it in use now, for fear it would be confiscated by a British soldier or other unwelcome

Whig official who walked in uninvited to look for contraband tea or firearms. She hid the tray in the bottom of the flour barrel and only brought it out to use for special visitors.

Baby Midge began to whimper and Alice stooped to gather her youngest daughter in her arms and dab away the perspiration beading upon the baby's face. The baby laughed when Alice blew into her neck, giving her kisses and hugs. Tears of despair welled up in Alice's eyes and she hugged the baby close. Why? Why must these children of hers be forced to suffer for the intolerances of the adults in their world? She found it harder and harder to keep a rein on her emotions. "Surely somehow we can smooth out our differences before there is any more violence!" she asserted out loud. She shuddered, remembering hearing of all the lives lost in the battle at Lexington last spring. She did not like any form of conflict and the very thought of violence between neighbors, and even against England, created a knot in her stomach. There had to be a way for adults to accept differences without fighting, even if animosity ran high. She held the baby closer until it struggled to get down and run with the older children.

Inside the house Josiah and Paul's voices rose in fiery argument. Then dire, grim silence. Paul marched out to the yard, his face red and set with anger as he took Elizabeth's arm, called their children to come and strode rapidly along the roadway. Elizabeth turned a puzzled look at Alice.

Again, Alice's children gathered around her. To shield them from any arguments or heated discourse by Josiah until the calmer voice of Franklin could smooth the air, she said with forced animation, "Let's go for a walk by the river," leading the way on the path around the barn. Soon the younger ones were skipping and running past her on this unexpected adventure. Ordinarily, because she was afraid of a possible drowning, she would not let them go to the river. They waved to boys poling past on rafts and threw stones to outdo each other in the size of splashes. They stood in silent awe as a bevy of geese honked and circled to find a night's resting place in the cattail-filled eddies before she led her own brood back to the house. It was nearing suppertime and life's routines must continue.

As they neared the house Alice saw Franklin sitting stiffly in the gig looking straight ahead. He made no attempt to notice nor speak to her before she walked inside and put on her apron. Why was he just sitting there? The room was empty. She shrugged. Probably the rest of the men were in the barn doing the evening chores.

"Good afternoon, Alice," a familiar voice wearily spoke from the kitchen doorway.

"You sound tired from your walk, Aunt Beth. Please sit down and have some buttermilk," offered Alice, reaching to move a chair forward for her.

Beth sat down heavily onto the chair, letting the fatigue of her long walk overtake her. It had been a dusty trudge back to this farm from her daughter's house by the river in town. Aunt Beth, as she was affectionately called by the Marsh family, lived on the farm as a general domestic. Her husband had died in an Indian raid when their daughter was a baby and to support themselves they had come to live with the Marshes. When Beth's daughter married John Twill and began having babies every eighteen months or so, there was not enough room in their small household nor money to support an additional member. Mother Marsh was an invalid by then and needed the help, so Aunt Beth stayed on at the Marsh farm, continuing to stay even after Mother Marsh had died and been buried in the family plot at the corner of the north field close to her husband and sons. Each Sunday Beth rode into town with the family to attend church, then spent the rest of the afternoon visiting her family, walking back before dark settled upon the countryside. As the years went on the distance from town seemed to grow longer and longer. When would the year come that she could not make it back by dark? Each year she hoped John would save enough money to buy a horse and wagon to bring her back, but often a new baby came instead. Thus far there had been eleven babies, of which eight still lived.

"Hello, Beth," Uncle Amos spoke. Carrying a small bundle tied with twine he limped into the kitchen from the back bedroom he shared with Gilbert. Alice was surprised to notice how frail and old he appeared as he stood before the women in clothes far too large for his frail frame.

"I am saying goodbye, Alice," he spoke wearily.

"Goodbye? Why? What do you mean?" she questioned, hoping he was not serious, but her racing heart feared that it was true.

"I am going into town with Franklin to stay with him for awhile. I will be fine," he said shakily.

"But why?" She moved to grasp his arms, trying to hold him in this place.

"It is better this way," he answered hoarsely, declining to give any explanation. "Goodbye, Beth," he said politely as he shrugged Alice's arms aside and headed toward the yard. Franklin helped him squeeze onto the gig's seat and they drove off slowly as the long shadows of a fall evening closed in upon them.

She leaned against the door frame apprehensively watching the empty road long after they disappeared, recalling the love she had for this favorite uncle and the stories he told catching the delicate shading of local twangs or the often surprising twist of words that made his stories favorites with everyone. Well, nearly everyone.

Aunt Dorcas could not abide his tales. "Disgraceful! Shocking! People should not laugh in this world. Life is too serious for laughter!"

For many years Uncle Amos had lived on a farm five miles farther out the pike. With no progeny to help carry the burdens and general bad luck, the farm became run down. A severe injury to his left knee when kicked by the cow and the death of his beloved wife were the crowning blows that finally forced him to sell his farm. He moved to the Marsh farm as a welcome helper to his grand niece, Alice, and her family, receiving in return the respect and affection he had always shown them. However, just this morning at breakfast, hot words had been shouted at him by her husband Josiah when Uncle Amos had spoken in favor of a reasoning argument put forth by the opposing political side. Ultimately, Uncle Amos was waiting to settle for whichever side won in the present political argument.

The clamor of hungry children drew her back to the present. No one spoke during the supper meal of cold meat and leftover vegetables. The tension in the air even stilled the usual childish chatter and questions as they finished off the meal with sweetened bread soaked in milk.

While Aunt Beth organized the supper cleanup and prepared the children for bed, Alice followed Josiah into the yard, grabbing his arm for him to stop and look at her.

"Tell me what is going on!" she demanded. Seldom did she speak in such a brusque manner to her husband, but so much upheaval had transpired during the past few hours that she had to know. "What happened to make Uncle Ezra leave so quickly?"

He hesitated, then spoke bitterly. "A mob broke into their house in town while they were gone and ransacked it in search for hoarded tea or firearms or inflammatory material. Then those darn Whigs set it on fire. Darn, darn Whigs!" He pulled away from her grasp and looked at Alice before continuing. "The rebels forced your father to give up teaching, claiming he was a traitor. Their house and everything they own was taken from them. Franklin thinks he and your mother managed to slip away to your sister's in Gloucester." He turned and began to walk away.

Alice gasped. It had been weeks since she had heard from her parents. Why had they not come here instead? Did they fear further severe persecutions if they came to this Tory house? Was it because of Josiah's extreme outbursts?

Following his retreating back she questioned again, "What about Amos?"

"In some instances Amos sides with those rebel Whigs. He is wishy-washy, wanting to wait and see which side finally wins out. I am persuaded it will be the British side. I will not have any hint of disloyalty in my house. It is best he left."

"But he is family," Alice protested. "You can't tell him to leave. He has never spoken strongly about it. He would never do anything to harm us. He would even defend us if he had to."

"I will not have it," declared Josiah emphatically, striding faster toward the barn.

"What about Paul?" she persisted, matching his stride.

"He is becoming one of them." The anger in his voice stilled him momentarily. "He has been persuaded that the colonies are right to want to separate from England," he continued bitterly. "I know England has the right to be here and should rule us under the king. Our safety is dependent upon them as a child to a father. We will have nothing more to do with those people across the road."

"But they're our friends," she protested.

Angrily he turned to face her. " I will not tolerate any disloyalty to me and that includes you!" he shouted, jabbing his forefinger toward her before turning to hang the lantern on a post nail and pick up a pitchfork.

She could not understand why he was so vehement about his point of view. His family had been in this new world for several generations. He had grown up with the freedoms from direct English rule in the colony. Was it because he had spent a few years accompanying Uncle Ezra to England learning the intricacies of trading, enjoying the stimulation of the cosmopolitan city of London? Maybe he would have settled there if his father had not ordered him home to take his place on the farm when all his older brothers had died in a flu epidemic. In recalling his experiences there, nothing back home seemed to equate to England. The more anyone tried to convince him of the rebels' cause, the stronger was his argument of the Tory side.

She hesitated. Should she continue? She looked at his angular features silhouetted against the stone wall by the lamp light. They expressed his personality, for there was neither softness nor ease in either. He expected perfection from those around him to meet a standard he had mentally created. Since no one, particularly his wife Alice, succeeded in achieving this criterion, he generally expressed displeasure and continually drove those around him to an ideal even he could not articulate. The increasing pressures to operate this farm short handed and the mounting animosity from friends and foes alike caused a deep-seated frustration and anger at his unfair lot in life that drove him with a savage intensity to relentlessly demand even greater perfection. She waited but he gave no further explanation. She finally turned and walked slowly back to the house, unmindful of the full, yellow moon just out of reach in the night sky.

Lifting her skirt she climbed the steep stairs to say goodnight to her children, ten year-old Jeremy and five year-old Horace in one bed, eight year-old Penelope (Penny) and three year-old Susanna (Susie) in another. She listened to their prayers, fluffed their feather pillows and kissed them goodnight.

"Mama," Jeremy whispered. "When is Uncle Amos coming back? We are supposed to go fishing tomorrow morning."

"I don't know but I'm sure he will come as soon as he can. He enjoys fishing with you," she replied, trying to be reassuring. She leaned down to give him an extra kiss.

She descended the stairs slowly and tried to calm the upheaval churning in her mind by vigorously sweeping the floor. Aunt Beth was already snoring in her bed in the kitchen. The rays of moonlight visible through the gaps in the boarded window drew her outside. She did not care at that moment if any rebels were lurking in the shadows by the road. She just had to get out. As she leaned against the trunk of the oak tree she prayed fervently to understand what was happening in her tiny corner of the world. This world she lived in seemed to be unraveling and she was fearful of the changes taking place.

It seemed days rather than hours since she had reclined on the quilt looking at the house before her. She had been daydreaming again of replacing this old house with a fashionable Georgian-style home. She had drawn a picture in her mind of a central door with a fancy brass knocker, a beautiful pediment over the door, two windows on each side, a matching second story and the newest style of sash windows that went up and down. Previously, when she had expressed this desire to Josiah he had declared, "After I buy that last piece of bottom land, then I will build the grandest house in the whole county." It had not materialized yet and probably never would. Instead, the beautiful dream had turned to harsh reality as she had looked intently at the building before her. This saltbox style house that held the accumulated treasures of many generations looked run down and worn for bleached shingles showed through; no whitewash had been brushed on during the summer months. There were boards nailed across the old-fashioned diamond-shaped panes of glass that had let warm sunlight into the house. No local store owner would sell whitewash or glass to this household. The hay meadow beyond the house was a blackened, scorched field; a suspicious fire had consumed the hay before it could be cut and stored. The corn stalks had been cut, but the corn lay piled in the yard and on a wagon bed, for no grist mill would grind it locally. Josiah would have to take it to a mill much farther out the pike to find any miller willing to do the job.

Last spring in May of 1775, when Massachusetts declared, "loyalty to him (King George) is now treason to our country," a Tory was no longer a political opponent to be coerced but a traitor to this country and legally subject to any kind of personal persecution including confiscation of all their firearms. This included anyone residing in the household. Traitors! How could they be labeled traitors? Their families had been developers and lovers of this land long before many of their opponents' families had arrived. Traitors!!! "No, 'tis not true!" Alice affirmed over and over again in her mind. With the exception of Gilbert, by the busiest chore time of summer, all the other farm hired hands had left by one's and two's, some stealthily, some by resigning, others fired by Josiah for disloyalty to him. As a result of his Tory stance Josiah was subject to increasing pressures to recant or be fined repeatedly and suffer increasing abuses. Even Alice had been spitefully told by some ladies of her church to "take your traitorous family and get out of the country."

To her family and friends Alice appeared a quiet, introverted woman, even timid — a flaw she openly admitted to herself. She felt compelled to stifle any strong emotions within herself rather than express them openly. Her fearfulness of conflict caused her to hang back or try to shun contrary situations. She had grown up in town, always conscious and constantly reminded of proper Christian goodness and comportment that was expected of her. Her father had been a respected schoolteacher, writer of letters for the unschooled and general advisor to many of the town's citizens until this awful news from Franklin. How could the rebels take away his teaching position? Why would they do that to him? She had been permitted to attend the common school where he taught and learned to read, write a legible hand and figure to the rule of three. At home her mother taught her to sew a fine hand, spin and play the recorder. Reading was her favorite pastime, drawing adventure and excitement from the lives of others recorded on the pages, heroic lives she longed to have but afraid in her timid nature to ever attempt.

At sixteen, after persistent wooing by Josiah, both their parents' encouragement, and her own romantic illusions of married life — as well as the fear of being an old maid — Alice had married Josiah and moved out to this farm, still owned and occupied by his parents. Josiah was ten years older than she and presented himself as being versed in and knowledgeable of the world having traveled far more than any young men she knew. Initially, she had been puzzled by Josiah's erratic reactions when she attempted to quell the anger welling up in him with words and acts of affection. After awhile she gave up trying, settling for the numbness of routine hard work that she imagined stretching far ahead into the future. She reflected that their marriage had become one without affection, full of strained physical and verbal communications as they moved separately through the daily demands of a farm. Generally, life flowed from day to day, week to week, season to season in the same pattern, happiness and unhappiness compartmentalized, a segmented existence. Once in awhile she experienced a yearning for the remembered noisier, quicker pace of town living but she managed to squelch these longings in the crush of chores that allowed her little time to involve her mind in regrets or the greater happenings in the world. However, each week she felt herself drawn deeper into this conflict against her will. Secretly she had agreed with many of the Whig's arguments, also seeing reason in the Tory's side. As her family and home suffered increasing abuses by townspeople, former friends and neighbors her anger began to build, forcing her to begin to hate the Whigs, no matter how reasonable their arguments. As her world closed her tighter into this isolated farm, she found herself filled with resentment, anger, frustration, loneliness and fear.

She shuddered. "Oh. Lord, please make this madness stop," she whispered in the night, touching her fingers to the rough bark of the oak tree, seeking the strength it manifested.

"Alice, where are you?" Josiah called, silhouetted against the open doorway. "Come in here to bed," he commanded sharply.

"I'm coming," she answered. Sighing, she let her fingers linger a moment longer against the bark, then turned toward the house.

2

ALICE PICKED UP HER SKIRT with one hand to avoid the heavy dew covering the grass and plants as she walked along the path of the herb garden gathering marjoram and thyme for the dinner soup. The morning sun was gradually burning off the dense fog that obscured the barn and road. She hummed a made-up melody of contentment. She loved this time of day. A new beginning. A new hope. Though it was still early in the day, farm life had begun hours earlier. Josiah and Jeremy were at the back edges of the fields gathering firewood and trimming brush. Gilbert, the last hired hand, was spreading manure over the burned field. Inside the house Aunt Beth was straining grapes for jelly and ketchup[1]. Penny and Horace were stringing beans with thread for drying. Susie was struggling to separate flax fibers for spinning. Midge, with her head encased in her pudding[2] cap, was playing on the braided rug with whittled blocks and Alice had just put butter-milk breads in the proofing box to rise.

She paused to deadhead some late blooming mums, then leaned over the clam-shell border to pick a tenacious weed or two or three trying to get a toe hold amidst the profusion of fading, withering flowers. She looked up to admire the last blooms on the hollyhocks growing straight and tall along the house wall, then reached to pluck off some seed heads and put them in her apron pocket. Later, if she remembered, she would store them in a packet till next spring's planting time. Maybe the sunny side of the barn would be a nice location. She fondly recalled her mother helping plant the hollyhock seeds from her childhood home when she first moved to this farm. Then Elizabeth gave this deep-red specimen to her last spring. "I'll plan to grow more of the red ones next year, though they do remind me of the red-coated British soldiers I saw on parade in town many times," she told herself. She chuckled. "And to believe I used to think they were so handsome in their uniforms." Hope lay in the seeds she plucked. Hope that by spring her world would be at peace.

"Mama." Jeremy broke her reverie as he came around the back edge of the house. "Papa wants me to get the sharpening stone. He said it was near the barn door but I can't find it." His young voice showed frustration. His father expected him to perform as an adult and he tried to, but he was still a child and afraid of his father's short temper and a box to the ear if he could not find the tool.

"I'll help you look," Alice said, setting her basket on the path and turning to walk back to the barn. Patting Jeremy briefly on his head, she experienced a catch in her throat as she thought of her first-born growing up so quickly. Momentarily she wished he could stay a child forever. She delighted in her children when they were babies and toddlers.

"Auntie Alice! Auntie Alice!" Screams interrupted their search.

Alice and Jeremy hurried from the barn and saw Abigail running into their yard through the lifting fog.

"Mama fell and won't get up," she wailed, pulling on Alice's skirt to draw her across the road.

"Where's your father?"

"He went to the blacksmith's early this morning with Peter." Abigail tugged harder on Alice's skirt. "Please hurry!"

Aunt Beth, Penny and Horace had also rushed out of the house at the sound of Abigail's screams.

"Aunt Beth, stay here with the little ones. Jeremy, come with me," Alice called after her as she ran along the drive with Abigail.

Elizabeth was lying on the floor amidst broken pottery and scattered peas. Alice knelt beside her, assured when she felt a pulse, but unable to revive her with smelling salts.

"Jeremy, run home to get your father and the wagon. We have to get Aunt Elizabeth to the doctor. Quickly! Oh, take Abigail to our house." She gave a reassuring smile to Abigail, then ordered the children, "Run!"

Alice wiped Elizabeth's face with cool, dampened cloths, calling her name, praying for a response.

Endless minutes passed before Josiah guided the wagon into the yard.

"I can't get her to respond," Alice said despairingly to Josiah. She was close to tears.

Without a word Josiah gathered Elizabeth in his arms and laid her in the back of the wagon on a quilt Alice yanked off a bed. She climbed in beside her, cradling Elizabeth's head in her lap, holding her hand tightly and crooning soothing words during the jolting ride as Josiah whipped the horse to a fast trot along the stony road, rutted from a recent rain. Speed was necessary over comfort.

"Whoa," Josiah ordered the horse to stop, pulling back on the reins in front of the doctor's house. He quickly gathered Elizabeth in his arms and strode up the walk as Alice hurried ahead to knock on the door.

"Matilda, we need the doctor for Elizabeth," Alice breathlessly explained when the door opened slightly and an unfriendly face peered at them. Quickly Matilda opened the door wide and led the way to the side room used for patients.

"Set her here," she commanded, motioning to a table in the center of the room. "I'll fetch my nephew," she said, glaring with intense dislike at Josiah as she hurried from the room. Matilda was an ardent Whig supporter but animosity with Josiah had begun over some town issue long before the present tension had arisen. This antagonism now included anyone in his household. Medical emergencies, however, required tacit acceptance into this part of the house.

Josiah stood by the table, awkwardly shifting his hat from hand to hand. "I will go find Paul," he said, hurriedly turning to leave.

"Abigail said they were at the blacksmith's," Alice called after him.

"What happened?" Dr. Hill quizzed Alice as he entered the room and bent over to listen to Elizabeth's heart and abdomen. The doctor had recently come to town taking over the practice from his uncle, old Dr. Pace, who had been Matilda's husband and had died earlier in the summer. Alice had seen the new doctor once at a distance but had not met him formally.

"I don't know!" Alice said. She took a deep breath to quiet her racing heart to explain. "Her daughter came to get me when Elizabeth fell and wouldn't get up. I don't know what happened," she repeated in a choked voice as she clasped and stroked Elizabeth's hand between her own, willing her to waken.

Dr. Hill's brown eyes glanced up at Alice sympathetically, briefly noticing the flour-dusted apron she was still wearing. Alice looked down, embarrassed to see the soil. In her haste she had forgotten to remove it.

At that moment, Josiah, Paul and Peter rushed into the house. Alice and Josiah left Paul to confer with the doctor in the examining room and took Peter into the parlor across the hall. Though the inside shutters were open for the day, the weak sunlight filtering past overgrown lilac branches outside the window did little to brighten the dark red, flocked wallpaper of the room.

Time slowed. Josiah paced back and forth. For once, chattery Peter sat wide-eyed and silent on a child's stool close beside Alice, sucking the thumb of his right hand, holding tightly onto her skirt with his left fist. Alice's thoughts flitted from memories of happy hours spent with Elizabeth during their growing-up years as next door neighbors to possible causes or outcomes of the present crisis.

Could she have realized something was very wrong that Sunday afternoon when Elizabeth kept rubbing her head? Could she have done something? Had she even thought about it in the crush of her own chores? She guiltily uttered prayers for the Lord's hand to be upon her friend.

Over a month had passed since Josiah and Paul had the argument that separated the friends. A haze of hostility seemed to rise with the dust along the road dividing their farms. No longer did the families wander back and forth. When they had met in the Anglican Church yard the following Sunday the men looked straight ahead, refusing to acknowledge the other's presence. Alice and Elizabeth looked at each other with anguish and then turned away, obeying the dictates of their husbands to break all association with each other. Penny and Abigail surreptitiously waved to each other from their pew boxes before their mothers' gloved hands stilled them. Penny had sat and stood through the long services, letting tears flow down her cheeks and an occasional loud sniffle punctuate the pastor's sermon and prayers. She then slammed the pew seat down in childish anger after the hymn.

"Penny!" her mother had admonished her daughter out loud.

The following Sabbath day the Dowds did not come at all. It was whispered they might attend the Congregational Church! Penny's tears flowed again each time she glanced over at the empty Dowd pew.

Unfortunately, animosity toward English crown supporters increased and their Anglican pastor, supported by the crown and fearing for his own safety, had returned to England ten days ago. After his departure the church doors were permanently closed and locked.

The Marsh farm became an island of isolation as contact with townspeople and neighbors became negligible. The last Sunday Beth had been to visit her daughter she had carried back the dreadful news of the Peters' farm being raided during the night by rebels who ordered everyone out of the house. Mr. Peters, in his all-together, was not even allowed to put on any clothes before they put him in a wagon and drove off to the Whig prison on Block Island. They warned Mistress Peters not to return to the house or they would take her too. When she realized one of the little children was missing she defiantly sneaked into the house, groping around without a light until she found her two-year-old boy. Then the house was sold, (given?) to one of the sheriff's friends. Beth had no idea where the family was staying now. Would the rebels do the same to the Marsh family?

Here in this shadowed room of Matilda's house, Alice prayed silently for the welfare of her dear friend and their own safety.

Uncomfortable in this somber silence, Josiah halted his relentless pacing in front of Alice. "We are leaving," he declared.

"We can't go yet," Alice stated pleadingly, startled he could be so insensitive. She looked at him accusingly, as if his unyielding, narrow-mindedness had caused the problem her friend was experiencing.

Josiah looked at her and at Peter, whose left hand had crept into Alice's. He was momentarily at a loss. "I will wait in the wagon," he finally said gruffly. "Come out soon," he ordered and left the room.

Shortly, Paul crossed the hall into the parlor. In the dim light Alice could not read the expression on his face. Relief yet anguish filled his voice as he spoke. "She is awake but can't speak or move. I will take her home. Can Aunt Beth stay with her until I get her mother or sister to come?" he asked, taking Alice's hand in his to emphasize his need for her to agree to the request.

"Of course," Alice said, rising and giving Paul an embrace filled with relief and caring. "We'll leave at once and send Aunt Beth right over. Let Abigail and Peter stay at our house until you get Elizabeth settled. In fact, Peter can ride home with us now." Hopefully, now the families would be friends again.

As Alice and Peter walked out to the wagon she noticed the back of a familiar figure limping along the rutted street, head down. "Uncle Amos?" she spoke softly, unsure if it was really him.

The man stopped, hesitated then slowly turned in response.

"Oh, Uncle Amos! I'm so pleased to see you!" she cried, rushing over to give him a warm hug. He felt small and fragile under his overcoat. She had neither seen nor heard from him since he left the house that dreadful Sunday.

He held on to her for steadiness. "Dear Girlie," he spoke in a whispered voice, calling her by the name he used in her childhood. His face was gaunt, emphasized by several days' growth of whiskers, his eyes bloodshot and yellowed, his hands trembling as he held her.

"Where are you staying? Are you all right? Why aren't you at Franklin's house?" Alice questioned, shocked by his appearance.

"I am fine — I am fine," he murmured, as if he could not quite understand her questions.

"You must come home with us." She began to draw him toward the wagon.

"No!" With a spark of energy he resisted her tug. "No," he reiterated, glancing at Josiah sitting stiffly in the wagon, then he pulled away from her and limped rapidly in the opposite direction.

Alice stood still, bewildered. What should she do?

"Get in the wagon," Josiah commanded. She handed Peter up then climbed up unassisted.

In a resigned voice Alice relayed to Josiah the arrangements she had made with Paul. He looked annoyed and started to rebuke her when a thud was felt on the side of the wagon. Bang. Thud. Another object hit Alice's arm and dropped into her lap. Startled, her reflexes pushed a rotten cabbage off as she looked up and back to see two boys chasing after them aiming to hurl more missiles. Josiah snapped the reins urging the horse to gallop. What had happened to this town, this place of her birth and life? The former familiar street looked foreign as they dashed toward home.

In the safety of their own farmyard Alice gently pried Peter's hand off her arm. She smoothed his hair and kissed his forehead then handed him down to Josiah. She took three big gulps of air to calm her beating heart. "I can't let them see me afraid," she whispered to herself as she climbed down to the ground, wavering slightly as she walked toward the back door of the house.

"Um. It smells good! Thank you for baking the bread I left in the proofing box, Aunt Beth," Alice exclaimed, entering the house.

"Paul will be bringing Elizabeth home shortly. It seems she likely had a stroke and will be needing help. He asked if you could care for her until her mother or sister can get there. Abigail and Peter will stay with us for a day or so. If you would rather stay here I can go instead," Alice explained.

"Of course not. I'll go," Beth answered firmly. She wiped her red-stained hands on her apron and moved about the room gathering her shawl, nightgown and clean apron. "The grapes should be done dripping by tomorrow. I'll come back to make the jelly when I can," she said, motioning to the crushed, cooked grapes bound in a torn piece of sheeting and suspended from a rod over a crock to collect the dripping juice. She was justifiably proud of her role as expert jelly/ketchup maker.

"Abigail and Penny, go with Aunt Beth to get nighties for Peter and Abigail," Alice ordered. Delighted to be together again for a day or two longer, the girls skipped around the room, tripped over Midge and ended in a heap of laughter and howls of protest on the floor.

When the midday dinner was over, Alice put Susie and Midge to bed for naps. Peter had already fallen asleep on the kitchen bed. She taught Penny and Abigail a new stitch for their needlework samplers then helped Horace practice writing his name. Finally, before beginning her spinning, she sat at the other end of the kitchen table to compose two letters. Her hand shook as she held the quill pen. A deep feeling of loneliness and despair washed over her.

> Dear Mama and Papa,
>
> How are you faring? How is Joan and her family? I have had no words from you and I am concerned about all of you.
>
> Today, by chance, I met Uncle Amos on the street in front of Dr. Pace's house. He left our farm a few weeks ago after a disagreement with Josiah, intending to stay with Franklin Fremont. I am greatly worried for he was thin and ill in appearance. It would be best if he could go to you but I do not know how he could get

there. He would not come home with me. I will try to contact Franklin to learn what happened.

We are still safe here at the farm. Please do not worry about us. These trying times have left us all in turmoil and uncertainty. Needless to say, I do not like it.

Elizabeth suffered a stroke today. My prayers are for her to recover soon. I am concerned for the baby she is due to have within the month. Please add your prayers for her recovery.

Midge is into everything and at the "no" stage. We miss you and hope to see you soon. Perhaps by Christmastime, or by next spring. I pray the conflict with England will be over by then and we can be together again. Please give my love to Joan and her family. We all miss you.

Your loving daughter,
Alice

Dear Franklin Fremont,

Today I met Uncle Amos on the street in front of Dr. Pace's house. He appeared quite ill and confused. Since he would not come home with me will you please tell me where he is living that I may try to help him? I am extremely saddened he is no longer living in this house and I implore you to help me make arrangements for his care.

Cordially,
Alice Marsh

Quickly she read over the letters, sprinkled them with pounce[3], folded and sealed them with wax, then placed them on the sideboard to hand to the next deputy mail rider to pass by on the road.

. . .

Disobeying Josiah's softened command of no contact with her friend, Alice managed to slip across the road for a few minutes every few days. She reported about the comical adventures of Porky's ongoing war with the squirrels, her progress of preserving food for the winter and a new recipe for boiling corn cobs with beans. She chatted about the weather and her efforts to contain Midge's curiosity. She helped the children press the last few colorful leaves to hang around Elizabeth's room. On some of the days Alice visited, Elizabeth lay still in bed watching with sad, frustrated eyes, unable to speak or move one side as tears slid down her cheeks. Other days she became agitated, struggling unsuccessfully to move or speak.

One day Alice happened to be backing out of Elizabeth's room, still chatting, as Dr. Hill walked in and they bumped into each other. The doctor put his hand forward on Alice's waist to lessen the collision. "I'm so sorry," Alice began to apologize, starting to blush at the pressure of his lingering hand upon her back.

"It is not necessary," he responded, reaching to shake her hand with a small squeeze and smiling warmly. "It is Alice, is it not?" he questioned, confirming her name from his memory.

"Yes."

"Elizabeth, I'll come back again soon." Alice waved to her friend and hurriedly left the room, still blushing and embarrassed by the warmth of the doctor's hand on her back and the friendly gaze in his eyes. Why had she reacted this way?

. . .

Alice kept intercepting the deputy mail rider on his twice-weekly rounds but there was no response from the letters to her parents or Franklin. In fact, there was no mail at all for the Marsh farm.

As Alice and Penny skipped along the road to demonstrate that intricate motion to Susie one afternoon on their way home from picking bay berries for candle wax, they were startled by the doctor driving his carriage out of the Dowd's driveway. He waved. Alice blushed with embarrassment at being caught in such an unladylike act. Suddenly she remembered — and felt — his touch and quickly raised her hands to her face to hide the mounting color. He reined the horse close by. "Good day, ladies," he said, tipping his hat in greeting. "How are you this lovely day?"

"We are well. How is Elizabeth today?"

"There is no change."

"Thank you. Goodbye," Alice said with reserve, quickly ushering her daughters toward their driveway. She did not want to prolong the conversation or he might notice her blushing. Could it be because he was sympathetic to the Tory beliefs that he was willing to converse with her in a non-medical situation?

. . .

Days slipped past. Few yellowed leaves clung onto the tree branches. There was the decided chill of approaching winter in the air. Overnight ice formed on the water trough by the barn. Winds, rains and shorter days dictated a hurried preparation to be ready for the rigors of winter; animals and people alike felt the urgency. Not only was the weather pressing them on, but it also seemed to communicate a rising nastiness around the farm. During the night rotten vegetables bombarded their boarded windows. Pumpkins slammed against the door with a startling thump, their broken pieces smashing upon the steppingstone slab. In the morning there was a mass of seeds and pulp to clean up and salvage for pig food. Some nights the attacks seemed to go on until dawn. A full night's sleep seldom occurred. Frequently the fearful cries of the children necessitated Alice's presence upstairs to calm their apprehensions. Some nights the children crowded in bed with their parents. No one became accustomed to the random attacks. Many nights Josiah and Gilbert patrolled the perimeter of the farmyard armed with pitchforks and clubs but the tormenting disturbances still happened after they went inside. When Josiah complained loudly to the sheriff he received a lukewarm "We will look into it" response, but his protests only seemed to escalate the attacks.

With the heaviest harvest chores finished, the boys walked two miles for the first day of school. When they arrived they found the doors locked. No classes could be held in the school that served the Marsh farm. When Mr. Greene, the teacher, had protested against the destructive actions of the Whig agitators, he had been asked (told?) to leave. He argued to stay on, but his salary was eliminated and the school doors padlocked. Finally, intimidation and physical threats forced him to leave town. As a consequence, Alice and Josiah debated what to do about Jeremy's schooling in particular. Alice hesitantly suggested they send him to live with her father for further schooling while Josiah insisted Jeremy stay home to help with the farm chores. Without Uncle Amos's help there was an even greater need for another pair of hands. In the end Jeremy remained at home and Alice tried to help him with reading lessons just before bedtime. Jeremy was secretly pleased. This was an opportunity for him to do manly things, even taking his turn guarding the perimeter of the property with his father or Gilbert. He wished there was still a gun around the house he could shoot at those rebels that threw rotten pumpkins at his house. His boyish anger was growing toward those rebels who had confiscated all the firearms on this farm.

One morning an outcry arose underneath the back window. Alice and Aunt Beth hurried outside to see what was causing the commotion. Horace and Peter were rolling on the muddy ground locked in flinging arms, twisted legs and bloody noses. The women pulled the boys apart, getting in the way of a few flailing fists.

"What is going on?" Aunt Beth and Alice asked in unison.

"He called me a darn Tory," Horace hollered.

"Well, you are," Peter yelled back.

"Am not."

"Yes, you are. Darn Tory! Darn Tory! Darn Tory!"

"That's enough!" Alice barked emphatically, leading Horace to the water trough, while Aunt Beth marched Peter across the road.

Alice dipped the corner of her apron in the cold water and wiped Horace's face. Between "ouches" and cold-water shocks Horace asked his Mother, "What's a darn Tory?"

How could she explain the political upheaval going on in the country that was affecting the friendships of two little boys who did not even understand the words? Now the escalating animosity of the fathers, the choosing of sides and the forgetfulness of shared lives was transferring down to the children.

As they were preparing for bed that night, Alice told Josiah about the boyish fight. "That settles it!" he declared. "You are not to have anything more to do with that family."

"But we need each other," Alice protested.

"You think so but we do not. As my wife you will obey my orders. You will never go there again. Never! Do you understand?" he spoke fiercely, standing in his hand-knit wool long johns and nightcap, pointing his forefinger at her to emphasize the order.

"Yes," Alice replied in a tiny voice, lowering her eyes to hide her distress. She climbed into the cold bed, lying still as Josiah erupted in talk, reciting on and on about the treachery that surrounded his life. She told herself that her husband had reasons and pressures that were putting this strain on him. No longer was he able to sell produce and hay to the British in Boston to augment their income. He neglected farm chores and left early in the morning. One day he loaded the finer pieces of household furniture onto the wagon and left, returning empty handed. Generally, he arrived home late after dark with no explanation. Maintaining and protecting the farm, coping with the frequent, sporadic attacks of vandalism, as well as possible personal attacks as he drove away from the farm property, were causing him to take his frustrations out on his family. Surely that was why he raged at everyone in the house over the slightest things and smacked the boys for imagined infractions of his orders. He did not hit the girls. He just chastised or ignored them. He snapped impatiently at Alice's questions or the children's efforts to talk with him. Usually Josiah was quite vocal: issuing orders, criticizing, expressing definite opinions, correcting others' ideas. Recently his behavior had turned to an ominous silence, frequently even refusing to communicate with Alice in the privacy of their bed. His uncharacteristic silence threatened the usual order of the household. He moved through the days as if the dark cloud of an impending storm enveloped him.

"Today I was stopped by the sheriff and handed a bill for overdue payment of property taxes that far exceeded the amount of previous years," he said, interrupting her thoughts. "I had never received any bill so how would I have known about it?" He swore under his breath.

"Why don't you pay them tomorrow?" Alice asked.

"We do not have enough hard money left," Josiah answered.

"We don't?" Alice asked, surprised at his answer. In the past he had never informed her of their financial situation. Instead, he always claimed they were poor yet was able to purchase land or livestock when he wanted to acquire more.

"You know that every time they brought me into court when I would not join their cause they made me pay the fines in hard currency, or threatened to throw me in jail. Every time I sold produce or wood or animals though I got paid in nearly worthless Continental paper money. I cannot even complain about their worthless money or I get fined! I have even sold off some of my land." He clenched his jaws in anger at this devastating blow to his self worth. "I will go see Franklin in the morning," Josiah said resignedly. "Now go to sleep," he added, turning over and shutting off the conversation.

Soon his regular breathing indicated he had fallen asleep, but Alice lay wide awake wondering what she could do to help. She knew the situation was fearful but not to this extent. The threats of this war were closing tighter around their house — her home. The lives of her family, even Aunt Beth and Gilbert depended upon this farm. She clutched the quilt tighter around her shoulders to shield herself from the approaching storm. Oh well — she yawned — surely she did not need to worry. Between Josiah and Franklin Fremont, their lawyer, the men would take care of this latest concern. As she drifted off to sleep she heard a faint, human-sounding scream traveling on the winds and rains beating against the house.

"Please ask Franklin about Uncle Amos," Alice reminded Josiah as he harnessed the horse in the morning. "He never answered my letter," she added.

"What letter?" Josiah asked suspiciously.

"After we met Uncle Amos outside the doctor's house, I wrote Franklin to ask him what happened," she confessed. "I also wrote

Mother and Father. Will you please look to see if there are any letters from them at the mail rider's house?"

Climbing into the saddle he looked at her and nodded, too preoccupied to chastise her for not mentioning the letters to him earlier.

The occasional smiles Alice had allowed to animate her face had ceased, replaced by two horizontal, parallel lines of frown wrinkling her forehead. The lines deepened as she watched him trot out of sight in the rain. Now the lack of money was another concern she had to think about. Why had he not told her about this sooner? Was he trying to shield her or was it his usual way of not informing her about his business?

In the house Alice pushed her worry to the back of her mind while cutting up a muskrat Jeremy had caught in a trap, putting the pieces to soak overnight for stew, and chopping vegetables for today's dinner soup.

"Mama, the doctor's carriage is in Abigail's yard," Penny announced as she walked into the house with a basket of freshly gathered eggs.

"He goes there frequently," Alice replied, half listening to her daughter's comment. She stoked the logs in the fireplace with the poker before swinging the iron kettle on the crane over the heat.

As she mixed cornmeal, molasses and milk for the dinner pudding a knock on the door interrupted her activity. Penny hesitantly moved to open the door a crack then stood still solemnly looking at the visitor. Alice wiped her hands on her apron and stepped by her daughter to see who was there.

"Dr. Hill," she said cautiously, surprised to see him. "Please come in."

"I will only be a moment," he answered, stepping over the threshold into the cozy room busy with children and family life.

As his eyes adjusted to the dim light, he looked around the room and then let his eyes stop to meet Alice's. "I came by to tell you that Elizabeth and her baby died last night. Her mother asked me to stop here on my way. I know about the tension between your families, but I know she loved you and cared about you. She missed your visits," he spoke softly.

No! She did not want to believe the words she had just heard. Time stood still as she gradually absorbed the news. Her attention riveted on the drips of rain sliding off his greatcoat creating a ring of wetness on the bare floor.

Penny moved close beside her and took her hand.

"Thank you," Alice finally whispered. She lifted her eyes to meet the doctor's and they stood silently looking at each other, communicating empathy and understanding.

"I will be on my way," he said softly, moving toward the door.

Alice reached over to open the door. "Thank you again," she said sincerely as he brushed past her into the gray storm. Aunt Beth came close and the two women held each other, sharing their sorrow. Death was a common occurrence but the pain of grief was no less hard to bear.

"I must go over," Alice said, putting on her wool cape.

"Can I go too?" Penny asked.

"No, not this time," Alice replied, leaving the warm room.

"Alice, please come in," Elizabeth's mother Hannah said, pulling Alice into the somber room and clasping her tightly as tears filled their eyes. This woman was as dear as her own mother. In Alice's memory Hannah had loved her as if she was truly Elizabeth's sister. Now they held each other in unspoken sympathy.

Abigail walked over and clutched Alice's legs. Alice knelt down to hold the child tightly in her arms.

"You are not welcome here," Paul spoke dully from the bedroom doorway.

"Paul, I'm sorry," Alice began, looking up at him as if she had not heard his statement.

He advanced toward her. "Sorry? Sorry? You should be. It is your fault she is gone!" His voice grew in fury. "She loved you and what did you do? You caused her stroke. You are a Tory devil. A witch. She fretted because you would not come over to talk with her but I know you stayed over there and cast spells that killed her. You just go on feeling sorry. I hope it kills you too! Now, get out of here you — you Tory witch!" he yelled down at her, spitting out those hateful words of anguish.

Alice looked at him in disbelief. "I," she began. She would not talk with Elizabeth? It was Josiah, and Paul too, who had laid down that dictate!

"Just go!" Paul pointed toward the kitchen door. He then turned and entered the bedroom, shutting its door firmly.

She rose awkwardly to her feet, looking perplexed at the closed door. Hannah reached over, putting her arms around Alice's shoulders. "There, there, dear, he doesn't mean it," she crooned.

"I'm so sorry," Alice whispered.

She left the house, grasping her cape tightly around her head to protect herself from the cold pelting rain, sometimes stumbling into muddy puddles as tears blinded her eyes.

The tears continued to slide down her cheeks, dripping into the pudding and onto the floor or table as she automatically went about her daily chores. The children worriedly watched her, each one trying to comfort her with pats or offers of help.

The daylight hours slowly passed. Late afternoon darkness came early and Josiah had not returned. After supper chores Alice kept her fingers busy knitting recycled wool yarn into a pair of socks for Gilbert, dropping a stitch or two as her eyes blurred with more tears. Her mind flitted from grief to worry about Josiah's lateness.

In the darkness Josiah rode into the yard and on to the barn. He walked into the house after bedding the horse for the night and took a seat at the table. Alice dipped him a helping of soup, cut off a slab of bread and stood by his side as he began to eat.

"Aunt Elizabeth died today," Penny told her father, then burst into tears.

"That is too bad," Josiah said unemotionally, resuming his eating.

The emotional strains of the day, the unrelenting rain and the chill of late autumn had tired everyone and there were few protests about early bedtimes.

Alice rearranged a blanket over Midge, sound asleep in the trundle bed by her parents' bed, then waited impatiently as Josiah prepared for bed. For him to be so quiet vocally still surprised her. She presumed he would speak when he was ready. Urging him on with questions would not help get the news she wanted.

Slowly, in whispers, he began to recite his day's experiences. "When I got to Franklin's office the room had been ransacked, the doors broken and boarded up. I found him at home. He cannot help me, for the courts will not let him read law because he is a Tory. We went to the town office and they said notices had been mailed to us. They would not directly say the mail had never been delivered but it did come out that no mail at all was to go to us, nor even from us, because it might be inflammatory! Any of our mail can be opened by them." He stopped to take a big breath as anger welled up in his voice. "Those thieves wanted the tax money by the end of the day. Franklin did not have any to loan me. The sheriff was standing there and he offered to buy this farm for a fraction of what it is worth. The old coot always did want this place. I will never sell!" Josiah exclaimed vehemently.

After a pause he continued, "I rode past your father's house in town. It looks rundown and unkempt with that new family living there. Next, I managed to slip over to Lynn to see Uncle Ezra. They are in a hard way there, too, living in a partially burned house." He sighed. Alice reached over and took his hand. He looked at her, surprised by this act of sympathy. He went on. "All of Uncle Ezra and Aunt Dorcas's children have moved in with them and there is hardly enough food for them all. Thankfully, Uncle Ezra loaned me the tax money and I signed a promissory note he requested. Then I brought the money back to town." His anger began to rise again in his voice. "When we stamp out this rebellion I will be able to repay the loan." Gradually he became quiet before adding, "the taxes for next year are due in two months." He put off concern about that payment as he turned over for sleep.

The beating rain emphasized the dreariness and despair of the long day.

"What about Uncle Amos?" Alice inquired.

"Franklin is searching for him again. He keeps wandering away and has been gone about three days now, who knows where. Now go to sleep," he ordered, shutting off any more conversation.

Tears flowed silently down Alice's face. Sadness and loneliness filled her soul. She realized how much she missed Elizabeth. She could not even tell Josiah about the shock of Paul's accusation. There was no one she could share it with, not even Aunt Beth. Now, the turmoil of war had moved closer to her life. She had cried so much today. How could there be any more tears left within her?

3

*S*URREPTITIOUSLY, Hannah had managed to send a note to Alice telling of the time and day of Elizabeth's burial. Alice debated over and over again within herself whether or not to attend until her love for Elizabeth had compelled her to dare be defiant, knowing Josiah would have refused to let them go. Guiltily, Alice had waited until he left the farm before ordering Gilbert to harness the horse to the wagon. Now she reined the horse to stop at the end of the driveway. Aunt Beth sat next to her with her cape clutched tightly around her shoulders as Penny and Horace sat huddled close together in the bed of the wagon. They waited, solemnly watching the hearse pull out of the Dowds' driveway, followed by wagons carrying Paul, Abigail, Peter, their grandmother Hannah and additional relatives. Letting them put significant distance ahead, Alice flicked the reins, keeping the horse far enough back from the Dowds to avoid notice. She did not want Paul to stop and deny them attendance at the burial. Only the grind of wheels on dirt and the squeak of an ungreased wagon wheel interrupted the magnified stillness. Even the wind kept silent. A threatening cloud shadowed the road adding another layer of gloom to the scene.

At the local cemetery the somber gathering assembled around the earthen hole as the minister recited scripture passages over the casket of Elizabeth and her unborn baby. Standing at the back of the crowd with her hood pulled forward to conceal her face, Alice bit her lip to force back tears pooling behind her eyelids. She vowed she would not cry in this place. She tightened her hold on Penny and Horace as they leaned close to her, grasping her gloved hands. The knowledge of death had been awakened in their young lives.

After the casket had been lowered into the hole, they joined the slow-moving line of mourners as it gradually advanced to Paul and the family. In hushed tones they said the insufficient phrase, "I am sorry." The women hugged Abigail and Peter. Penny and Abigail sobbed audibly into each other's shoulder. Remembering Paul's outburst, Alice hesitated. Pulling her hood farther over her face and bending her head she extended her hand to shake his. Blinded by grief, he failed to recognize her or remember their past meeting. Hers was just another hand among many. As she reached to embrace Elizabeth's mother, Hannah placed a locket in Alice's hand, curling her fingers around the case. "'Tis a lock of Elizabeth's hair," she whispered.

Choked with grief, Alice whispered, "Thank you." For the first time today tears emerged from her eyes. She turned away and saw Horace and Peter facing each other, hands stuffed in pockets, eyes cast down to shoes twisting holes in the freshly turned earth. She reached over and took Horace's arm, pulling him gently. He looked relieved. He could not figure out what to do or say as he stood before Peter.

Alice's hushed murmurs of greeting to townspeople were returned or ignored depending on political leanings as they all slowly moved toward the wagons. Unexpectedly, Alice realized that Dr. Hill and Matilda had fallen in step with her. Matilda looked straight ahead, pursing her lips in a taut, thin pencil line while the doctor and Alice nodded to each other but spoke no words. He helped Matilda into their carriage, then took Aunt Beth's and Alice's elbows to escort them to their wagon. As he helped Alice onto the seat he squeezed her hand before he let go. Feeling a blush rising she managed a weak "Thank you" as she turned away quickly, grateful for the rising, penetrating, cold wind bathing her face. She snapped the reins urging the horse to ignore the twirling leaves blowing in frenzied patterns before it. In a rush of noise, fierce, biting raindrops pelted their bodies, stinging faces and hands. The horse needed no further command from Alice to gallop toward home and the shelter of the barn.

The dreary mood of the cemetery service lingered into the late hours of the day. The demands of food preparation, sewing, diffusing children's arguments and lesson instructions filled the hours, yet all the while Alice kept listening for hoof beats trotting into the yard that would indicate Josiah was home.

After a supper of porridge and egg custard sweetened with grape jelly, the girls huddled close by the warm fire as Alice read a story. A downdraft of wind blew smoke back into the room, forcing coughs and teary eyes from everyone. Midge dropped off to sleep in Alice's lap while Susie snuggled against Aunt Beth's bosom.

The door banged open as a sudden rush of wind and raindrops pushed Gilbert, Jeremy and Horace stumbling into the room with armloads of wood. Night chores were finally done, the livestock watered and bedded for the night, the barn doors closed and bolted.

Alice dressed her sleepy babes in nightshirts warmed by the fire. Even Jeremy's drooping eyelids told her he too should be off to bed. The weather was too nasty for their nightly parade to the outside privy so chamber pots would have to do for tonight. Prayers were mumbled between yawns.

As Alice bent over to give her daughters a good night kiss, Penny reached up to encircle her mother's face with her childish hands and asked softly, "Mama, what are Abigail and Peter going to do without a mother?"

"I'm sure they'll miss her very much, but I expect sometime Uncle Paul will find another mother who will love them and care about them," Alice responded softly.

Penny squeezed her hands tighter on Alice's face and whispered fiercely, "Please don't die, Mama!"

Alice enfolded her daughter in a long, comforting embrace, rocking her in her arms and kissing her curly head. Finally, she released her arms and laid her daughter gently on the pillow next to Susie, already asleep, and kissed both on the cheeks. "Good night, my dear ones," she said softly as she picked up the candle and went downstairs.

She put another log on the fire, sat down in the mother rocker, as the children called it, and picked up her latest perpetual knitting project. Porky yipped in dreams on the hearth. Aunt Beth snored in the kitchen bed as Gilbert joined in with competing snores from the back room. The wind howled. Flying branches hit the house. She shivered as a cold draft blew through a broken window. She realized she had dropped a stitch three rows back. Her mind could not concentrate. Where was Josiah? He usually returned much earlier. What if something had happened? What if the horse threw him off and he was lying hurt in a ditch? What if he had been waylaid by drunken Whigs? What if he had been tarred and feathered? She shuddered, imagining that horrible scenario. Questions. Prayers. More what-ifs with no answers.

Even Alice's eyelids began to droop in sleep as time passed. A knitting needle dropped to the floor with a clatter, startling her awake. Should she go to bed?

Her answer came as Josiah pushed the door open accompanied by the wind and rain. He looked tired yet somehow more relaxed, as if he had made a decision.

"Did you eat?" Alice asked.

"I ate earlier," he replied, moving toward their bedroom behind the fireplace.

Alice stirred the morning pudding cooking by the fire, banked the coals for the night, then joined Josiah in bed, closing the curtains to contain some warmth.

Her husband reclined stiffly against the bed pillows as if he was going to talk. Alice waited apprehensively.

"I am going away in the morning," he finally stated.

"Going away?" she asked. "Why? Where? For how long?" She felt her voice and body tighten, anticipating hard answers she did not want him to give.

"I am leaving for New York where the British are in control. It will be safer for me there. Here the rebels are lying in wait to tar and feather us loyal men or throw us in prison or worse."

"But you said you signed the Association form recently and practiced marching at the militia gatherings. Weren't you declaring your loyalty to their cause so they wouldn't persecute you anymore?"

"You know it was simply a sham, a way to save myself from any more fines or jail. I am not going to pretend any more. I have just been biding my time. Today I learned that Paul has been telling everyone it was just a lie. My safety is in jeopardy. I have to go!" He settled back deeper against the pillows. "They will not bother women and children, so you will be safe here. The fall cleanup is done, so Gilbert and Jeremy can handle the chores."

"But Gilbert is a man too. Won't they harass him?"

He shrugged. "He is just a gimpy-legged, dumb hired hand," he said dismissively.

"He's the only one who has stayed to help you. You can't believe he is of no account," Alice said heatedly, not surprised but still appalled by Josiah's attitude.

They lapsed into silence.

A thousand questions rushed through her mind. "Where will we go if they confiscate the farm and throw us out of the house as they did with the Peters?"

"They will not."

"But what if they do?" she persisted.

He was trying to formulate an answer. "Well, if that should happen you can try to go to New York or your sister's."

"What about the taxes?" she finally asked. Ever since the tax problem arose she worried how Josiah would pay them.

"I promise to be back with money before they are due. This rebellion will be over by then," he said. "You have got food here so you will not need any money. Oh, and by the way, you cannot ask for any help from Uncle Ezra if you need it. He and his entire family have already left for New York. Stop worrying. I am sure the British soldiers will soon crush those rebels." There was a gleeful tone in his voice as he imagined the rebels being ground into the dust of the earth — those rebels that used to be his friends and neighbors.

"But what am I going to do for money if I need it for the taxes or something else in the meantime? Prices keep rising higher every day," she pointed out. "Can't you leave me some of the money you got for the furniture?"

"No. There is not much left and I am sure I will need it all. I told you not to worry. But just to ease your mind, I promise to send some back to you when I get to New York," Josiah said in a placating tone. "One more thing. Do not let the farm go to that greedy sheriff," he warned her.

"How can I stop that?" Alice asked, frightened with this burden.

"You will have to find a way."

He continued giving orders to Alice, many which she could not remember. Her mind filled with the details of managing without him. She often resented his excessive orders, though they had always given her direction. Now, she felt relieved there would be some days without his constant commands, days to do what she felt needed to be done without his voice always in her mind. But could she manage without him? He had always told her she could not, yet now he was leaving her. Undoubtedly he would come back soon and point out her failures. On the other hand, she, Aunt Beth and Gilbert could manage perfectly well for a little while. She hoped.

Josiah hurriedly satisfied himself sexually on top of her then rolled off and turned away, his signal for ending any more conversation.

Though she had been so tired before he came home, now she could not sleep. Her mind kept fretting about the whole situation looming before them. She listened to his breathing, heard hoof beats passing on the road and automatically steeled herself for the thud of rotten food striking the house. Her head ached and she realized she had developed a cold. It was far into the night before she finally dozed only to awaken with a start well before dawn. Maybe she had dreamt Josiah was leaving.

She turned and saw he was sitting on the edge of the bed bent over fastening his shoes in a flickering candle glow. She stretched her legs beneath the warm covers, relishing the comfort they provided and not at all eager to put her feet on the cold floor. With an audible sigh she prodded herself to get out of bed and slip on her dress and apron.

"Please don't go, Josiah," she whispered. "You're needed here." She stood before him and put her hands on his shoulders, physically trying to keep him in this place.

"I am not going to stay here and be attacked. You will be perfectly fine. I will send for you when things get settled. Now pack my bag," he ordered, removing her hands and standing up to go to the kitchen.

Alice moved about the room gathering two woolen shirts, some socks and one pair of long johns, carrying them to the kitchen to arrange in the saddlebag. She stored some hardtack, dried soup and a wooden bowl and spoon in a second saddle bag.

Josiah sharpened his razor on a strap behind the door as Alice dipped some warm water from the kettle into a pan and handed it to him. They did not speak. Their actions were born of habit and the strain of the moment.

When Josiah finished shaving he went to the barn to speak to Gilbert and harness the horse, returning with Jeremy. Wakened by the activity in the house the other children sat at the table ready to eat.

"I am going away for a few weeks to help in the fight," he told them, flashing Alice a warning look. "Mind your Mother while I am gone."

"Can I go with you?" Jeremy asked expectantly.

"No, you stay here to help take care of the farm," his father answered. He looked at each one of them. Jeremy bit a trembling lip. Susie and Horace sat still with uplifted spoons. Propped on Alice's left hip Midge sucked her thumb. Aunt Beth challenged Josiah with a fierce look. Yesterday the two of them had had a loud argument during which Josiah threatened to send her to her daughter's. Only loyalty to Alice and the children kept her from leaving right then. Alice looked away. Penny ran over and clutched his leg. "Don't go, Papa!" She held on tighter.

"Where can I reach you if I need you?" Alice asked, looking back at him for some soft look of concern for his family.

"I will send word back," he said, releasing Penny's grip. He picked up the saddlebags and walked out the door without any goodbye kisses or further words. Jeremy and Penny stood in the doorway waving goodbye as he rode past the barn and turned west into the woods just as the faintest blush of dawn crept into the sky.

"Coward!" Aunt Beth hissed, turning to stir the porridge.

"Oh, no," Alice protested, having overheard the comment. "'Tis not safe for him here anymore. You heard him say he was going to help in the fight."

"He just said that for their sake," Beth replied, pointing her thumb toward the children. "You know he's a staunch Tory no matter what he told the magistrate. He's leaving so he won't have to contend with the Whigs or take care of us and this farm," she said accusingly.

Alice did not reply. She did not want to admit to herself that Aunt Beth was right; that he was more concerned about his own safety than the family's.

. . .

Even with the nuisance of a stuffed head and dripping nose, one day, then two, passed with a relaxed routine. The sunshine even emerged to cheer them. There was laughter, singing and happy hours before bedtime as Gilbert entertained the children with his dancing puppet — Horace fascinated as usual by its motions. The random night attacks had stopped as well. Alice felt the tension in her shoulders releasing. Perhaps the management of the farm would not be so difficult.

Nevertheless, on the third morning the sheriff's wagon drove into the yard. He approached the unlatched door and walked in uninvited, startling Alice as she was bent down to push a trivet over coals in the fireplace. Porky snarled at the intruder's feet.

"Mistress Marsh, where is your husband? He has failed to attend militia training. Now he is subject to fines amounting to two pounds. I'm here to collect."

"I don't have that kind of money," Alice gasped, straightening up.

"Either he appears tonight or you must supply a substitute," he said leaning his big hands on the table across from her.

"A substitute? How can I possibly do that?"

"You have to find one. And remember, if that person doesn't fulfill his obligation, or acts up, then you're liable for his fines." He spoke with a smugness that implied he knew Josiah was not in the area and she would be unable to fulfill the substitute order. "Have him at the green this evening by six," he ordered. Turning, he left the house whistling "Yankee Doodle" as he spurred his horse to a trot.

Alice stood at the table in shock. "Aunt Beth, where can I find a substitute?" she asked in a small voice. "I don't have any money to hire one nor do I know anyone who could possibly do it."

Beth answered matter of factly. "The only ones are Gilbert or Jeremy."

"But Jeremy is just a child," Alice protested, "and I don't want to ask Gilbert with his bad leg."

The women discussed alternative solutions. In the end Alice walked out to the barn to find Gilbert sharpening the saw on the grinding wheel. She stood quietly watching the long fingers test the sharpness on the saw teeth.

Gilbert Daye was of indeterminate age, long on silence, long legged, long armed, long necked and as loose-jointed as the wooden puppet he danced on a board to entertain the children on winter evenings. Though hampered by crudely-set broken legs as a youth, he was the steady, one-speed, hired hand who had been with the family for twenty years. Even now they knew little about his background or family, for he never went to visit anyone, nor was he much for talking. Talking seemed to be a labor for him. He expressed himself with big, rough hands that could fix a harness, shape an ash ax handle into a work of art or guide the oxen by subtle movements of his long fingers.

"Gilbert, why do you stay? Every other man has joined the rebels or gone to help the British," she said quietly.

A blush began to rise up his neck and face as he looked at her. He averted his eyes. "The farm needs a man," he answered gruffly.

"I — we deeply appreciate the work you do here and I feel we have not said thank you often enough. I do thank you," she said shyly. She watched him set the grinding wheel spinning again in the trough of water before she hesitantly continued. "The sheriff was just here demanding we pay money because Josiah has not been at militia training. We are to supply a substitute in his place. Do you know anyone in town or on another farm who could take his place?" Alice asked, hoping he could supply an answer.

"No."

Alice could not bring herself to ask him to do it. She looked at the unbending leg extended at a strange angle as he sat at the wheel. "Thank you," she said quietly and turned to leave.

"I'll go."

"But you're too old and ..." She looked at his legs, too embarrassed to say it.

"Lame," Gilbert supplied the word. "No matter. I'll go."

"Are you sure you can do it?"

"Yes."

"Thank you, thank you. I will never forget it," she said with obvious relief.

. . .

After two weeks had passed, Alice hoped each day would bring some word from Josiah. There were no signs the war between England and the colonies had ended. Josiah was capable of taking care of himself and they were getting along all right on the farm. Truly she did not need to worry. Travel to New York often took weeks. Possibly he had not even reached there yet. Maybe he did not have any money to send her. If he did return he would surely be imprisoned or worse and she did not want that to happen. However, she could not help worrying: What would happen to all of them if the war went on for years? Would Josiah be able to help her or must she fend by herself caring for the farm and her family?"Lord, I can't do that. I don't know how. Please, send him back," she begged.

On Horace's sixth birthday a loud thump and sharp cry of pain interrupted Alice as she mixed a pumpkin cake for his celebration. Aunt Beth and Alice dashed out the door to find Horace crumpled on the ground under the oak tree. A makeshift ladder lay on top of him.

"Ow! Ow!" he cried as the women untangled him from the pieces of lumber. His left forearm lay askew, bone piercing through the flesh — the break too ragged to fix at home.

"Penny, run and get Gilbert and the wagon," Alice called out to her eldest daughter.

Alice and Gilbert lifted Horace onto the wagon bed and, in spite of a possible bombardment of rotten vegetables or rocks, the three were soon off to Dr. Hill's to the tune of Horace's constant moans.

Alice comforted Horace as much as possible while waiting for the doctor to finish with other patients. It seemed so very long ago that she had sat in this same room waiting for word about Elizabeth. The wait finally over, Alice forced herself to hold Horace still on the table as the break was set and strapped in place.

"How did this happen, young man?" Dr. Hill asked, handing Horace a piece of hard candy.

Between subsiding sobs and sucks on the candy, Horace related the details. "I wanted to fly. I was climbing up the ladder I made when it broke and I fell. It's my birthday, you know. Look, I have on my big boy clothes, too." Another big sob erupted from him, as much from disappointment at his unsuccessful venture as from pain.

"Thank you so much," Alice said, as Dr. Hill helped Horace off the table. "How much do I owe you?"

"The charge will be one pound," he said.

Alice blanched. She did not have any money. "I'll get the money to you as soon as possible," she promised.

"I know you will," Dr. Hill replied, taking her hand and giving it a lingering squeeze of comfort as Matilda stood watching from the doorway with her perpetual glare. "I will stop by in a few days to see how Horace is doing. Give him some paregoric for pain."

"Thank you again," Alice said, aware of Matilda's presence. She pulled her hand from his and escorted Horace past Matilda.

"Good day, Matilda," Alice said sweetly. There was no response. As the door closed she overheard Matilda chastising Dr. Hill, "What are you thinking about, flirting with that married Tory woman?" Alice did not hear his reply, but her cheeks burned red with embarrassment. As she climbed onto the wagon a peal of Matilda's laughter echoed in her ears.

At home Horace became the center of attention, showing off his set arm. He regaled the girls with details of how he planned to fly. He repeatedly bragged about the sweetness of the hard candy he had been given, then whined to lick the cake batter bowl as a birthday treat.

"Here it is, you little scamp," Aunt Beth said, handing him the bowl.

"Someday I'm going to be a doctor," Horace announced between finger licks off the bowl.

"Why?" Penny asked.

"'Cause I'll get to have candy anytime I want," he declared, with a superior air.

"That's enough" Alice said, shooing the little girls into bed for naps. She put Horace to rest on the kitchen bed, though he kept asserting he was not tired. It was not long before his long eyelashes rested on his freckled cheeks in sleep.

No sooner were the children asleep than a loud banging on the door broke the quiet. Aunt Beth lifted the latch just as the tall, bulky sheriff prepared to bang again. He was accompanied by two equally large, unsavory-looking men.

Porky had risen from his usual sleeping space by the fire, barking and barking at these strangers.

"Hush!" Aunt Beth commanded.

Obediently, Porky stopped barking, changing the tone to a low throated, intimidating growl.

"We're here to inspect for contraband tea and arms," the sheriff said as they walked in without an invitation.

"We don't have any. You've looked before and didn't find any so get out," Aunt Beth proclaimed, standing firmly in their way.

"Maybe you lied," the largest one said, pushing past her to begin the search in drawers of the few remaining cabinets, then tramping down to the root cellar and demanding the key for the tea caddie, which was not even locked. It too was empty.

Alice stood against the fireplace wall, her heart pounding in her chest in fear. Were these men going to throw them out of her house? Direct confrontations such as this made her want to fade into the wall.

The men made no attempt to be quiet or careful as Aunt Beth followed them from room to room. "I know you, Tom B. Don't you wake our babies," she scolded the largest man. "We don't have any tea, so get out."

The sheriff closely examined every room then stopped in front of Alice. "Where's your husband?" he asked, leaning close to her face.

"He's not here." She croaked out the words.

"Where is he?" he asked again, leaning even closer, looming tall above her.

"I don't know." She could only whisper this time. Breath-stopping, paralyzing fear!

"Beth, where is the master?" the sheriff asked, continuing to lean into Alice, his breath hot against her face.

"I don't know. We haven't heard since he went to sell some animals. Maybe you know what happened to him," Beth said in feigned ignorance.

"He went to fight with the British," Horace chimed in from his position on the bed. The two women looked at him with surprise.

"I see," the sheriff said, signaling the men to withdraw.

The men stood in the open doorway, letting in a cold wind as they talked. Disappointed they had not found any contraband, they were satisfied however, that they had their answer about Josiah. They finally left and Aunt Beth pushed the door shut and bolted it. Then she went to the back door and bolted it as well. Porky continued to pace by the door giving an occasional warning growl.

Alice slid her shaking body onto a chair at the table, afraid and ashamed of her cowardice.

"Thank you, Aunt Beth," she whispered.

By now Susie and Midge were awake, frightened and clamoring for attention. Penny slowly emerged from under the table where she had taken refuge. Alice told Penny to play a game with Susie and Midge while she finished preparing Horace's requested birthday supper of Scotch broth. Aunt Beth had come to the rescue again, having finished the birthday cake while Alice was at the doctor's.

That night, Horace frequently moaned or cried out in pain in his sleep. To comfort him Alice put him in her bed. She slept fitfully. Questions repeatedly worried her during periods of wakefulness. Where was she going to find the money to pay the doctor? Would the sheriff return soon to put them out of the house?

. . .

Another week passed. The usual chores in the barn and house occupied the daylight hours. Darkness arrived earlier in the afternoon. The wind blew fluffy snowflakes around the sky. The nightly attacks had resumed again with increasing fury. Sound sleep was elusive.

Alice hoped Josiah would send her money by way of a reliable acquaintance but no visitors, friendly or otherwise, came to the farm. She needed money. She searched the house and barn in every nook and cranny she could imagine hoping to find some forgotten coins. There was nothing but dust, mouse droppings and a lost stocking.

As Alice walked toward the house with Penny carrying a basket of eggs early one morning, Dr. Hill drove his carriage into the yard. She smiled a welcome to him as they walked into the house. "Good morning, Dr. Hill."

"Please, call me Brewster," he said, returning her smile.

"Will you stay a moment and have some buttermilk?" Alice asked as he finished examining Horace.

"I would like that," he replied.

She pulled a chair close to the fire and scurried to pour buttermilk into a green glass tumbler.

"Please sit with me," he said, pulling another chair close by his for Alice.

"Thank you," she said, sitting down by him. Midge toddled over and climbed onto her lap, reaching over to pull on Dr. Hill's coat buttons.

"I hear Josiah is gone. How are you getting along?" he asked solicitously.

"We are doing well," Alice replied without much conviction.

"Are you expecting him soon?"

"Possibly."

"I am sorry to see you had to give up the lovely floor clock," he said sympathetically as he looked around the emptier room. She glanced at the space where the clock had stood. It had been a prize possession of Father Marsh's. The children called it the hiccup clock for the unusual catch in the mechanism as it struck the hours.

"Thank you," Alice responded. She had resigned herself to less furniture in the room.

Dr. Hill lingered for some time relishing the warmth of the fire and the company, giving horsy-back rides upon his knees to Susie and Midge. With obvious reluctance he stood up to leave.

"It has been so pleasant by this fire," he said, emphasizing the word this, as Alice helped him slip on his bulky fur coat. "I must be on my way. I will stop back again soon to check on Horace. He is coming along fine," he reassured her. Dr. Hill smiled down at her, holding her hand between his. "Goodbye. For now," he said, stepping out into the gathering snow flakes.

"He's sweet on you," Aunt Beth commented with a chuckle.

"Oh, no," Alice blushingly protested. She smiled in spite of herself. It was so nice to talk with a man without being criticized or lectured. Better still to have a man pay attention to her, especially one so handsome and accomplished.

As a new day dawned, Alice woke with a cold nose indicating a low temperature outside. There was stillness in the air, a sign an early layer of snow had fallen during the night. An answer had come to her about money. She would sell her silver tray to pay for the doctor and more medicine. Relieved to have come up with a solution, she hurried out of bed to the kitchen to stir the fire and heat water. As she moved about the room she explained her idea to Aunt Beth.

"Why sell the tray? Why not some chickens?" Aunt Beth asked.

"We might need the chickens for food if Josiah doesn't come home soon. We can't eat the tray," Alice replied.

"But you prize it so," Aunt Beth said.

"I know," Alice sighed. "I want to go to town this morning," she continued, before she changed her mind.

"Let me come with you," Aunt Beth requested. "It's been so long since I've seen my daughter and I need to check on her. I can visit with her while you do your business. Gilbert can tend the children."

"Of course," Alice said, reaching down into the flour barrel to pull out the cherished tray. She noticed the flour level in the barrel was getting low. Should she buy some more? Or more cornmeal? Josiah had never managed to get the corn ground before he left.

When Gilbert entered the kitchen with a pail of fresh milk, Alice explained that the women wanted to drive the wagon to town and needed him to watch the little ones. He silently nodded his head in agreement, turned around to return to the barn and hitched the remaining horse to the wagon.

Alice wrapped the tray in an old shirt, fastened on her cape and hood, finished giving instructions to Penny and Jeremy and left the house with Aunt Beth.

The weather was too cold for talking on the ride to the daughter's home by the river. Alice stayed in the wagon watching as Aunt Beth hurried in the door of the run-down house that backed up to the dark, rushing river. Then she drove on to Franklin Fremont's house.

After several knocks Isabel, Franklin's wife, opened the door.

"Why, Alice Marsh," she exclaimed, surprised to see her on this cold day. "Come in. Come in." She drew Alice by the arm to a seat by the low fire.

"Thank you. Is Franklin in?" Alice responded, untying her cape.

"Did I hear my name?" Franklin boomed. He smiled at Alice as he entered the room and shook her hand.

Alice warmed her hands around a mug of hot weed tea as she answered questions about the children.

"Have you heard anything from Josiah?" Alice finally asked.

"No, where is he?" Franklin asked with surprise.

Alice briefly explained Josiah's absence, leaving out his reason for leaving to protect himself.

Franklin said, "I will try to find out anything I can for you."

"Thank you. I would appreciate that. Now, I need your advice. I want to sell my silver tray and I need to know the best way to do it, or how to get it turned back into coin without being cheated." She unwrapped it to show them.

Franklin took the tray from her then handed it over to Isabel. "Money is tight everywhere these days," he said. "People are not buying luxuries, I am afraid."

Alice felt a surge of disappointment.

"I'll buy the tray," Isabel said. "I've always admired it. Let me get it from you. Someday, when I'm tired of looking at it, you can buy it back." She placed the tray on the table where the weak morning sunlight flashed a bright reflection off it.

"I can't let you do that," Alice mildly protested, noticing the depleted larder and the frayed coat cuffs Franklin wore. They were not well off either.

"Yes, you can," Isabel declared, leaving the room to gather some coins.

Franklin looked after her with a smile, then shrugged his shoulders at Alice. "She is in charge of everything inside the house," he said, totally agreeing with his wife's action.

Isabel returned to Alice's side, placing five Dutch silver dollar coins in her hand and closing her fingers over the cool coins.

"Will this do?" Isabel asked. She glanced at Franklin, who nodded assent.

Still protesting their generosity, tears of gratitude filled Alice's eyes as she accepted the money.

Shuffling footsteps were heard approaching the room.

"Oh, Uncle Amos," Alice exclaimed, rushing to greet him as he entered. He looked smaller yet healthier than the last time she had seen him. She had fretted he had been lost or dead yet here he was at last, safe in Franklin's house. Smiles of pleasure greeted her in return.

"Shall I take Uncle Amos home with me?" Alice asked. She felt that she should be caring for him, not the Fremonts.

"I think it best if he stays here," Franklin said. "You do not know when Josiah will return. Amos is used to our ways now and does not wander away anymore. Besides, we love his stories, do we not, Isabella?"

Smiling at her husband's affectionate use of her name, she assured Alice, "That we do. Let him continue to stay with us."

Alice recognized the wisdom of their words. She spent a little while longer enjoying their company, catching up on the local news and the progress of the war. Franklin and Isabel tactfully avoided any reference to the hardships they were experiencing as loyalists. Franklin's attitude was one of disdain for the Whigs. He felt they were rabble, far beneath him, just hoodlums and mobs of unsatisfied riffraff looking for ways to steal under the pretext of a political separation from English rule. She learned that Franklin had never received her letter about Uncle Amos. Also, she was not surprised to hear that Abigail and Peter were staying with their grandmother Hannah down the street. There had not been any sign of the children at the farm across the road for days.

As Alice rose to leave, Franklin gave her a few back copies of the Tory paper, Rivington's *Gazette*. She had not read any for a long time. The news it carried was always so dreadful, filled with dire predictions and rumors of Whig savagery. She gave each friend a hug and then walked through thickening wet snow to the wagon. The coins weighed heavy in her skirt pocket.

Her next stop was the doctor's house. Matilda opened the door a crack.

"Is Dr. Hill in?" Alice asked.

"No, he isn't," Matilda replied sharply.

"Will you please give him this money for fixing Horace's arm?" Alice asked, reaching in her pocket to pull out a one dollar coin and hand it to Matilda. Matilda grasped the coin and shut the door with no further words, not even a thank you.

Alice drove to the apothecary to purchase some more paregoric. She had debated with herself about purchasing more corn flour but decided to wait as long as possible before spending any more money. The last stop was to pick up Aunt Beth.

She hitched the horse to the broken gate post in front of Beth's daughter's house and stepped over holes in the porch to knock on the door.

Aunt Beth drew her into the dim light of a tiny, cluttered room smelling of sour milk and other peculiar odors.

"I can't go back with you," she said in distress. "John joined the rebel army and has not returned yet. Another baby is due soon and my daughter needs my help." She waved her arm around the crowded room including many half-dressed children. It was obvious Aunt Beth had begun to clean up the mess of soiled clothes and dried food littering the floor.

Alarmed at the statement, Alice looked at Aunt Beth's distraught face. "What will I do without you? You've been like a mother to me," she spoke. Ashamed of selfishly thinking of herself first she reached over to touch Aunt Beth's arm. "I can't keep you from helping your family, though. Whenever you can, please come back to us," she implored.

"You are strong and you will manage. Believe it," Aunt Beth said encouragingly as she pulled Alice into her arms. The two women clung to each other.

"I'll get Gilbert to bring your things," Alice whispered. "Goodbye for now."

As Alice turned the horse toward home her mood was sad as she realized how much she would miss Aunt Beth's help and companionship. She had been her supporter, her strength and her friend. Alice touched the coins in her pocket, relieved that she had been able to pay the doctor. At last she had some money of her own if she needed it. She shivered. Was it the wind, or the growing realization that Aunt Beth possibly was gone from her forever, or fear she might be pulled off the wagon and tarred and feathered before she could get home? She snapped the reins and uttered a prayer for courage.

4

THE COLD, BITING DAYS OF EARLY WINTER settled over the land and penetrated throughout the house. The older children huddled together in one bed to share their shallow body warmth under heavy homespun quilts. Gilbert moved from the unheated back room to the kitchen bed. Alice kept Midge in bed with her. Overnight, ice formed on top of the water in pails set on the kitchen table.

It became a test of fortitude for Alice to face another day. As she wakened she snuggled closer to Midge's warm body. She mouthed prayers of thankfulness that filled her thoughts: thankful she was not pregnant again, thankful they had not been evicted during the night. She prolonged lying under the warm quilts as long as possible before duty spurred her on to arise from the warm bedcovers, slip on her dress and run across the cold floor as quickly as possible to the kitchen and the blazing fire Gilbert had usually stirred into life.

Each morning Alice half expected to see Aunt Beth kneeling by the fire arranging apple pies to thaw for breakfast. How she missed her presence and all the work she had done to operate this house!

When Gilbert delivered Aunt Beth's clothing, he learned that her daughter's husband John had been wounded fighting with the rebels, then died shortly after from an infection. Aunt Beth explained her duty was to be with her family and she could not consider returning to the Marsh farm, at least not in the foreseeable future. He relayed a message from her warning Alice to be careful. There was talk that the wives of Tories were going to be tried in a court and punished.

Many more weeks had passed since Josiah had left for New York. Still no news from him. No notice from any source ever came. How did he plan to get money to her?

"Jeremy," his mother called up the stairs one morning in late December. "Time to get up, son." A creak of the bed signaled he had heard. When he stepped down the stairs, Alice spoke softly to her first born. "Happy Birthday." She kissed him lightly on his uncombed brown hair and hugged him. "I'm so proud of you," she added. She was pleased with the efforts he made to assume a man's role on the farm.

It was still early that same morning when Franklin knocked at the back door, calling out Alice's name.

"Do come in," she answered, glad to see a friendly, familiar face. The children rushed to search his pockets for candy treats.

"Get back to your chores," Alice commanded after their successful search.

She handed over a cup of cider.

"Thank you," Franklin said wearily, amply filling one of the chairs pulled close by the low fire. He reached into his wallet and pulled out the tax bill, handing it to her without comment.

Alice read the due date on the bill. "Two weeks left!"

She had spent two of the coins on medicine, cornmeal to fill the kitchen barrel, shoes for Jeremy, lamp oil and, perhaps foolishly, repairs to a pot by a passing tinker. She was trying to be as economical as possible but there were only two coins left. She sighed. She was not managing well enough to have any money for this latest demand.

"What am I going to do?" she asked fearfully, not expecting

THE HOLLYHOCKS WILL BLOOM AGAIN

Franklin to have a ready answer, but hoping for one to suddenly appear. Of course he had no answer. She could tell by his slightly baggy clothes that life was not too easy for him either.

Franklin patted the seat on the bench close by him motioning for her to sit.

"All I could find out was that Josiah had been in New York and then likely had gone to England," he stated quietly.

"England?" Alice asked in surprise. "What about the farm? The money for the taxes? His promise to send for us? When will he come back?" Fear gripped her soul.

"I do not know," he answered sadly yet honestly. "Very likely it is just a rumor."

She swallowed to push down a bile of anger mixed with panic that rose in her throat.

"Perhaps Josiah sent some money for the taxes before he left, if he did leave the country," Franklin said hopefully.

Alice looked at him with tears in her eyes and shook her head slightly in a negative motion. Would it not be here by now if he had?

"I am so sorry I do not have it to give to you," he said woefully.

"Thank you. I appreciate the thought," she said, trying to sound brave. She smiled weakly and rose to gather four eggs from the basket on the shelf, tying them in a napkin and handing them to Franklin. "Please take them for Isabel to use."

He protested lamely but Alice insisted. "You've been a dear friend," she said, patting his arm gently.

"Thank you," he answered. "Keep up your spirits," he encouraged her as he walked heavily out to his gig to a chorus of childish "Byes."

"Mama, did Papa really go to England?" Penny worriedly asked, having overheard the conversation in the small room.

Before Alice could respond, Gilbert entered the kitchen carrying a pail of milk. "Mistress, there is no more feed for the animals," he said hesitatingly.

Alice looked at him with surprise. This seemed the longest sentence Gilbert had ever uttered in her presence.

"Oh, my!" Alice said with a catch in her throat, not wanting to acknowledge one more need. However, she could not let the remaining animals die of starvation. "When you are ready, please go to the feed store in town. I'll get some money for you," she added, going to the bedroom to pick out one coin from her hiding place. Her meager supply was almost gone. Should she send some of the extra eggs for him to try to sell or should she keep them for their own food? The chickens were not laying too well just now. She did not like having this kind of dilemma. Why must she? How could she?

Gilbert worked in the barn, then split blocks of wood for the fireplace, ordering Jeremy and Horace to bring it to the house. Thus it was early afternoon before he left with the wagon. A nagging worry flickered on the periphery of her mind. "It's just the gloom of the impending storm," she told herself, looking out at heavy, low-lying snow clouds gathering on the horizon.

Alice kept the children busy during the remaining afternoon hours with chores and lessons.

The snow began to fall with a whisper, then with increasing density. The sunlight disappeared and so did any visibility of the road as Alice and Jeremy trudged to the barn to tend the animals for the night. She did not usually milk the cows but all available hands were needed in the barn and Gilbert was not back yet.

As if he had read her mind, Jeremy called down from the loft above where he was sweeping sparsely scattered shafts of hay down to feed the cows and oxen, "Mama, shouldn't Gilbert be here by now?"

"I'm sure he's on his way," she replied loudly, trying to be reassuring. "Maybe the snow is much deeper toward town. Don't worry. He'll be along."

In answer to her statement they heard the movement of the horse outside the barn door. When Gilbert failed to bring the animal in Jeremy went outside to help. "Mama," he called. "Come quickly."

The horse, still hitched to the wagon, stood patiently waiting by the door. There was no sign of Gilbert. The seat where he would have sat was covered with snow. What had happened? Where could he be?

Jeremy unfastened the harness and led the horse to the stall where it calmly stood while its two caretakers worked silently to dry the animal and tie on a blanket. It began to lick the floor for stray whispers of hay, thoroughly satisfied to be home in its own stable. After the wagon was unloaded, feed ladled out to the animals and the barn doors bolted, Jeremy and Alice trudged to the house through blowing, drifting snow that had accumulated at least six more inches since the afternoon, worry accompanying each action and step. The family gathered round the fire for warmth and light as Alice tried to keep her voice calm as she read the Christmas story from the Bible. That special day of Christ's birth would soon be here. She missed attending the regular church services, especially during Christmastime. How would they celebrate this year?

The nightly ritual began as Alice listened to urgent prayers for Gilbert from bended knees, tucked the children in bed together, kissed them tenderly on their sleepy heads and piled on an extra quilt.

"Mama, where is Gilbert?" Jeremy whispered again before she left the loft.

"I don't know. I'll go to town in the morning to find him," she told him, trying to sound reassuring but afraid to make such a trip.

Downstairs she gathered her knitting needles and yarn, starting a new pair of mittens for Jeremy. His hands were getting icy blue from the cold work in the barn.

A faint knock interrupted her worried thoughts about Gilbert. Porky ambled close to the door to emit a rumbling growl. Alice tensed, fear rising in her limbs. Who or what was out there this time? Were the rebels here to evict them from this house? It could not be Gilbert or Porky would not growl and the rebels would have knocked louder. "It must be the wind," she spoke to Porky, trying to assure herself as well as the dog.

The second knock was louder and not a figment of her imagination. Grabbing a poker she moved close to the door without opening it. She was not going to let any rebel into her house! "Who's there?"

"Alice, it is Brewster. Dr. Hill. Please open the door," the voice outside the door called.

"Brewster?" Here on a night like this?

"Yes."

Alice lifted the latch. Standing before her was Dr. Hill, covered in snow. She could see his shay collecting snow by the oak tree. Gilbert was not with him. Where was he?

"Dr. Hill. Brewster. Please tell me what happened. Where is Gilbert?" she asked, shivering slightly.

Brewster walked in, hung his coat on the rack, piled logs on the fire and pulled the bench close by the warmth. Alice poured two mugs of rum, dropped in some butter, inserted a poker into the hot coals in the fireplace then into the liquid. She handed one to him and sat beside him, cupping her hands around the second mug for warmth. Watchful Porky sat, his rump resting on her feet.

Brewster sat silently warming his hands around the mug then spoke. "Gilbert was on his way from the feed store. As he passed by the tavern a group of rabble rousers who had drunk too much too early in the day happened to come out and see him. They grabbed the horse and pulled Gilbert off the wagon, dragging him behind the building. They stripped him, covered him with hot tar and feathers and propped him on a rail, which they proceeded to carry past the stores and houses, your obedient horse following behind. No one tried to stop them." He shook his head in puzzlement. "I think they planned to put him in your wagon and send it home as a warning, but by the time they got near my house they realized he was severely burned and injured, so they dumped him in the snow near by. It was just by chance a kind passerby saw him and helped him to my house. Aunt Matilda and I tried to get off as much tar as possible but he has lost so much skin I am afraid he will not make it. Usually they do not use so much hot tar." He sighed with the memory of the pain he had seen.

"But why Gilbert?" Alice asked, tears forming in her eyes, as she visualized the pain he was suffering.

"Because he worked for a Tory, I suppose," Brewster answered simply.

"But he's been doing militia training," she protested.

He shrugged, unable to give an explanation.

"Can you bring him here for us to tend?" Alice asked, quiet sobs clouding her voice.

"I medicated him heavily. Wait a few days yet. Then we can see how he is doing," Brewster answered.

They were both silent for a long moment as they contemplated the sad course of the day.

"I do not know where the horse and wagon are," he stated.

"They are here." Alice filled him in on the horse's appearance without its driver.

Brewster aroused himself. "I must be on my way," he said, getting to his feet. He extended his hands to Alice's work-worn ones, helping her up to stand close to him. Keeping her hands in his he pulled her to himself then wrapped his arms around her. For a moment she let herself relax against his body, relishing the feeling of protection, care and strength. "Good night, dear, beautiful Alice," he whispered, leaning down to kiss the top of her head.

He struggled with his heavy fur coat. "I will see you in a few days," he said, smiling and lightly touching his fingers to her face. Then he walked out, closing the door behind him.

Alice leaned against the door, giddy with a feeling of euphoria at the thought of being held, kissed and told she was beautiful. The moment passed as guilt crept into her thoughts. "I'm married! Why did I let him hold me?" She slept fitfully all night. A question jolted her mind. Would Jeremy have to be the militia substitute for Josiah and Gilbert now? Thoughts from sorrow to joy to worry intermingled. "Oh, Lord, please help me. I feel so vulnerable and I'm afraid, afraid of my feelings, afraid for Gilbert and afraid of the future."

When Brewster drove into the yard and knocked the next day, Alice and Penny were cutting vegetables to put in with chicken bones simmering in the pot over the fire. As Alice opened the door she could tell the news was not good by the shake of his head.

"Gilbert died this morning," Brewster said quietly. "I have notified the undertaker. Does he have any family about?"

"I never heard him mention any," Alice replied. She leaned against the table for support as the sorrow of another life lost saddened her mind. Horace came and stood beside her, putting his hand in hers. He had always been fond of Gilbert as Gilbert was of Horace. She looked down at her son with tearful eyes and squeezed his hand in response.

Dr. Hill leaned down to examine Horace's arm. "The mend is just about complete. Keep the strap on for two more weeks. But no more flying. Agree?" he teasingly commanded Horace. "I will send the undertaker by," he added, turning to leave.

"Thank you," Alice said softly.

To lessen the children's tears Alice dressed the younger ones in warm coats, hats and mittens and took them outside to play in the snow while she shoveled a path to the barn. The sunshine sparkled on the pristine whiteness. The children tramped around making patterns of footprints in the uninterrupted expanse of white snow. They flopped down to make snow angel patterns and threw handfuls into the air to see them shimmer as the flakes fell to earth again. She paid little attention to their spontaneous laughter filling her ears. How quickly their delight eased their sadness in these moments.

Alice and Horace walked into the barn. "Jeremy, Gilbert died this morning from injuries he received yesterday," she said sadly. He was shoveling manure into the pile in the center of the barn. He looked at his mother with despair, lips trembling. Slowly a look of resolution came into his eyes. He tightened his jaw and straightened his body to its fullest height. "I can handle the farm," he spoke with brave, eleven-year-old assurance.

"And I will help, too," Horace added, struggling to take another shovel off the wall hook with one free arm.

"We'll do it together," Alice said. She wanted to hug them, but the look in their eyes told her they did not want to be treated as children anymore. They were so young to take on men's roles. Oh, why did Josiah not come back or send for them?

In the midst of the dinner meal in early afternoon the undertaker drove his sleigh into the yard. Earlier, Alice had finished going through Gilbert's meager belongings in the back room. There were no papers, no remembrances of his earlier life. Only some faded clothes and his dancing puppet man.

"Good afternoon, Mistress Marsh. The doctor said Gilbert had no family hereabout. Do you want to assume responsibility?" he said, standing just inside the door, hat in hand.

"Yes, of course. He was part of the family," Alice answered.

"You know he can't be buried in the church lot. He wasn't a member there," the undertaker added.

"I know." Alice sighed. She could not seem to think straight.

"Why not set him by Grandmama and Grandpapa in the north field?" Jeremy chimed in with his idea. "He was part of this farm, wasn't he?" Gilbert was not family by blood but he was in all other ways.

"What a good idea. Yes, we'll do that," Alice said with relief. "But we can't dig the grave ourselves," she added with concern.

"I'll bring out some men tomorrow morning and we'll bury him then. The ground won't be all frozen yet." The undertaker spoke with practicality. "Do you have some clothes to put on him?"

"I'll get some," Alice said, turning to get clean work clothes from Gilbert's sparse pile.

"We'll see you in the morning, Mistress," he said, turning to leave. "I'm sorry for your loss," he added kindly, awkwardly tipping his hat to her.

Early the following morning, the undertaker drove his sleigh hearse into the yard followed by a sleigh with two men. Jeremy and

Horace climbed aboard guiding the way to the family graveyard in the north field.

Alice dressed the girls and herself in warm clothes. Carrying Midge, she led Penny and Susie by walking in the sleigh tracks to the north field. The men had just finished digging the burial hole in the still unfrozen earth when they arrived.

"Do you want to say a few words, Mistress?" the undertaker asked. The men removed their hats; the children stood in solemn silence.

"Yes," Alice answered. She took a deep breath, seeking inspiration. "Lord, here is one of your children, Gilbert Daye. He loved your land and your animals. He was a faithful, hard-working member of this, his adopted family. Look kindly upon him and fill his heart with peace. Amen."

The family Gilbert had embraced as his own for over twenty years stood together while the plain pine box was lowered into the grave. As the dirt was shoveled upon it, Horace spoke for all of them. "Goodbye," his sad young voice rang out. This silent man had always been a part of these children's lives.

The family turned and walked back to the house while the men finished closing the hole. Shortly, the sleighs drove to the house and stopped. The undertaker came to the door, hat in hand. "That was a nice prayer, Mistress. The charge is one dollar," he said.

Alice gasped, thinking how little money she had left. "Just one moment," she said, entering the bedroom to retrieve the last coin.

"Thank you, Mistress," the undertaker said, as he took it from her hand, put on his hat and turned to leave.

"You're welcome," Alice said, shutting the door then turning to look at the familiar room. The loss of Gilbert's presence on this farm struck her with full force. Today of all days. The day before Christmas. Her children's solemn gaze emphasized the loss. She just wanted to crawl into bed and sleep away the challenges, problems, anger and fear.

"I'm hungry," Susie said, coming over to take Alice by the hand and pulling her toward the fire and leftover simmering stew. She must go on. "One step at a time," she whispered to herself.

"Sit down, children," Alice ordered, beginning to ladle the stew into the everyday wooden bowls. "Penny, please tie napkins on the little ones. Wait a minute till we say grace." The children could barely wait to fill their tummies. Alice busied herself around the kitchen, eating little so the children would have more. She was too full of misgivings to be hungry today anyhow.

Before they left the table, Alice went into the back room and brought out the dancing man.

"Horace, Gilbert would want you to have this," she said, putting the toy into his hands.

"Thank you, thank you!" Horace said over and over, rubbing his hands across the wood. "Someday I'll make him dance as good as Gilbert did," he promised.

Christmas morning shown bright and clear. Alice rose early to gather pine cones, pieces of pine boughs and nuts from the back room to place around the kitchen table. Before each child's plate she set newly-knitted mittens, scarves and hats, the last one only completed a few hours before. As she was finishing decorating, the children rushed down the stairs.

"I'll get Midge," Penny called, running into the bedroom to help her little sister.

They stood admiring the Christmas greens of ivy, holly and laurel used to decorate the kitchen, stairs and doorway. They had chosen them with care yesterday afternoon from the woods. Unable to afford the traditional Christmas Eve supper of oyster stew, they had eaten a substitute stew of rabbit that Jeremy had caught in a trap. Before bedtime they had gathered together close by the fire singing Christmas songs between verses of the Christmas story. When Horace made the wooden man dance they clapped and cheered. It had been a celebration of Gilbert's life as well.

Milking and animal-tending chores still needed daily care even if it was Christmas.

"Be good and mind Penny while Jeremy, Horace and I do the chores," Alice reminded the little ones. It bothered her that she had to leave them unattended while she was in the barn. It was either that or take them all with her each time. Once, before Penny (often called Little Mother) could stop her, Midge burned her fingers trying to retrieve a block that had rolled into the fireplace flames.

The rest of the morning echoed the cheer of the day with the children singing, laughing and playing. At dinnertime Franklin, Isabel and Uncle Amos drove into the yard for a surprise visit.

"Merry Christmas!" Franklin boomed, standing in the open doorway.

"Merry Christmas!" the children hollered back, rushing to hug him and search his pockets for candy.

"Come in. Come in," Alice urged them, greeting them warmly as they came through the door.

The guests took time to admire the fresh smell of greens and listen to each child's chatter. Alice was grateful she had set their last ham on the spit to cook and had mince pies warming in front of the fire for this special day. Now there was enough food available to serve her family and the unexpected guests.

"Children, did you know observing Christmas here in Massachusetts was outlawed by the Puritans in England in 1643?" Franklin asked as they sat relishing the meal. "You would have been fined five shillings for observing Christmas. It was even against the law to have mince pie on Christmas."

"I'm sure glad we have it in our family now," Horace exclaimed, licking mince off his fingers.

"Jeremy and Horace, you are doing such a fine job with the animals. Will you show us?" Franklin asked after dinner. "You women sit here and chat. We will take the girls," he said helping with coats and all the hats, mittens and scarves needed for the cold day. "Lead the way, boys."

"How are Abigail and Peter and their grandmother," Alice asked at one point. It was comforting to sit quietly with another woman friend. She missed this kind of sharing companionship.

"Doing fine," Isabel answered.

"I haven't spoken to Paul since the funeral." Alice sighed. She grieved for the loss of her friend and the friendships of neighbors.

Again the reoccurring questions. Why must men fight each other? Was it for glory? For power? For someone else's land? For money? Why can't we continue to live as helping, caring neighbors instead of tearing each other apart?

"How are you getting on?" Isabel asked. She leaned across the table to take Alice's hand in hers.

The warmth of this loving touch brought tears to Alice's eyes. "I'm afraid," she admitted. "Without Gilbert I don't know what's going to happen if Josiah doesn't come back soon. I am so harried trying to care for it all," she sniffed, waving her arm to include the house and farm. "Jeremy and Horace work so hard in the barn and Penny in the house. Even Midge tries to help. They all do but there is still so much to do. Every day I keep worrying the farm will be taken from us." For a moment she indulged in feeling sorry for herself then she wiped her eyes with a handkerchief and blew her nose. "We'll manage," she said determinedly. "Now, how are you doing?"

There was quiet between them. Alice sensed Isabel was framing difficult words to speak. "We are going to try and leave town for New York this week. In fact, we're sneaking away!" The shame of this indignity made her cheeks burn. She continued, "Franklin hasn't been allowed to practice law. He can't even speak or write legal opinions anymore and the town keeps demanding money we don't have. We had to turn the office over to them for back taxes and now they'll get the house, too." She hesitated. "I don't know if Uncle Amos will be able to stand the move."

"Let him come back here," Alice spoke at once. "It would mean so much to me and the children."

"He's not physically able to do much," Isabel explained. "And he forgets a lot."

"That's all right," Alice said. "Even staying in the house with the little ones while I'm in the barn would be such a help." The two women smiled in relief, having solved this problem so effortlessly.

The families hugged and kissed each other goodbye as they prepared to move out of each other's lives, uncertain they would ever see one another again.

Winter

A cold coming we had of it,
Just the worst time of the year
For a journey, and such a long journey:
The ways deep and the weather sharp,
The very dead of winter.

— *Journey of the Magi,* THOMAS STEARNS ELIOT

5

ALICE TRUDGED FROM THE BARN to the sparsely-furnished house carrying a bucket of milk. It was soon after dawn. Bone-weary tiredness and worry kept her from noticing the glistening, newly fallen snow. Truthfully, she hated it now. Snow meant cold and cold meant firewood supplies decreasing, cold, blue hands and shivering bodies. Jeremy remained in the barn feeding one cow, one pair of oxen and one chicken, the only animals left after Alice had sold the rest. In the last two weeks she had sold more furniture too, far below the true value, to raise more money for the taxes being demanded by the town and due today. This morning the cow was to go to the next farm down the road. She had felt forced to accept the pittance the owner offered at this last moment to add to her collection of coins. In the back of her mind was the constant pressure to obey Josiah's admonition not to lose the farm.

Alice portioned a small amount of the precious milk over the breakfast of cornmeal mush for each child and Uncle Amos. She recalled the little amount of meal left in the barrel when she mixed the batter last night. The root cellar and smoke house provided most of the sustenance for their meals but these supplies were growing slim also. They had only been partially full after harvest season. How much longer could they go on this way? Soon there would be nothing left to sell. Then how would she be able to come up with money to supply their needs or the demands sure to arise? Still no word nor money had come from Josiah. Was he in New York or had he really gone to England? Why had he not told her? Was he even alive? This uncertainty filled her with both anger and anguish. The sporadic night attacks had increased in frequency. More windows had been broken. Uncle Amos and Jeremy had ripped boards from the horse stalls to cover the holes and stuffed the cracks with cut-up sheets to keep out some of the snow and cold.

A knock interrupted the meal. Alice walked over to unlatch the door.

"Morning, Mistress Marsh," said the estranged, long-time neighboring Whig farmer, peering into the room. "I'm here to fetch the cow."

"Just a moment," Alice replied stiffly. "I'll get my cloak." She did not invite him in but shut the door to keep out the cold as she retrieved her cloak. They walked to the barn in silence.

At the cow stanchion the farmer began to tie a rope around the cow's neck.

"Please pay me the money," Alice said, holding out her hand.

"Here it is," he replied, digging coins from his grubby pocket and dropping them on the dirt floor. "Oh," he said with a feigned look of surprise.

Alice quickly bent down, gathering them into her hands and counting as she picked them up.

"There are only eight shillings here," she said, looking up at the smirking man. "The price was for ten."

"You must have missed some," he said, preparing to move out the door with the cow.

"Wait, let us look for sure," she begged. She called to her son, "Jeremy, please come here and help me look."

"I gave them all to you," the farmer belligerently replied, quickly moving out the door.

"Wait!" Alice hollered after him, frustrated and angry as he left. Could she prove he did not give her the ten agreed upon?

Alice and Jeremy searched the dirt, raking and sifting the packed earth, bits of hay and scatterings of dried manure, but no more coins were found. They had been cheated.

During the cold walk back to the house she listened silently as Jeremy expounded on creative, imaginary methods of revenge. Momentarily her mind joined in the act of retaliation. She wanted some way to vent her anger too. She picked up the broom and began to whack icicles off the roof edge. When she had hit all the ones she could reach, she drew a deep breath, entered the house and went directly into the bedroom. She gathered all her coins and paper currency from her hiding place, spread them over the bed-covers and counted them into piles. There were not enough! Just one more silver dollar was all she needed.

Uncle Amos came to the doorway, watching her search all the drawers and the secret compartment of the dresser one more time for some she might have overlooked. There were no more.

"I need more." Alice looked at him beseechingly, as if he could reach up and pull some from the ceiling. She felt ready to cry.

"Perhaps they will give you an extension on the rest," he said encouragingly, coming over to hold her awkwardly. She let herself rest briefly in his arms, then pulled away and began to drop the money into her black pocket bag. She pulled on her winter cloak and gloves, all the while giving orders to the children.

"Let me come with you, Mama," Jeremy insisted.

Her first reaction was to say no to save him from a possible tarring or other dire threat but why not let him come along as company and protection, from what, she was not sure. "I'd like that," she replied, smiling briefly at his growing maturity.

They hitched the oxen to the sleigh wagon and were soon plodding on the road to town. Protectively holding a stout stick in his hands, Jeremy sat up as tall as his height allowed beside Alice. Paul and an unknown woman dashed past them in a fancy sleigh. "I wonder if she'll be the new wife?" Alice pondered aloud. Paul gave no sign of recognition to them. This lack of acknowledgment felt like the pain of a sharp knife slicing into Alice after all the years of friendship between the families. She still grieved the loss of Elizabeth, as she imagined Paul, Abigail and Peter did as well.

Alice and Jeremy walked along the foot-tamped path into the town office. Crowds of reluctant homeowners filled the benches in the overheated, steamy, wool-smelling room waiting their turn to pay the tax bills. Alice and Jeremy were forced to stand leaning against the back wall for the better part of an hour before it was their turn to take their place in front of the collector.

Alice stood in front of his desk, emptied the coins and paper currency from her black bag and counted them into neat piles. "This is all I have, though it is not enough for the entire bill I know. I'm requesting an extension to come up with the rest. Please?" she begged nervously. It was the first time in her life she had to transact business in this intimidating situation before town officials.

The collector counted the money, looked at his ledger filled with columns of English pounds, shillings and pence recordings, noting a check mark beside the Marsh name. He pushed back his chair scraping the floor, got up from his desk and walked into the adjoining room. The sound of voices in deep discussion penetrated from behind the closed door. Long moments of anxiety washed over Alice before the collector, followed by the big, smirking sheriff, finally emerged from the room.

"We can't grant you any extension," the collector said, avoiding her eyes. "You pay it all today or we take the property, including the animals and household items and auction it off."

Alice could not believe what she had just heard.

"Why?" she managed to ask.

"That's the law," the sheriff replied coldly, leaning forward and pressing his bulky hands on the collector's desk.

"What's to become of us if you take the farm?" she managed to whisper.

"Well, there is the poor farm," he answered callously, knowing they had no immediate family living in the area to house them. His dark eyes were full of spite and avarice.

"I know you just want the farm for yourself," Alice accused the sheriff.

"Either pay it all today or the sheriff comes to put you out tomorrow," the collector spoke with bravado.

Alice felt faint standing before them. The hot, steamy room seemed to whirl around her, the voices in the room fading away. Grasping the edge of the desk for support, her eyes fastened upon the coins stacked neatly in a row. Her coins. The coins they had labored for, sold their animals and possessions for, including all but one of her expensive brass pots, even scrimping on food to collect. For what? Only to lose it all? She drew in a deep breath, leaned over and began to put the money into the black bag.

"Oh, no," the collector protested, reaching over to stop her.

"They're my coins," Alice said determinedly, pushing his ink-stained hands aside and scooping the last pile into her bag. "Come, Jeremy," she commanded, gripping his arm and turning to march out of the room with her head held high, her heart thump, thump, thumping in her chest.

"Hurry away from here," she urged, handing the reins to Jeremy. Where had that burst of defiant courage come from? She put shaking hands to her face. What do we do now? Over and over that question ran through her mind, but she was too numb for any answer to penetrate past the repeated question.

"Jeremy, please stop by the doctor's house," Alice suddenly ordered. Last week Brewster had promised he would help her if she needed it and she surely needed it today. Just one more dollar.

"Whoa!" Her son reined the animals to stop by the stepping stone in front of the doctor's house. Alice climbed out of the sleigh wagon. "I'll just be a few moments," she said, walking shakily up to knock on the door.

Grim-faced Matilda answered.

"Matilda, may I see the doctor, please?" Alice asked, a note of begging in her voice.

"He is busy." Matilda began to shut the door, then a malicious gleam came into her eyes. "However, do come in and wait," she said, moving aside for Alice to step into the dark hallway. "I will tell him you are here," she added in falsely sweet tones, leaving Alice alone.

Matilda returned shortly, followed by a slim young lady. "I want you to meet Hannah Smith, Dr. Hill's betrothed. She is moving here from Connecticut. They will be married in a fortnight," Matilda spoke with a tone of glee as she took the young lady's arm, pulling her forward to Alice.

The dim light of the room obscured Alice's startled look. "How do you do," she managed to get out, extending her hand for a shake.

At that moment Brewster walked into the hallway, startled then embarrassed as he recognized Alice.

Alice looked at him questioningly. Discomfited, he lowered his eyes.

Silence filled the closing walls of the entry hall. There could be no help from him. How could she extricate herself from the awkward moment? She coughed. "I," then cleared her throat. "I stopped to see if you had any medicine for a bad cold Uncle Amos contracted," she spoke at last, imagining the story sounded as false as it was.

"Just a moment," Brewster said, relieved to leave the room.

With folded arms and a malevolent smile Matilda stood back watching Alice and Hannah waiting in awkward silence.

Brewster returned shortly with a vial of dark liquid. "Give him one teaspoon every four hours," he instructed professionally, handing her the bottle.

From a back room a clock began to chime the hours. One (hiccup), two (hiccup), three (hiccup). Alice looked at Brewster as recognition registered. It was Father Marsh's clock. She would recognize that distinctive hiccup anywhere. Why had he not told her he had the clock in his possession?

Finally, she managed to mumble a faint, polite "Thank you" then turned to leave this gloomy entry without asking the cost. Brewster was obviously relieved she did not prolong the encounter as he followed to shut the door behind her without a goodbye. She could not look at him again.

Alice's cheeks burned with shame as she climbed into the sleigh wagon. "Jeremy, please let's go home," she whispered. She told herself, "Of course, he would get married. He had no ties to me. I was a fool to think we could ever have anything between us. But why hadn't he told me last week when he stopped by one night? The night he told me he loved me, cherished me and kissed me on the lips. Oh, why did I let myself begin to care for him so?" Hot tears slipped down her burning cheeks. In a rush of horror she questioned. Was he truly a Whig and just using her? Was that why he was always asking about Josiah? Just to learn his whereabouts? How naive she had been. Her heart lay on the floor of her chest, shattered once more into a million pieces, first by Josiah and now Brewster.

Deep shadows fell upon the landscape. More snow seemed imminent. Alice could not concentrate on the house nor the children. She wandered around the half-empty rooms looking yet not seeing, tears blurring her vision. She was quiet, only half listening to the children's subdued chatter and arguing. Her mind raced helter-skelter searching for an answer to their dilemma. Outside in the cold air she mechanically chopped off the head of their last chicken, savagely plucked off the feathers, letting them fall to the ground or fly off with the wind now swirling blinding snow. She jammed the fleshy parts in a pot of hot water with turnips and carrots for an early supper.

Shortly after dusk she tucked Uncle Amos and the children into bed. Uncle Amos loved this family but had no solution either. She sat in the mother rocker mechanically moving to and fro, no knitting in her hands this time. Over and over the words poor farm entered her thoughts. The idea of them all being sent to the county farm for being poor and indigent appalled her. The children would be separated, the boys hired off and the girls and Alice sent to work as indentured servants. Uncle Amos would be unable to mentally or physically cope with the degradation and she would be doing menial work forever and ever, unable to earn enough to keep them together as a family. She had failed. Josiah's predictions about her presumed failure as a mother, wife and manager of the farm had come true. When he realized she had lost the farm he would be furious. There could be no telling what he would do then. What more could she have done? Over and over she reviewed each transaction she had made. The answer was always the same. Nothing more. The pop of an errant spark startled her so that her heart began to race.

A noise outside awakened Porky. He moved from Alice's side to growl by the door, beginning to paw the wood in an attempt to get at the cause of the noise. His fury increased. Alice grabbed a poker and stood trembling by the door ready to hit anyone daring to break in. This was her house for one more night and she would protect it. All became still. She waited and waited. No more sounds. She tiptoed into the bedroom and peered through a crack in the boards. She could not discern any unusual shadows nor movement in the limited visibility of the snow storm.

"They've gone, Porky." She knelt down hugging his muscular body and burrowing her head in his neck fur, clinging to his strength. She released the dog, patting his head one more time and sat down again by the fire, too wound up to even try going to bed. Porky sprawled by the door occasionally emitting a low growl. When it was time for him to pee, she cautiously opened the door a crack to see if anyone was outside in the blowing snow. Porky nudged the door wider, dashed out, racing on his short, stout legs toward the oak tree. Growling, barking, snarling, he fought fiercely with a faint shadow. A cry of pain. A sharp yelp. Silence. The shadow disappeared.

"Porky! Porky!" Alice called for Porky to return. No response. Grabbing the poker she ran out the open door toward the tree.

Porky lay bleeding on the trampled snow. Blinded by whirling snow flakes she struggled to hoist his fat body into her arms and carry him toward the house.

Awakened by the ruckus, Jeremy appeared by her grasping a stout stick in his hand. He stooped to help carry the injured animal in to his favorite spot by the fire. The beloved dog, sensing home, love and warmth, gave a sigh and died. Tears ran down the cheeks of Jeremy as Alice held him close, her grief blending with his.

Somehow, the shock and rage of this attack on Porky cleared Alice's mind. She knew what she would do.

"Jeremy, we're leaving for Aunt Joan's tonight, as soon as we can get ready. I will not let us go to the poor farm," she exclaimed fiercely. "Please pull the trunk down from the loft. I'll start gathering clothes. Let the other children sleep for now," she said, turning to begin the task.

Quietly yet quickly she moved about the house gathering clothes and packing them in the trunk around the big Bible with its listing of family members.

"What about the oxen and sleigh?" Jeremy worriedly whispered. "Won't they come after us if we take them?"

"We need them more than they do. I think they're making out very well without them," Alice replied. She did not feel any guilt taking the animals, sleigh wagon and their personal clothes.

Uncle Amos stirred with the noise of their whispers. Alice spoke softly to him, telling him what she planned to do. "You've been there before and you know the way," she said, desperately hoping he would be able to guide them. Frequently, his mind was living in the past. Tonight the sense of urgency brought him into the present. He got up, put on extra warm clothes and turned to limp to the barn with Jeremy who carried Porky. While Jeremy dug a burial hole for the animal in the packed earth of a stall, Amos moved about in the dim light of the lantern. His eyes seemed to see into the dark corners, knowing exactly where to find the tools they might need in the future. He placed them in the bed of the sleigh wagon, layering over them their remaining small supply of hay that would be food for the oxen as well as insulation and softness for the passengers. Over that he spread an old matted bear skin.

Jeremy and Uncle Amos hitched the animals to the sleigh wagon, drove them to the rear of the house, loaded the trunk to fit under the seat, then helped the sleepy children onto the vehicle. Horace hopped off and ran into the house, scraping his shin as he stumbled up the stairs to reach under his bed, returning with the dancing man in his hand. Alice handed out all the pillows, quilts and blankets off the beds to pile upon the younger children.

"Jeremy, tie some rags around the clappers on the oxen's bells. We can't let anyone hear us as we go," Alice ordered.

Together Jeremy and Uncle Amos carried out the heavy iron kettle partially filled with corn-meal mush that would serve as their breakfast.

Alice hurried back to gather some pewter spoons, wooden bowls and the remaining prized brass pot. One last time she entered their home. For many generations this land and house had been home to the Marsh family. Now it was being taken away from them because they were on the opposite political side. She looked around at her pretty dishes, her mother rocker, the few remaining pieces of furniture and the stain on the hearth where Porky died tonight. She had failed to save this home for her children and their children. "But I have to keep us together," she protested aloud in the emptiness. Glancing around one more time she noticed the favorite China blue and white cup and saucer of Mother Marsh, one Josiah had brought her from England. She lovingly took them off the shelf, wrapped them in a towel and added them to the odds and ends in her ample pockets. Tucking three recorders into her knitting box and touching her waist to make sure she had the black bag with its coins firmly tied around her, she left this home of so many memories, latching the door behind her.

The biting wind drove large snowflakes across the landscape, piling them deep against the house in the short time since the storm had begun.

"It will be hard to see where we're going," Jeremy said worriedly, climbing up to sit on the bench beside Uncle Amos.

"All the better to cover our tracks," Uncle Amos replied. "Let me have the reins. I know all the roads about and the best way to avoid the night watchman in town." He seemed energized by the activity of the past few hours.

The oxen methodically plodded through the mounting snow as they pulled the heavy-laden sleigh wagon. Alice turned to look back one last time, yet before they had ridden onto the road the house had disappeared from view in the fury of the storm. She snuggled underneath the quilts with the younger children, reassuring them about the big adventure they were embarking upon, holding them almost fiercely to her shivering body yet all the while worrying they would be intercepted.

Under the protection of the storm they rode unobserved mile after mile through the snowy night, stopping frequently for the oxen to rest. The fear of being caught subsided imperceptibly and her shivering lessened. By daybreak they had reached beyond Salem. Uncle Amos guided the animals to a farm house and barn situated back from the main road, nestled in the folds of shadowed fields of white obscured by the continuing storm.

An elderly man emerged out of the dimness carrying two buckets of milk balanced on a wooden yolk over his shoulders. He walked toward them warily, then broke into a smile. "Amos, you old coot. What are you doing here?" The two men, being distantly related by marriage, greeted each other with old familiarity.

"We're on our way to the coast," Amos explained. "My nephew is mighty ill and we need to get there to help. I . . ., we'd appreciate it if we could stop and rest here awhile."

"Of course. Of course. Come in. Come in," the farmer said, leading the way into the house. "Put the oxen in the barn," he called back to Jeremy

Alice woke the sleepy little ones and they were lifted down from the sleigh and carried into a warm kitchen. The house held several generations of this family, hospitable yet wary of committing themselves as Whigs or Tories. Alice, sensing the general message Uncle Amos had relayed, spoke in generalities as well. She cautioned Jeremy with a look and slight negative shake of her head when he began to tell why they had left their home the night before. After being awake all night and worn out by the extraordinary activity, Uncle Amos soon dozed by the warm fire.

"Please, let me help," Alice offered, as the women of the household prepared vegetables and breads for the day's meal. She retrieved some of the thickened cornmeal mush from her kettle, cut it into wedges and fried it in bacon grease. It was all she had to contribute to the meal. Soon there was the chatter of children playing, brief conversation, the scraping of utensils and the bustling about the room of everyday activity.

The stomping of the owner's feet clearing off snow woke Uncle Amos. It was the afternoon dinnertime. The adults sat at the scarred trestle table and the children stood silently along the wall as the older man spoke a lengthy grace invoking the Lord's blessing upon them all. Alice whispered "amen" to that.

The wind and snow intensified, again blanketing the earth, bushes, trees, closing in visibility. It did not take much persuasion for the Marsh family to spend the rest of the day and night within the snug walls of this home. The travelers slept on their own quilts by the fire. Alice dozed fitfully, occasionally resetting a quilt over one of the children, frequently feeling her waist to be sure the coins were still safe and secure under her dress. She dreaded their possible loss.

In the morning a bright, clear day beckoned them to continue the journey. All were refreshed and eager to be going. Even the oxen seemed enthusiastic to lead the way. A profusion of "thank yous" accompanied the reloading of the sleigh wagon. In an air of anticipation and excitement they were off, the children chattering and singing songs. At midday they stopped by a grove of trees to eat the last of the cold cornmeal mush and stretch their legs.

The farther they traveled, the more the strains and griefs of the past months gradually began to lessen their grip on Alice's mind.

She caught herself smiling and even joining in the singing. Hope for a brighter future beamed from the sky on the sun's rays.

The increasing smell of salt air beckoned them onward.

Darkness had moved in from the east as the sleigh wagon with its now-weary occupants pulled into the yard of Alice's sister and her family in Gloucester.

"We're here," called Uncle Amos. He had visited once years ago to help Joan and her husband build this house.

Alice jumped down and ran to the door to knock.

Her sister cautiously opened the door. She looked amazed as Alice sagged into her arms in relief. "Mama, Papa, come quickly. Alice is here," Joan called joyfully. The families reunited with hugs, kisses, tears of joy and explanations all babbled at once.

After a warmed supper of finnan haddie ladled over potatoes, Alice tucked the children together in a loft bedroom upstairs they shared with their cousins. Again the fatigue of the journey and the warmth of the room soon lulled Amos to sleep on the couch in the kitchen.

In the flickering light of the fireplace Alice's parents and her older sister Joan sat around the kitchen table listening as she briefly whispered the circumstances that compelled her to make the long journey far from the Marsh farm. Far into the evening they spoke in hushed voices, catching up on the latest news and rumors.

"What do you think I should do now?" Alice asked, primarily wanting her father's advice.

He looked around, envisioning this tiny house with a multitude of people living together. "Let us think about it tomorrow," he replied. "You are tired now. Let us all get rest," he said, rising and helping pull his arthritic wife up off the chair. They both kissed Alice good night and went to bed in the back bedroom.

"Alice, sleep in with me tonight," Joan ordered. She banked the fire, checked the door latches, picked up the candle and led the way to the front bedroom. Joan's husband Elisha was absent for long periods of time fishing. Each journey he made brought apprehension to his wife and family. They feared he might be fired upon or seized by an enemy warship, yet he felt it necessary to continue his livelihood.

"I'm glad you're here," Joan said, squeezing Alice's hand as they lay side by side.

"Oh, so am I," Alice fervently whispered, squeezing back. She yawned, silently thanking Providence for their safe deliverance to the arms of loved ones. As she began to relax, tears slid from her eyelids. Josiah, Elizabeth, Paul, Abigail, Peter, Hannah, Aunt Beth, Gilbert, Franklin and Isabel, Uncle Ezra and Aunt Dorcas, the pastor and congregation, beloved Porky and yes, even Matilda and Brewster, and the farm had all gone from her in these past months leaving her alone with her precious children who were dependent upon her for their survival. She had not realized how deeply the immense sorrow of these losses had weighed her spirit down. Only now in the warm welcome of her parents and sister did she recognize how low her spirits had sunk. Another deep yawn. Her parents were here and they would protect her and care for her as they had done when she was a little girl. Her childhood trust in them lulled her mind into a heavy night's sleep.

6

ALICE OPENED HER EYES to unfamiliar surroundings. She felt terrible. Her head ached. The room swirled around. The bed undulated up, down and sideways across a choppy sea. The gray bed curtains moved in opposition to the bed. She closed her eyes to stop the motions and drifted back into sleep and disjointed dreams.

Alice realized she was sitting on a snow-covered tree stump in the north field of the farm. The tax collector standing before her reached for the black bag with its jingling coins. The sheriff gripped one of her arms and her cheating neighbor the other to keep her from protecting the bag. She twisted around, pleading with Josiah to come help her. Rowing across the field in a boat, he lifted one hand off an oar to point his forefinger at her, then resumed rowing.

She fought to twist again, loosening one arm to reach for Brewster as he danced past in a reel with his arms around his fiancée and Matilda. Heavy-set Franklin whistled *Yankee Doodle* in his gig as he threw legal papers out, first one side then the other. Gilbert

85

sat in his coffin dancing the puppet on an ax handle. Uncle Amos limped in the field, hand casting seed corn in circular patterns. Her father sat on Father Marsh's gravestone and lectured Horace on philosophy. Even Jeremy did not stop to help as he raced around Uncle Amos's circles, flying a kite in the falling snow flakes. Every way she twisted she saw a male too busy to help free her.

She struggled and wrestled but the bag slipped from her grasp. The tax collector pulled all the coins out of the bag and tossed them into the air where geese flying south caught them in their bills. Sobbing, she covered her face with her apron and slipped off the stump onto the ground.

"Alice, dear, wake up," her mother's voice carried over her sobs.

Alice opened her eyes to see her mother's concerned face bending over her. Turning she saw her sister Joan on the other side of the bed. They helped raise her up to drink some herb tea. Alice smiled weakly at them, lay back on the pillow and felt a cool, damp cloth placed on her forehead as she sank into sleep again.

Now there were no men around. There was no one, neither children, nor women nor men. Alice stood alone in an empty room enclosed by bare walls. She walked around and around to find a door. Not on this wall nor any wall. There was no door. Strange, but there were no windows either. Here she was. Alone. Trapped. By herself in a room with no way in or out. Panic began to make her heart race. How could she get out? Did she want to? Oh, yes! She looked up the high walls and saw blue sky. There was no ceiling on this room. That was the way out. Surely there must be a ladder or furniture in here to climb. A search of the room once more proved it was empty. Nothing. She despaired of ever getting out. Slumping to the floor, Alice hugged her knees, rocking to and fro, to be forever teased by the inviting sky.

High above, a bird flew across her vision. That's the way! I'll become a bird and fly out of here. I can't fly. But I *must* if I'm ever to get out. I *will* fly. She stood and raised her arms to the light. Up, up she rose past the high walls, over their edge to settle with panting breath and beating heart on a nearby tree branch. She was out.

Scared but out. The grass looked so green, the leaves so brilliant, the sky so blue. How wonderful the world appeared. She was free! Tentatively she moved her feet down the trunk from one branch to another. With each movement she felt more confident.

"Alice," her father's voice called from far away. "Please sit up and drink."

Alice opened her eyes to see him sitting by her side holding a glass. She smiled at him. He looked beautiful. She ran her tongue over her cracked lips as her father helped her sit. She gulped the herb tea down as fast as possible. The taste of that liquid was an elixir.

Lying back on the pillow again she said hoarsely, "Thank you. How are the children?" she inquired.

"They are all well," her father told her.

"That's good." She yawned and closed her eyes in sleep.

Alice was not a bird anymore. She was still alone. So alone but this time walking along a tree-shadowed, seldom-traveled pathway toward a bend obscured by intertwined branches. Though sad and fearful that she would only find danger or loneliness around the bend she kept traveling forward. As she moved closer someone gently took hold of her left hand. She turned to look into the face of a man whose kind eyes conveyed to her that she was safe, deeply loved and cherished. Abundant love and peace filled her soul as this face she identified as Jesus silently conveyed to her she was worthy of love because she was a child of God. Exuberant, bubbling-over joy filled her soul! He led her by the hand around the bend toward the path ahead bathed in brilliant light. There was no danger there that she could not handle with him holding her hand. As they walked closer to the light that was God her companion let go of her hand. She wanted to hold on to it forever. How could she enter the future alone when she had been so fearful in the past even with people around her? His look told her she would be all right if she always remembered that his spiritual presence was with her, loving, reassuring, encouraging and believing in her. He disappeared and she turned to slowly walk along the illuminated path toward the next bend with quivering courage. In the past, she had prayed 'words' taught by her parents and church hoping for answers to her petitions, yet not really believing there was a source. Now there would be no doubt in her mind.

Alice let out a big sigh and opened her eyes. Penny was sitting on the edge of the bed stroking her mother's hair.

"Hello, sweetie," Alice whispered. "I love you," she said, reaching up to caress her daughter's pretty face.

A rush of joy turned Penny's serious look to one of smiles. "I love you, too, Mama," she whispered back, laying her head on Alice's shoulder.

"Penny, come out of there," hissed Joan, peeking between the curtains.

"I'm awake," answered Alice.

"How do you feel?" Joan questioned, opening the bed curtains.

"Hungry."

"That's a good sign," Joan said, smiling with relief.

"How long have I been asleep?" Alice asked.

"Three days."

"Three days! Why didn't you wake me?" Alice exclaimed guiltily, trying to rise up and get out of bed.

"Calm down, Sister dear. You had a fever. Sometimes you tried to get out of bed, sometimes thrashing about and crying. You kept us deeply worried for awhile," Joan answered. "The fever seems to be gone," she added, feeling Alice's forehead.

"Can we see Mama?" Susie asked, peeking over the edge of the high bed.

"Of course, baby." Alice reached forward to help her little daughters up beside her.

"Me, too," chimed in Horace.

Soon all Alice's children were on or beside her, laughing, kissing and explaining their activities while she was ill. When they heard the laughter, her parents, Uncle Amos and Joan's children quickly crowded into the small room as well. It was a grand time of rejoicing.

"Surely, I'm rejoicing the most. Thank you, God,." Alice whispered the prayer. These loved ones surrounding her looked especially beautiful and precious.

"Enough, enough," Mother Lewis commanded, shooing everyone out of the room.

"Please help me up, Mama. I want to go out to the kitchen and eat," Alice requested.

Her mother steadied Alice on the walk to the table in the kitchen. Joan set a bowl of fish chowder before her sister, watching carefully for any signs of fainting.

Alice sat for an hour or so listening to the news of the past three days. Then she began to yawn.

"Back to bed you go," Joan ordered.

"I guess I'm more tired than I thought," Alice admitted, not protesting the order.

Alice woke after a short nap. Her mind recalled the dreams that had been so lucid. She thought about the meanings they would have for her life. As she absorbed this wonderful knowledge and joy, she thought about the people in her life as well as the infinite number of people in the world. She knew that whenever she looked at them she would always see the same love she had received reflected in their eyes. She felt relaxed and reassured that whatever happened in the days and years ahead, she would be able to cope. All she needed was courage. Nor would she ever be truly alone.

. . .

Once Alice began her recovery she progressed quickly into the active life of this enlarged household.

The house was tiny; three rooms on the first floor and one unfinished room above that was divided into two sleeping sections by blankets strung between the rafters. While Joan's husband was at sea, Alice shared the downstairs front bedroom with her. Their parents slept in the back bedroom, Uncle Amos on the couch in the kitchen and the nine children upstairs; five of Alice's and four of Joan's. They could manage the sleeping arrangements.

Father had become a victim of the war. He was so dismayed and traumatized by the actions of some of the former townspeople toward him, people he had taught and helped, that he now refused to leave Joan's house. He refused to associate with anyone other than family. If a visitor, even a child, stopped by he retreated to the back bedroom. However, he could not check his love of teaching, so he was delighted to teach his grandchildren within the house.

Alice gradually doled out the money in the black bag to help pay for food. The coins were going quickly. The oxen were sold. Prices were rising and the paper money minted by the Continental Congress had little value.

It was left up to Alice and Jeremy to stop the outgoing flow of coins. Jeremy got a job sweeping, hauling water and operating the bellows at the blacksmith shop. Alice left the house early most mornings and walked along snow-covered streets to the center of town. There she went from business to business, even reluctantly tavern to tavern, offering to work for any kind of pay. Day after day she returned to the tiny house, discouraged by the discrimination of sometimes being labeled a loyalist yet hopeful for success another day.

One morning Alice stopped once more in the butcher shop. As she waited for the butcher to finish with a customer, she could not help but overhear the conversation between them. The well-dressed lady was lamenting the sudden departure of her cook just when this special dinner had to be prepared for prominent people today. Could not the butcher cook the meat and send it over?

"Pardon me, Mistress," Alice chimed in, surprising herself by her boldness. "I couldn't help but overhear your dilemma. I would be willing to do the cooking for you. If you like what I do then perhaps you would hire me to be your cook," she said hopefully.

The lady frowned as she looked Alice up and down. "I do not know you," she said. She looked to the butcher for some encouragement. He nodded slightly. "However, I am desperate. We will try it for today," she continued with some reluctance.

"Thank you. I will do my best," Alice replied, excited there was a possibility of work even for today. "How many people will be dining? At what time? What had you planned to serve?" Alice asked a barrage of questions.

The lady appeared flustered by all the questions. She explained there were to be twelve people dining at 2:00 p.m., but she seemed unfamiliar with the kitchen or its supplies. She usually left all those details to the cook.

Alice looked thoughtful. "Perhaps it would be best if you buy this roast here," she said, indicating one the butcher held in his hand. "I will go with you to your house and see what you have on hand. If I need something more I could come back to the stores to get it."

"That sounds acceptable. And what is your name," the lady asked.

"Alice Marsh," Alice replied with a smile.

"I am Mistress Talbot. Let us be on our way," she commanded.

The women left with the roast in hand. There was little conversation between them on the way to the Talbot home. As Mistress Talbot cautiously watched her, Alice examined the kitchen and its contents. She mentally calculated the time and ingredients available, then stood before Mistress Talbot and explained what she could do to present a suitable dinner for the guests.

Mistress Talbot seemed relieved and readily accepted the suggestions.

"I do have another question," Alice added. "Who will do the serving and cleanup?"

"I will have my housemaid Cora do the serving. You will have to do the cleanup," Mistress Talbot explained.

All through the morning and early afternoon Alice worked efficiently to prepare the meal. Occasionally Mistress Talbot stepped into the kitchen critically observing her progress. Alice's unfamiliarity with the location of items and utensils was her greatest frustration, yet she managed to create a hearty meal ready to serve by 2:00 p.m.

Once during the morning, Alice was able to send a message back to her sister by way of the gardener, explaining why she would not be home until late in the day. As it was, darkness had already settled over the town when she finished wiping out the last pot. Mistress Talbot again stood in the kitchen doorway watching.

"My compliments on the meal. It was delicious and there was much praise over it. Please come by in the morning and we will discuss your employment as our cook," she said, turning to leave.

"Thank you," Alice replied. She was tired yet excited about finding work.

On the walk to her sister's home, Alice breathed in the crisp winter air mingled with sea saltiness. "Thank you. Thank you," she shouted to the heaven above sparkling with a profusion of early evening stars. She was grateful, so grateful that she hummed a joyous melody and skipped along the deserted snowy roadway.

Day in and day out Alice walked to and from the Talbot kitchen accompanied by Penny, who helped her mother prepare three meals and tea every day, six days a week. Alice had persuaded Mistress Talbot that she needed Penny's hands to accomplish all the cooking and baking required. Besides, every little bit of income was helpful.

Joan's husband Elisha periodically returned with the fishing boat and in the spring Jeremy had cajoled Alice to let him go with his uncle and Joan's two oldest sons. Now Alice's eldest was working on a fishing schooner at sea and she prayed daily for his safety. Each time they docked back home she was amazed how much taller and more robust Jeremy had grown since the last docking.

The family woke one morning in early summer to find Uncle Amos had died during the night. Just the night before he had lain awake until Alice returned, wanting to talk, mostly about the farm life he had shared with his wife. Now he had joined his beloved. The family mourned his passing but deep grief was assuaged by their gratefulness for his life.

. . .

Six years slipped past as the Marsh family settled into this new life. Alice watched as the children's personalities were becoming more and more evident. A worrier, seventeen-year-old serious Jeremy assumed the weight of the world. His Uncle Elisha channeled that energy into hard work on the boat. Little Mother Penny, now fourteen, bossed the younger children, who were grateful she was at work during the day. Twelve-year-old Horace was quite accomplished at making the puppet dance on the board as well as excelling at his studies, though chopping wood took up all his spare time. Besides eating, ten-year-old Susie loved to read, often letting her spinning slow to a stop while daydreaming about the current story. She and Horace frequently had long, sometimes loud debates with Grandpapa Lewis about some philosophical idea. Midge, now eight, had lost her baby fat by running around outside trying to be helpful even when the chickens did not appreciate it. She was far more interested in gardening and animals than "girls" inside work. Joan's family increased with the birth of two more children.

These years in Gloucester were full of hard work and sparseness yet filled with happy family companionship and caring. There were many evenings and Sunday afternoons when recorder music and singing filled the air. Except for Sundays, card playing was a favorite pastime, especially for Mother Lewis. Coping with the deprivations of the raging war swirling around throughout the country as well as a persistent, nagging fear of Whig retaliation, drew them closer together as a family. These were years of waiting in this tiny coastal town. The waiting sleep of winter. Waiting for the rebirth when the war would end.

One evening in late 1782, after an especially tiring day, Alice and Penny walked home in the winter night air. The bitter cold caused their shoes to squeak on the packed snow. It was even too cold to talk.

Nearing the house, they saw an unfamiliar horse and sleigh hitched to the stone post in front. Alice quickened their pace, fearing some crisis had happened to her family. As she entered the room she saw them sitting solemnly around the table. Horace, Susie and cousins were peering down the stairs from the loft. A stranger had his back to the door. He stood and turned to face her as she and Penny stepped inside.

"Papa!" Penny cried, dashing over to throw her arms around his waist.

"Josiah?" Alice could not comprehend that her husband stood before her. His face appeared pudgy and sallow and he had put on considerable weight. The leanness of his farming years was gone.

"Hello Alice," Josiah said. He did not move to help her as she removed her cloak and gloves, hanging them on the hook by the door.

Alice's cold hands shook slightly as she sat beside her sister on the bench. She glanced at her parents seated across the table. Her father kept his eyes downcast on a book. Her mother sat stiffly in a chair, her lips pursed tightly in a disapproving manner, glaring at Josiah. Thousands of questions replaced the initial numbness of shock as she sat and stared at this strange man, the father of her children, the man she had shared intimacy with in their bed for eleven years.

Josiah sat down heavily. He looked at Alice as if mentally rehearsing the best way to explain his absence. Soon the old bravado emerged as he told a tale of going to England with Uncle Ezra and Aunt Dorcas, their families and slaves before moving on to more affluent quarters. Weaving a tale of intrigue, interspersed with titles of earls and dukes, he related a story of high living without actually explaining what he did. Why he had returned to this country before the war was officially settled was a mystery he never explained except to hint at a secret mission. When he had disembarked in Boston he chanced to meet an old acquaintance who told him the Marsh farm was occupied by the sheriff's family and the Fremonts no longer lived in town. He had traveled here to Gloucester to see if Alice was here with her sister, or to see if Joan knew where she might be.

"And here you are," he said, reaching across the table to take Alice's hands. She tried to pull them away but his grip was hard. The courage she thought she had gained drained out of her and the old response to Josiah returned. She lowered her eyes, letting her hands remain unresponsive in his.

"Tell us more," Penny begged. She stood with her arm across her father's shoulder, thrilled with the story he told.

Alice interrupted. "Penny, 'tis time for you to go to bed. Morning comes early."

"Can't I stay longer?" she pleaded.

"No," Alice spoke sharply. "Horace and Susie, get in bed. Now!"

"Oh, all right," Penny pouted. She made her way around the table giving each adult an obligatory good-night kiss, lingering to hug her father last. His response was brief and cold. Penny looked hurt as she stepped back and headed for the loft above.

"It is time we all went to bed," Father Lewis declared, rising and helping his wife off the chair. "Good night, Josiah," he spoke formally.

Joan rose and looked at Alice questionably. Alice's eyes pleaded with her. She did not want to go to bed with this man tonight.

"Josiah, you can sleep out here on the couch for tonight," Joan declared, taking a candle and heading for her bedroom.

"I'll be right along," Alice said, thankful for Joan's handling of the situation.

"Stay and talk with me," Josiah said, keeping a firm grip on Alice's arm. They sat silently until the house was still in sleep. The low fire in the hearth was the only light flickering against the shadowed walls.

"Why did you let the farm go?" Josiah whispered at last.

"I didn't have the money for the taxes," Alice replied.

"You should not have lost it," he spoke accusingly.

"You didn't come back or send the money as you promised," Alice spoke defensively. "I could not sell enough furniture to cover the bills and the animals were already sold."

For the better part of an hour Josiah reverted to his former ways, berating her for the wrong choices she had made and for losing the farm. And surely on top of that, she must be doing a miserable job raising the children. On and on the litany expanded. *It*, whatever it was, was all her fault.

"But you never even let us know if you were alive," Alice interjected, protesting the harangue. Only a vague excuse of hush-hush work came forth from Josiah. He paused as the torrent of imagined failures slowed to a tickle.

"They killed him, you know," Alice spoke in a sad whisper after a lengthy silence, looking down at her work-worn hands in her lap.

"Who?"

"Gilbert Daye, your hired hand. You remember him. The mob tarred and feathered him so badly that he died. All because of you," she said accusingly, looking up at this man before her.

"I had nothing to do with that," he defended himself.

She rose. "I need to go to bed." She had no energy to argue.

He rose and pulled her to himself, wrapping his heavy arms tightly around her.

"Please, let me go," Alice whispered, worn down by the events of this evening. "I have to go to work soon."

Josiah gave no additional objections as Alice moved to extricate herself. He leaned over to give her a kiss but she slipped away from him and left the room quickly. She did not even undress, but pulled a cover over herself and lay awake on the bed until dawn's light penetrated the curtains. She berated herself for her lack of courage to stand up to Josiah. What might be ahead of them in the future? "Oh, Lord, I need your presence now," she whispered, extending her left hand to the empty space beside her.

Soon after dawn Penny and Alice moved quietly through the kitchen gathering their cloaks as they prepared to go to work. Each was lost in her own thoughts during the walk to the Talbot house. Even the usual chit-chat between them during the day was absent.

Alice felt deeply tired after work finished for the day. She dreaded the return to her sister's house. She even hoped Josiah might have left. Life was going along nicely without him. Why did he have to come back and complicate it all? The sleigh remained parked in the yard.

. . .

Each day followed the same pattern. Josiah stayed, spending his days storytelling, sleeping and eating with a rare trip around town in the sleigh. When Alice asked him about his secret mission he declared that it was in progress. For all his talk of high living he contributed nothing to the upkeep of his family or himself. Often acting as a stranger he was moody or remote. Other times the old familiar discontent with those around him produced criticism and demands to be waited upon. Since Alice and Penny were gone for hours on end, Midge outside caring for the animals and Horace either at studies or chopping wood, it fell to Susie to stop her spinning and cater to his wants. He seemed content with this life of leisure. Even Joan's outspoken criticism of his laziness affected him little other than causing him to put more pressure on his own family. The two of them were at an impasse.

He persuaded Joan he should sleep in the front room and insisted Alice sleep with him. Alice dreaded this fierce, painful contact as much as the sight of his daily presence. She worried about another pregnancy. It was difficult not to revert to her old reaction to him. She could not quite believe his professed love for her and his family nor could she see any evidence of it.

When news arrived in the spring of 1783 that the British had recognized the American independence with the Treaty of Paris, Josiah became depressed, his bravado now replaced with anger; anger against the Americans for winning and anger against the British for losing.

"I will not have us living here. We will leave on the first available boat for England to settle there," Josiah declared.

Alice dismissed the statement. It was full of hot air as so many statements had been. There was not enough money available for such a journey. Thus, she was doubly surprised to return home one night to be greeted by Horace exclaiming, "We're going on a boat. Papa said I could stay on deck and watch the sailors." He jumped around the room pretending to hoist sails and cast off ropes, ordering the younger girls to "look lively."

Alice looked at Josiah questioningly. Josiah shoved boat passage tickets into her hands to a place called Nova Scotia. They included ones for Josiah and Alice, Penny, Horace, Susie and Midge. There were none for Jeremy, Alice's sister Joan and her family nor their parents.

"Why this Nova Scotia?"

"Because I can get free land there."

"I don't want to go. Why do we have to?" Alice protested.

"Because we are not welcome here in this country," he answered. "I will not stay where I am not welcome."

"How can we go without Jeremy? Or my parents, or Joan and her family?" Alice was beside herself fearing this move to a strange land with Josiah.

"We will get settled and send for them later," Josiah pacified her.

"Where did you get the money for the tickets?" Alice asked suspiciously.

"From the drawer where you keep your money," he replied bluntly.

Alice walked into the bedroom and opened the drawer where she kept her extra money. Josiah had taken it all. Her shoulders sagged. She thought of all the day-in and day-out hours of work it took to earn these extra coins after she had paid Joan for food and necessities, extra that was allocated for emergencies and shoes for the children. She gripped the sides of the drawer.

"How could you take the money without consulting me?" she asked, trying to contain her anger.

"That money belongs to me as your husband," he said. "I do not need to consult you." Hurtful words but true.

"I don't want to go to that wilderness land. I'm needed here." Alice tried to change Josiah's mind.

"You are subject to my wishes. But — if you stay here the children go with me."

Alice gasped. The reality of his statement clutched her heart. Legally the children belonged to him and were subject to his rule. She could not let them go without her. They were still young. A debate raged within her. "What are my choices? I can stay here where my family has already suffered and been ostracized because we are labeled loyalists. It might even get worse for years, or maybe even generations. They need my help, too. Or do I go to this far off Nova Scotia with my children and work to create a new life and resurrected marriage with Josiah? He is my husband and I am expected to obey him and follow his direction. He is the father of the children and they are legally bound to be with their father for his support. Can our life together be better in that place? God, lead me, please," she begged silently. Angry tears rolled down her cheeks.

"Can we build a happy marriage in that place?" she asked.

"Of course. That is what I have wanted all along," he tried to reassure her. He put his heavy hands on her shoulders. "Alice, honor me in my decision," he commanded.

Still doubtful, Alice searched his eyes for the truth of his words that he truly cared for her and their children and that their life would be all right in a foreign land. She sighed, feeling tired and beaten. "I will," she whispered.

7

"*JUST LISTEN TO THIS ACCOUNT* by the King's Rangers of the Island of St. John," Josiah said enthusiastically, beginning to read from a pamphlet. "'The soil is good, the harbors spacious, safe and numerous. The waters abound with shell and fish. The taxes are few, the government mild and the lands finely situated and reasonable in price. Cattle are plentiful.' That story about starvation is nonsense."

"Starvation!" Alice exclaimed.

"That is just a scare tactic by the Whigs," Josiah explained. "With all that fish, no one will go hungry. Besides, it says here 'the mere necessities for subsistence are there.' There are great business opportunities for saw mills, especially to set up a lumber business with the West Indies, or fisheries just waiting to be started. Cattle and poultry are cheaper than on Long Island," he continued reading. "We will even get paid by the British government."

"Is that where we are going?" Alice asked, still doubtful.

"We'll go to Nova Scotia first. It should be about the same. If not, we'll move on," Josiah responded.

Alice and Josiah talked far into the night. Hundreds of questions and details regarding the move to Nova Scotia occupied the entire conversation. Josiah kept reassuring Alice that everything would go well. "There will be plenty of work for me in a growing settlement. You will see. Do not worry," he said.

Alice was still reluctant. "There's ice in the rivers. 'Tis still early spring. What will we do for money? Where will we live? Why are you in such a rush? We should think it over carefully."

"I have thought about it. It is the best move to make," Josiah replied crossly. "Stop worrying," he repeated. "Just go to sleep," he said, turning over to end the conversation.

"Do not worry," Alice repeated sarcastically to herself. She lay rigidly, thinking about what she had to do. Her thoughts became tangled as the weariness of a long day of work took over her body and sleep won the night.

Wednesday morning Alice and Penny walked to Mistress Talbot's house, entering the kitchen via the back garden entrance. Alice instructed Penny to begin peeling potatoes and carrots for pot pie, while she went upstairs to advise her employer about the startling change of plans. She knocked on the door to the bedroom.

"Come in," Mistress Talbot called.

Alice entered the room where her employer sat at her desk writing in her journal. "Good morning, Mistress Talbot. I have some distressing news. Penny and I will be leaving for Nova Scotia this coming Friday. My husband purchased tickets for the boat. Today will be our last day." She took a deep breath. "I am so sorry to leave you on such short notice."

"Leaving? What am I to do now?" Mistress Talbot exclaimed, annoyed. She had come to rely fully on Alice to plan, prepare and present three tasty meals and a bountiful tea every day.

"I am so sorry," Alice repeated the apology. "I have no other choice." Feeling a deep sense of obligation to the job she began to waver in her decision. She was close to tears. "Perhaps you could ask Mistress Hardy. She has helped me sometimes when we've had to prepare for a lot of guests," she suggested.

"I will try," Mistress Talbot said with a pout, closing her journal with a snap.

Alice returned to the kitchen and stood beside Penny busy chopping onions on the table. She gave her daughter a kiss on the cheek then put on a cape and took the pail off the hook to draw water from the outside well. The cold air felt good on her hot cheeks. Much as she would like to linger, she hurried back into the house, for there was so much more she wanted to accomplish.

All day and far into the evening mother and daughter worked steadily, cooking and baking. Alice prepared as many dishes as possible in advance to ease the strain that would be caused by their leaving. Late in the afternoon Mistress Talbot came into the kitchen with Mistress Hardy who had agreed to take over, at least temporarily.

When Penny finished scrubbing the last pot, hung the tea towels on the wall hook and picked up the broom Alice again left the kitchen to find Mistress Talbot.

"We are leaving now, Mistress Talbot," she said with a catch in her voice. "I have prepared food to last you for a few days. 'Tis in the spring cooler. I have truly enjoyed working for you and I thank you for giving us the work. I wish you well in the future," she added, preparing to leave.

"We thank you," Mistress Talbot said. "You have kept us well fed and done an admirable job. Please take this," she said, putting coins in Alice's hands. "It is your last pay — and a little extra," she added, giving Alice's hands a tight, grateful squeeze. "I wish you well, too," she said in uncharacteristically warm tones.

"Goodbye," Alice whispered, turning to leave the room quickly. This family had been kind to her. She put the coins in her pocket and went back to the kitchen to join Penny for the walk home. It had been a long, tiresome day.

A late spring snowstorm drifted down upon them, obscuring the homes beside the road. Even the trees appeared as ghostly shadows. It seemed indicative of her emotions. This was the moment of transition — the instant in time during change when one is leaving the old and entering the new.

The house was dark, the family asleep as Alice and Penny tip-toed through the kitchen. Each found their way to bed and to quick sleep. Tomorrow would be an even busier day sorting and packing for the trip ahead.

Morning came early as each family member rushed around to demand Alice's attention. "May I take this?" was the usual question. No's and yes's were the short answers. Horace wanted to be sure the dancing man was packed and his father said no. "Why not" was answered with the loud words "because I told you no." Alice felt like a defendant's lawyer pleading before a judge on the bench. Josiah prevailed. He also reminded Alice to hand him their last pay coins.

By evening the packing had been completed. A hearty supper preceded early bedtimes for they needed to rise well before dawn. Alice sat up with a start, reached for her wrapper and got out of bed.

"Where are you going?" Josiah asked.

"I've got to write Jeremy," Alice whispered. She felt her way into the kitchen, lit a candle and sat at the table with paper and pen.

April, 1783

Jeremy, my dear son, how I long to see you. When you return and read this letter, your father and I, Penny, Horace, Susie and Midge will be in Nova Scotia. The arrangements are made for us to leave on a ship sailing tomorrow, Fri. I wish you would join us there. However, you are a man now, doing a man's work and the decision must be made by you. You do have a home here with your aunt, uncle, cousins and grandparents who love you and care for you dearly. I am so proud of you. Always know your family loves you. Remember what I told you when you left for your first sailing trip: Before you go to sleep imagine that I am sending a good night kiss across the miles to you, my dear boy. I will continue to send you my love and a kiss every night until I hold you in my arms again. God will keep you safe

Your loving Mama

In the morning last-minute scurrying to gather all their goods threatened to delay the ride to the dock.

"Hurry up," Josiah called, seated next to Joan's third son on the wagon.

Numerous hugs, kisses and tears added to the delay. The possibility of a likely permanent separation gripped Alice and Joan as they embraced, patting each other's back, trying to be stalwart for the other. "I'll see you again soon when you join us in Nova Scotia," Alice whispered hopefully. Would they ever meet again?

Too emotional for words, she embraced her father, kissing his cheeks and rubbing tears from her face on his long leisure coat.

Mother Lewis insisted on riding with them, holding Midge tightly in her lap.

As Josiah supervised the loading of the trunks on board the 30-ton vessel bound for Portland, Maine to pick up more passengers, Alice clung to her mother. Would she ever see her again? She looked frail and aged as she kissed her goodbye.

"I want to stay with you, Grandmama," Susie cried, clinging to her grandmother's waist.

"You just go along with your Mama, dear. Grandpapa and I will try to join you before summer ends," she pledged, her eyes misted with tears, as Alice pried Susie's arms from their tight grip.

Herding her children like sheep before her Alice prodded them to walk up the gangplank of the ship. Even Horace's exuberance diminished as Alice and the children stood against the rail waving goodbye to her mother, who stood rooted to the dock waving and waving until they left her sight.

The family was directed to climb down a ladder to cramped quarters below deck. Josiah led the way to a cleared section amidships where their trunks had been placed. Other families and single men continually climbed down the ladder and claimed a spot of decking for themselves. Lanterns hung from the rafters at sparse intervals to provide some weak lighting. The largest square of natural light came from the opening above the ladder. Josiah took Horace up to the main deck to observe all the activity of boarding and casting off while Alice directed Penny, Susie and Midge to lay quilts down for sitting and sleeping. She placed the food hamper, prepared by Mother Lewis, next to the trunks.

The girls soon became acquainted with two other young girls, Maryann Collum, seven, and her sister Joyce, five, who settled next to the Marshes. Alice introduced herself to their mother, Mary, a small plump woman. She listened as Mary chattered on and on about her family's life on Cape Cod where John, her husband, had managed a sawmill. They were fortunate to have relatives already living in St. John, Nova Scotia who were going to shelter them and help them become established.

Alice noticed that Mary kept her hands in the pockets of her skirt. When she needed to use them it was possible to see there was some deformity, some gnarling of the bones. Politely trying not to notice, yet ashamed she was aware of it, Alice soon forgot to think about it. It just became part of this new acquaintance.

Bells rang, the call to "heave ho" sounded, the wood and roping creaked as the ship swung away from the dock. Frightened by the unfamiliar movement, Susie and Midge clung onto Alice. Alice lost her balance at the unexpected movement and all three fell sideways over the trunk. She had never been on a ship before either!

At noontime Josiah and Horace descended the ladder, zigzagging their way between a boat half full of people. Their faces glowed from the fresh air exposure, eyes dancing with excitement of the adventure they were embarking upon. There was so much to tell.

Introductions were made with fellow passengers and with John Collum, a large burly man with a bushy black beard. Heads nodded in recognition as similar versions of the same hardships they had suffered as Tories were recited.

"I worked for the crown in the duty office and was harassed or beaten every day until I was rescued by a family who hid me on their farm," one said bitterly.

"We were provincial soldiers in the regiments," chimed in several.

"Our property was confiscated and sold. We never received anything for it."

"My husband was put in the horrible Simsbury mine prison in Connecticut."

"Well, my husband was hung!" a woman chimed in with a sob.

"We owned some property the local sheriff wanted," Josiah said harshly.

"Me? I was loyal to the British crown and church," spoke another, "and proud of it."

"Hear Hear," were echoing refrains.

"What about you?"

The litany continued. They were all bound by a common purpose: to escape from the pressure of being Tories in America. They would settle in Nova Scotia, a place where they could practice their own beliefs in the rightness of the king to rule and the Church of England as well as receive land to replace property they had lost.

"I'm hungry," Susie whined, pulling on her mother's skirt.

"So am I," chimed in Horace.

"'Tis time to eat," Alice acknowledged.. "Sit here," she commanded, motioning to the quilts laid on the decking. She opened the hamper and took out bread, cheese and dried fish, cut off some pieces and handed them to her family before passing the brown jug of cider. She herself did not feel much like eating as the ship moved to and fro. Thankfully the noise of reverberating voices had diminished as more people took time to eat.

By mid afternoon Midge yawned as her eyelids drooped. Alice sat leaning back against the trunk and pulled Midge's head onto her lap, covering her little one with a quilt. Alice closed her own eyes. She was so very tired and did not want to listen to the chatter of the Collums and Josiah, or any other passengers, as they recounted their life stories. Besides, her stomach was not very happy with the side-to-side voyage it was getting.

· · ·

In the crowded quarters of the passenger deck, families looked after each other. Routines of eating and sleeping became regular. The constant hum of voices during the day and the obnoxious smell of puke and unwashed bodies assaulted the senses. The men gathered together, embellishing their stories, while the women and girls kept busy with hand work or cleaning up after vomits or emptying chamber pots out a porthole into the ocean. The little children roved about freely unless going topside with a parent (generally frowned upon by the crew). Privacy was minimal.

Late on the third day out, as Alice reached into the bottom of the food hamper, she felt a hard object wrapped in one of her old aprons. When she unwrapped it she found the dancing man.

"Oh, dear Mama," she whispered, tears blurring her eyes. She remembered her mother had insisted she alone pack the hamper. It had been her opportunity to circumvent Josiah's dictate and express this act of love for her grandson. Alice rewrapped the toy and placed it carefully in the bottom of the hamper again, vowing not to speak about it even to Horace.

She sat on a quilt, wrapping another around her shoulders. Tears flowed down her cheeks. Spasms of grief swept over her. She missed the old life at the Marsh farm even with all the hardships and worry. She missed her family back home. Most of all she missed Jeremy. Before, they would see him when he returned home for a few days after weeks at sea. Now they had left him behind. Would she ever see him again?

"Are you all right?" Mary Collum tenderly inquired, bending over Alice.

Alice looked up at her. "I'm not feeling too well," she admitted, blowing her nose and wiping the tears away. How could there be any more tears within her? It seemed she had already cried an ocean full in her thirty-four years. "I miss my son, my parents, my sister and her family. I miss home. I miss dry land, sunrises, work, everything." Alice felt miserable.

Mary sat down beside Alice, putting her arm around her shoulder. Alice looked at her, surprised by this empathetic act, then let her head rest on the extended arm.

"Just go to sleep," Mary crooned. "I'll watch the children for you."

"Thank you," Alice whispered, as she curled up by the hamper and closed her eyes.

She was aware off and on of Mary shushing the children. She even thought she heard her shush Josiah when he wanted Alice to do something.

When Alice awoke, daylight was gone. High above the deck opening stars twinkled in the night sky. Midge lay curled beside her sound asleep. Alice could see the other children and Josiah seated by the Collums. She twisted around and sat up. Her hand had fallen asleep and begun to tingle. Her movement alerted the rest of the family and they moved aside to make room for her to join them.

The next day she took advantage of the ship docking in Portland to join Mary on the deck above for a breath of fresh air.

"Sometimes I feel like one of those scorched timbers," she confessed, pointing to the upper reaches of the town where the lifting fog revealed blackened remnants of buildings still evident from the burning by the British in 1775. "Burnt but still standing."

"Um," Mary responded, tucking her arm around Alice's waist.

Alice turned to look at her. "You don't seem to be as upset at leaving for a wild place as I am," she said enviously.

Mary thought a moment then replied. "Not really. As long as I'm with John and the girls I don't mind where I am. Besides, my aunt and uncle will be there and they are my family, too. They raised me since I was six when my parents died."

"How fortunate you are to have them," Alice replied. She turned to look at the new construction of rebuilding evident in the town, reminding herself that she too could rebuild her life again with God's help. A ray of sunshine bursting through the fog turned the water around them to twinkling jewels and she smiled in response. "Thank you," she spoke out loud, smiled at Mary and squeezed her arm.

. . .

Five days later the ship docked in the harbor at St. John, Nova Scotia. The unloading process of people, animals, luggage and freight occupied hours. In the close confines of the crowded quarters of the ship the Marshes and Collum families had developed a quick friendship, a friendship that encouraged the Collums to invite the Marshes to stay with them in St. John.

"Follow us," John Collum shouted, motioning toward a wagon farther down the dock. Alice and Josiah struggled to keep the children close by them in the confusion of unloading booms, shouts, jostles and the crush of wagons milling about the dock.

A large elderly man stood by a hay wagon holding the lead horse by the reins. He greeted the Collums warmly then turned expectantly to be introduced to the Marsh family.

"Mary and I insist again that you stay with us for a few days till you get your bearings," John determinedly said to Alice and Josiah. "You agree don't you, Uncle John?" he questioned the driver, already assuming a positive answer.

"We accept," Josiah said, ignoring Alice's reluctance to be so dependent upon this family. He was already hoisting trunks and hampers and the youngest children into the wagon bed. The women crowded in as the men and Horace walked alongside.

"Giddap." Uncle John snapped the reins and the two horses began a slow walk away from the dock toward a house a mile away. Recent rains had turned the streets to slick mud rivulets, making the trip doubly difficult for the animals and walkers alike.

"Come in. Come in," Mary's Aunt Martha — quickly covering her surprise at the unexpected number of people — greeted them all with warm hospitality just as if Alice, Josiah and their children were members of her own family.

"We don't want to impose," Alice began.

"Nonsense," Aunt Martha overrode Alice's politeness. "Just call me Aunt Martha."

"My name is Martha, too," Midge chimed in.

"Well, aren't we lucky to have the same name," Aunt Martha replied, putting her arm around Midge's shoulder as they walked into the house. "You stay here as long as you need," she continued, leading the way up narrow stairs.

"Thank you," Alice replied warmly as they were led to a bedroom under the eaves. She arranged quilts on the floor for the children to sleep on close by the small bed she and Josiah would occupy. Mary and her family were to occupy a similar room next to theirs.

At the children's bedtime Alice listened to their prayers. She added a prayer of thanks for their warm welcome to St. John. She had been dreading the unknown more than she thought she would.

The adults spent the evening listening to the stories recounted by Uncle John and Aunt Martha. They had evacuated from besieged Boston in March, 1777 aboard a fleet of ships carrying 900 people to Nova Scotia. They were cared for in barracks, given fuel, furniture and even some money till they were able to purchase this property. It had been a hard existence at first in this harsher climate but they persisted, though many of the original group had become disillusioned and left. In the intervening years they had created a home surrounded by young apple orchards, "You can make it work if you continue to put in the effort and do not let yourself be discouraged," Uncle John advised them.

Josiah and John left early the next morning to secure work. It was late in the day when they returned.

"We were hired on by a company leaving tomorrow for a new settlement up river at St. Ann's Point. There is plenty of carpentry work there," Josiah explained to Alice.

"Are you well enough for that kind of work?" Alice asked, as she looked at Josiah's poor physical condition.

"Of course, I am," he responded, surprised she would even question it. "Besides, former Provincial soldiers will be given acreage, tools and food at St. Ann's Point. When I get there and secure my land I will send for you. It should not be long." He spoke excitedly about the prospects for the future.

"But you weren't a soldier," Alice stated worriedly.

"No, but the help I did in England will be reckoned on," he reminded her. Alice had not seen him this excited for many, many years. It gave her hope for bright days ahead. "I'm glad," she said doubtfully, yet truly pleased he was enthusiastic again. She opened the trunk, took out his clothes and tied them together with a rope. She rummaged in the bottom of the trunk pulling out a hammer, drill, saw and plane, tools Uncle Amos had been wise enough to retrieve from the barn when they left the farm.

"Do you have any money left for food?" Alice asked.

"I have what is left of your pay."

"May I have some to pay for food here?" Alice questioned.

"I should keep it with me for board and food till I get some money ahead," Josiah replied. "You will be fine here until I can bring you to me. You are entitled to food from the government so rely on that."

"I feel badly imposing upon John and Martha," Alice said with a worried look.

"They have offered so let them help," Josiah said callously.

His grasping attitude surprised her. She was still trying to reconcile this husband of hers to the man she had married. Before, he would have been reticent about accepting any favors. Now his attitude seemed to be that life owed him anything and everything he was able to get.

The men left and the days settled into a crowded routine.

. . .

"Mama, I don't feel well," Susie whispered, shaking her mother's shoulder one morning before dawn. Alice stirred, trying to open her eyes to see her daughter.

"Crawl in bed with me," she said. Her daughter felt hot with fever. Alice lit the candle and checked Susie. Red spots covered her body. Measles!

Within two days all the children in the house were fussing with fevers from measles. They must have contracted them from someone on the boat. Aunt Martha, Mary and Alice trotted repeatedly up and down the stairs tending the children with cold compresses, water, homemade lotions and food frequently augmented from street kitchens. Uncle John ran errands and drew continuous pails of water from the well. Some children were sicker than others but the whole household suffered.

Just as the worst seemed over and recovery was almost at hand another round of illness began. This time it was mumps. First one child, then another. Except for Midge it passed among all the children.

In late June Alice woke early one morning to the chirping of birds in the orchard behind the house. She looked over at her children sound asleep by her bed. No fussing, no rashes, no swollen glands. It was over. She eased out of bed, put on her dress and tiptoed down the stairs to the kitchen. Uncle John had stirred the fire and put a kettle of water on to boil.

"Good morning," he said with a low voice.

"Good morning," Alice whispered back.

"I thought I heard you come down," Mary whispered from the doorway. "Can you believe it? They're all well."

"Seems too good to be true," Alice said. "We should have a party to celebrate."

"Why not? Let's have a picnic," Mary spoke enthusiastically. "We could all use an outing."

Aunt Martha soon joined them and the three women talked excitedly, planning a picnic for later in the day. Even Uncle John added his ideas.

The children trooped down stairs one by one, wakened by the sun and energized with well being, unaware of the conspiratorial activities of the women.

Near noontime Uncle John shouted from outside, "Who wants to go on a wagon ride?"

"We do!" the children shouted back, racing to dash out the door.

"Be careful," their mothers called, waving to them. "You older ones watch the little ones," Mary cautioned.

"We will," Penny called back.

"Off we go," Uncle John shouted, flicking the reins as the horses moved down the lane.

As soon as they were out of sight, the women loaded hampers with food, plates and cups and walked to the far end of the orchard, spreading their surprise under the developing apples.

The excited voices of children heralded the approach of the wagon. The pitch rose higher when they saw the food laid on the blankets.

"A picnic! Hooray!" the younger ones shouted, climbing down and racing over to join the women.

Everyone had a wonderful time sitting together and eating. During a moment of lull after the meal, Alice opened their hamper and took out the object wrapped in her old apron and handed it to Horace. He unwrapped it hurriedly then gasped with delight when he saw the dancing man. "Oh, Mama," he said in surprise. He held the man lovingly, slowly beginning to make him dance. Everyone began to clap accompanying the rat-a-tat movements as the tiny man danced faster and faster.

Eventually, Alice asked Horace to cease. His eyes glowed with pleasure and contentment as he gently wrapped the dancing man in the apron, holding it close. He shyly slipped his free hand in Alice's as they walked back to the house. "Thank you, Mama," he said softly.

"Thank Grandmama Lewis," Alice said, smiling at her son. She was proud of his talent and his loving reaction. Maybe she should have been forthright with Josiah about the toy but she felt Horace needed to have it and she was glad she had it to give him. The double surprises of the day filled her with joy.

· · ·

The summer passed with no word from the men.

Returning dusty and hot from a September day spent picking apples, they were surprised to see John and Josiah seated in the kitchen. In the confusion Alice noticed Horace retrieve the beloved dancing man from a shelf and slip out of the room. She understood his concern to hide it from his father.

"Papa, when did you get here? What's the word about our home?" Multiple questions bombarded the men.

"Whoa, one at a time," John held up his hands in mock defense. "We came to take you up river to St. Ann's Point to your new homes."

A barrage of more questions ensued. The details were finalized for a move in two days up river to this new place, John explained. "I am entitled to a lot of 100 acres and 50 extra acres for each additional family member as a civilian refugee. We have been granted building materials: an ax, a spade, a hoe and a plow and we have ten years without paying rent to make it work," he explained further. In their off hours from work at a saw mill, he and Josiah had quickly cleared just enough land to build a small log house for John's family. Then he and Josiah had begun to fell trees on the property granted to Josiah as a former soldier. In the future John would help on that house.

"What is the place like?" Alice queried Josiah.

"Well, it has plenty of acres with a nice view close to the river south of the town that is being developed. I have three years to clear the land, get a house built on the property and begin farming. For now we will use a tent until I can build a house," he answered. "You will soon make it a home," he reassured her. The thought of owning land, and a lot of it, fueled his energy. He never referred to his acquiring land in the guise of a former soldier and Alice did not pursue it.

Once again, the men piled the baggage on the wagon for the trip to the dock. What other supplies did they need? What about a food source? There were hundreds of questions with few answers. The unknown loomed over the preparations.

It was particularly difficult saying "goodbye" and "thank you" to Aunt Martha and Uncle John for their generous hospitality. Reversing the journey of the previous trip five months before, Uncle John urged the horses to carry the full wagon to the dock. The balmy autumn weather, leafy trees in various shades of brilliant colors and yielding garden crops indicated the passage of time.

The two families found places to sit on the river sailboat amidst building supplies, trunks, boxes, animals and assorted miscellaneous odds and ends. Alice held Susie and Midge tightly by their hands. She feared they might fall overboard if she let go for even a moment. She begged Josiah to watch Penny and Horace. This trip did not seem to be an adventure worthy of excitement.

Five days later they tied up at a landing at St. Ann's Point where the two families parted. Josiah led his family, weighed down with two trunks and a wicker hamper, along a rutted road past tents or houses under construction. Alice and the children asked at each, "Is it this one?" The answer was always "no." Nearly two miles down the road Josiah at last stopped before a lot thickly covered with trees. A tiny clearing had been cut away to accommodate a large white army tent slightly askew from a recent wind storm.

"Here we are," he said, proudly waving toward the lot with its lopsided tent. "Come, let us go in." He led the way, lifting the flap and stepping inside.

It took some moments before their eyes adjusted to the dim light.

Alice slowly turned around, her eyes taking in the cobwebs in the corners, the dirt floor, the slugs clinging to the walls. A shivering shudder ran through her. "I hate slugs," she announced to no one in particular. A dust-covered table top set on two saw horses enclosed by two benches stood near the middle by the upright center pole. She looked dismayed at Josiah.

"It will be home for just a little while until I cut enough logs to build us a grander place," he said, anticipating Alice's concerns. "And there is a good brook running through the lot," he added.

"Mama, you should see back here," Horace stuck his head under the back flap of the tent. "There's some great trees for climbing back here."

Alice looked at his excited young face. She had a choice to make: to create a cheerful home or a bitter one. She smiled back at her son. "Just don't try to fly from one of them," she reminded him.

"Penny, girls, help me get this place cleaned up. Horace, go help your father bring in the trunks and hamper, then fetch wood and water," Alice commanded, moving briskly to remove her hat and gloves. Another involuntary shiver ran through her as she surveyed the slugs. "Ugh! God, why slugs?" she whispered the question before she added a "thank you" for their safe arrival.

Josiah looked at her with relief. "Come, Horace, let us do as we are told," he said, leading the way out the entrance.

8

"HALLOO," A VOICE CALLED, preceding the figures of Mary and her daughters walking across the rough ground from the road. Alice straightened up from the patch of green beans planted in irregular furrows between the tree stumps, wiped the perspiration off her face with her arm and clapped the dirt off her rough hands.

"I'm so glad to see you, Mary. And you too, Maryann and Joyce. You're growing up as fast as these beans," she said, motioning to the garden patches. "Susie and Midge, Maryann and Joyce are here. Come on out," she called. Her younger daughters dashed out of the tent, delighted to stop their chores. "Run and play," Alice waved toward the stumps. "Mary, what's wrong?" she asked, noticing her tear-stained face, diminished figure and pale complexion.

"I'm hot, with child again and furious!" Mary said vehemently, letting more tears run down her cheeks. "I've already lost four babies and I'm scared this might be the fifth."

"You have two that survived. This one might too," Alice said, trying to be encouraging.

"I know."

"Let's have a drink of switchel," Alice said. She linked her arm with Mary's and led the way to the open flap in front of the tent.

"Penny, will you please bring out the switchel and the dipper," Alice called. She watched her oldest daughter come out of the tent. Nearly sixteen, Penny was no longer a child but not yet a fully grown woman either. Her arms and legs were long, her skinny body moving awkwardly in a dress far too short for her. "I must get some material to sew another dress for her," Alice thought to herself. Funny, but she had not noticed before how much her daughter had grown. She always seemed too busy to really notice any of the changes in the children.

The women sat on a log placed across two stumps before the tent and watched the children play tag across the stumped lot.

"Why are you so angry?" Alice asked after a few moments of silence.

"Would you believe that the pastor met us on the way over here and scolded me for not having my hands busy as I walked? I know we're supposed to, but he never even asked me why. 'Idle hands are the devil's workshop' he kept repeating." She sighed. "I can't do sewing or knitting or tatting or even mending very well and my hands ache all the time." Looking at the gnarled hands in her lap she wailed, "If I could just get a few hours to let them rest!" Trying to regain her composure, she said, "Ummmm, this switchel is delicious. What do you use to make it?"

"I mix water, sugar, molasses, vinegar and ginger together in a jug, then we store it in the brook to keep it cool," Alice responded.

"Can you believe we live in New Brunswick now instead of Nova Scotia? Uncle John's efforts to create our own province separate from Nova Scotia really worked and we are actually living in the capital of the new province. Anyway, I want to see how the new house is coming along," Mary said in a better mood. She pointed to the horizontally planked walls of a post-and-beam house partially constructed next to the tent on the property.

"Come and I'll show you," Alice said, pulling her friend to the entrance of their house in progress. "This will be the everyday room," she explained, waving her arm toward the empty space with a stacked stone fireplace in the center. "The fireplace has a brick side oven too. Over here will be a bedroom." She walked off an invisible wall with a doorway. "The loft stairs will curve up here around the fireplace and there will be two rooms above, the larger for the girls and a smaller one for Horace and Jeremy, if he comes," she said hopefully. "We'll have a back door as well and ten windows in all. I'm hoping Josiah gets it roofed and shingled before winter comes, even if we do not get the glass in the windows. At least we can live inside with a fireplace and more room. There will even be a well near the back door," she exclaimed enthusiastically. "We already have the lean-to built for the cow and pig behind the house."

Alice was eager to get the house completed. Josiah was not content to have a log house that could be built quickly. He wanted to have a modern post and beam one. She recalled one Saturday afternoon in the spring when as many as twenty fellow workers and neighbors had appeared ready to hoist the rafters and lift the ridge pole in place. At the successful positioning of the ridge pole the men pounded on the frame shouting, "calling for wood." The master carpenter in charge of the raising cut down a young conifer and carried it back to the house where it was hoisted up and nailed in place on the beam. A prayer honoring the sacrifice of the wood was proclaimed by Josiah.

A limber fellow sitting on the ridge pole called down, "What will its name be?"

"Reunion," called Josiah, throwing up a bottle of rum.

"Reunion it is," the ridge sitter declared dramatically, ceremoniously smashing the bottle on the pole.

Even though the government furnished plenty of nails to finish the job, since that day Josiah's attitude toward developing the property and completing the house was erratic and lethargic and John had given up trying to help. Alice tried to be patient with Josiah, for she realized he was tired from working all day at the lumber mill to earn money, but she was impatient and there were many times she wished she was a man so that she could do the house building herself to complete it. Surely the house could be finished before winter came again. It would be too hard on all of them to spend another winter in the tent as they had this past year.

The past winter had been especially arduous. It had been particularly difficult trudging a path through the deep snow and breaking ice in the brook to draw a pail of water. Snow had been piled against the tent to keep out the wind, though she had worried it would get too heavy and collapse the tent. She and Josiah had taken turns heating boards by the fire to put under the children for warmth as they slept. It took constant energy to keep a fire going inside the tent. Beside that, food was scarce and they were always hungry. Many people in the settlement died of hunger or exposure. Josiah had to help dig graves with an ax in the frozen ground.

Horace gained expertise making the wooden man dance, entertaining them some evenings as they huddled around the fire. Josiah did not grumble too much at Alice about the toy her mother had slipped in the food basket, conceding Horace was good. When possible other relief came by attending church services.. At one nooning[4] break between sermons she had boldly spoken up in protest when people had railed against new arrivals to the area who did not adopt the beliefs and stance they held. "Did we not have to leave our homes because of attitudes just like this? We should act better than they did and welcome everybody," she had stated. There was no one who spoke up to agree with her, including Josiah, who chastised her for being so bold. Even this soon after arriving in St. Ann most people banded together jealously guarding their old thoughts and habits, closing ranks in this community against strangers. She had to keep reminding herself to be patient, to keep a bright outlook on the future.

As soon as snow had melted in the spring the children helped her scrape the accumulated dead leaves off the ground in order to break the packed earth with the hoe, for there was no room for a plow to operate between the stumps. During the summer her garden work, as well as the usual family-keeping duties, kept her busy every day, leaving little time to interact with people even if she had had the opportunity. For the most part there was minimal contact with friends and neighbors.

"By the way, I came to invite you and Josiah to our house for tea next Saturday after work to meet the new owners of the mill," Mary said, interrupting Alice's reverie as they walked back to the tent.

Alice looked surprised. "I didn't know the mill was sold. Josiah never mentioned it."

"They arrived last week. Their name is Hollis, and they have a young son who will take over one day, I suppose," Mary explained. "The tea invitation is for all of you," Mary said excitedly. "All the workers and their families will be coming I expect. Hopefully the weather will be nice for the children to play outdoors." She hesitated. "I wonder if you would bring a few batches of your delicious scones. They are so tasty and it would help me out so much. Also, would Penny be able to help serve?"

"I'll be glad to bring the scones and I am sure Penny can serve. Horace can help watch the younger ones outside," Alice said. How exciting it would be to go to a party. Providing some of the food was the neighborly thing to do. "Penny, would you be willing to help Mistress Collum serve tea next Saturday?" she called to her daughter.

"Yes, Mama," was the reply.

"Fine. Penny, if you can come by noon I would appreciate it," Mary said. "Thank you for the drink. It was a cool treat for this hot day. Come children," she commanded, starting the walk up the dirt road toward her home, her girls kicking up dust clouds as they skipped alongside her.

Alice walked into her tent home. She stopped and looked about in the filtered light. Within this limited space she had tried to create a home, a place of welcome and security for her family. With quilts strung on ropes she divided it into sleeping and living sections. The sleeping sections were separated into adult and children's quarters.

Susie's tall spinning wheel stood in the living section, along with the scrubbed and heavily waxed table. She had spent many spare minutes waxing the cherry wood with oil from sweet marjoram and lavender. It had been a way to bring a touch of elegance to this tent home. Two candles in tin holders sat on the table. A bench stood on each side. A separate bench along one wall held dishes, wooden utensils and bowls, two cast-iron frying pans, her brass pot, the family Bible, a pail of water and a jar of wild flowers picked by Midge. The trunks held their clothes. Someday they would be able to sleep on beds in the new house, but for now more quilts provided a soft place to sleep. Usually they were too tired at the end of the day to care if they were sleeping on the ground or a bed. Once the weather turned warmer she and Penny cooked on the fire pit outside the front flap, and she admitted to herself that they produced miracles with it.

Working together to survive in this wilderness seemed to break down the barriers between Alice and Josiah. There was an ease in their relationship that had never been there before. Even Josiah's demands and criticisms lessened and Alice began to believe their future would be brighter as a couple.

During the winter she became pregnant again but realized something was wrong. One morning she either fainted or slipped on an icy patch at the brook, striking her head on an obscured rock and losing consciousness in the snow. It was some time before Penny came looking for her and helped her struggle back to the tent. Soon after she miscarried the baby. It was early spring before she began to feel well and even now she was overly tired some days.

When Josiah came home Alice told him about the tea. He said he had forgotten to tell her about the new owners. He said it did not make any difference to him as long as he had a job, but today he was still morose and angry because John Collum had been promoted to the position of foreman two weeks ago and not he, Josiah; the fact that John had more experience meant little and the more Josiah spoke of it the angrier he became.

"We are not going to any tea at the Collum house," he stated vehemently.

"You can stay home, but the children and I are going. Mary needs the scones and our help. It is the least we can do to repay her family for all the help they have given us," Alice declared.

Josiah looked at her with astonishment. He seldom saw this display of independence that Alice had acquired while he was away during the war. He was not pleased with it.

"Do I have to go?" Horace questioned when told of being volunteered to help watch the young children. "I don't want to watch a bunch of noisy girls," he protested.

"Yes, you must," Alice said firmly, closing any further discussion about it.

Early afternoon on the day of the party Josiah arrived home from work and washed up. He agreed to accompany Alice but informed her that they would only stay long enough to put in an appearance. It was late afternoon when the family walked in silence up the road to Mary and John's house. Penny had left earlier, carrying the scones in a pine needle basket. Her dress was still short even after Alice had let down the hem as far as possible and trimmed it with ribbon to hide the old fold line.

Inside the Collum log home the late afternoon sunlight was transferred to the softened candle lights hung on wall sconces. The smell of sweets and the hum of many voices gave an air of excitement to the scene. John introduced them to the Hollises. Mr. Hollis appeared to be a reticent man as he stood stiffly by the fireplace giving only perfunctory greetings to the guests. Alice sensed Josiah's mood change as Mistress Hollis turned around and looked at them. Before them stood a slender figure dressed in a pale green watered silk dress that enhanced the blond curls framing a fair-skinned face and wide, green-blue eyes. Her face showed surprise, then a smile of welcome as she looked at Josiah. Her eyes turned smoky blue as she said a cool "hello" to Alice, glancing at her dress almost with disdain, before she turned her eyes again to Josiah.

Then, putting her arm through his, she led him to the punch table. It almost seemed they knew each other.

Alice felt a wave of jealousy and inferiority rise up within. She had spent an hour late last night turning up the hem to hide the frayed edges of the best dress she had, a gray dress handed down from Mistress Talbot. As a result the skirt was too short to be fashionable and revealed her dusty black shoes. She felt dumpy, dowdy and abandoned. She stood briefly with Mr. Hollis before the awkward silence propelled her to find Mary and offer her help, anything to get over this mixed-up mood she was in.

The hours passed. Alice expected Josiah to declare that they must leave soon, but each time she caught his eye for that indication he only shook his head no and turned back to listen to something else Mistress Hollis was saying. The Marshes were the last to leave. All the way home Josiah raved about the many fine attributes Mistress Hollis possessed, ones that Alice would do well to acquire. His reaction irritated Alice, yet at the same time she was most angry at him for being so flagrant about this quick infatuation.

For the next few weeks Josiah worked zealously on their house, somehow invigorated and inspired. Outside, the rest of the wall clapboard planking was nailed in place and the roof shingled. Inside, vertical planked walls enclosed the fireplace and chimney wall separating the rooms upstairs and down. A small entry way had been created at the foot of the steep stairs and a door placed to close off the bedroom. In the future they might be able to afford to plaster inside on the exterior walls. That wish was second in line to window glass. For now, greased paper and shutters would keep out the rain and cold.

By the end of September they marched as a family in single file from the tent into their new space, each one carrying their own favorite item. How spacious it seemed after the confinement of the tent. "I'm so happy to have the fireplace for cooking inside," she exclaimed to the girls. "Look, even the rope beds are in place." She called out the door, "Josiah and Horace, please bring in the table and benches and put them here on the floor." She was lucky to have a wooden floor, not just a packed earthen one. It was one thing she had insisted upon before they moved in.

Alice and the girls lovingly spread the family quilts around. She opened the trunks and handed out their clothes to hang on pegs attached to the walls. A moment of fond remembrance came over her as she lifted out the blue and white teacup and saucer that had belonged to Mother Marsh. She recalled the many items and furniture sold or left at the farm when they fled in the night so long ago. Why did she have to be the one to lose everything? She sighed. It was a choice she had made to keep her family together. Even if they had stayed they would have lost it all to the tax collectors. Her family was far, far more valuable than any piece of shaped wood. She lovingly placed the teacup and saucer in the middle of the table, now with permanent legs.

"Wait!" Penny ran to get a tatted doily she had finished for her hope chest returning to spread it under the saucer. They stood admiring the elegant picture it made on the highly waxed table. Midge retrieved a bottle with fresh flowers from the tent and placed them on a windowsill. This new house began to look like a home.

Alice went back to close the chest in the bedroom and spotted a folded piece of paper in the corner. Before casting it aside she unfolded it and discovered it contained dried seed pods of their Massachusetts hollyhocks. The sight of those seed pods brought back the memory of the day Elizabeth had had her stroke. Tears blinded her eyes as she grieved for that dear friend. Even though it was autumn Alice went outside and began to dig holes for the seeds on the south side of the house, all the while crying pent-up tears of grief and loneliness that dropped onto the turned earth.

. . .

One afternoon a knock on the front door startled Alice who was in the midst of remodeling a winter coat for Midge. She was surprised to see Mistress Hollis standing on the slab step with a small jar of store-bought pickled onions in her hand.

"Come in, please," Alice hesitantly said, trying to hide her surprise while stepping aside for her visitor to enter.

"Thank you," Mistress Hollis replied politely, awkwardly extending the pickle jar. Her sharp eyes swept over the room full of signs of living: material lying on the table, bits of thread scattered on the floor, trays of scones cooling, a pot of soup simmering in the pot hung over the fire, the hearth unswept. Alice felt a moment of embarrassment at the untidiness.

"Please sit down, Mistress Hollis." Alice motioned to a bench by the low fire in the fireplace. "Let me pour a cup of cider for you." She busied herself, feeling awkward and countrified in the presence of this finely dressed woman.

"Please call me Agatha," Mistress Hollis requested, sitting stiffly on the edge of the bench and making bland chit chat as she drank the cider. Alice kept feeling there was more the woman wanted to say.

After a long moment of silence Mistress Hollis leaned forward and asked, "Did Josiah tell you we had met a few years ago in London before I married Mr. Hollis?" She looked at Alice to see her reaction.

"No, he didn't," Alice spoke guardedly.

"I was very shocked to see him at the tea party," Agatha explained. "We have so much to talk over about old times and mutual friends that I am inviting you both to our home for dinner Sunday after church. Please bring your children. How many do you have?"

"We have four with us here," Alice replied.

"Oh, my! That is good. They will be company for Mr. Hollis's son Will. I will expect you next Sunday after church. *Josiah* knows where we live," she said, emphasizing his name. She rose, fastened her cloak about her and quickly left to her waiting carriage.

Alice stood leaning against the door flustered and angry. Why didn't Josiah say he knew her when she questioned him about it on the way home from the party? He had evaded answering her and she had not pursued it further, maybe not really wanting to know. Since that day there had been a subtle coolness in Josiah's attitude toward her.

When she confronted him about his acquaintance with Agatha Hollis on his return from work at the end of the day his answers to her questions revealed little other than the acknowledgment that he had met her briefly while in England.

After church services on Sunday the Marsh family sedately walked up King Street to the fanciest house. During the meal, Agatha continually spoke to Josiah, reminiscing about their many times together in London and the people they knew, negating Josiah's claim of a brief meeting. Occasionally she would ask Alice a question but barely wait for an answer before involving Josiah in another anecdote. Josiah beamed at the attention. Alice tried to engage Mr. Hollis by asking questions about the mill or his life in England but he replied only in monosyllables, keeping his eyes focused on his wife. Will, a little older than Penny, once in awhile whispered with Horace as the children stood against the wall to eat, but the girls were shy and silent.

The uncomfortable afternoon visit dragged on, relieved only when they finally left the house. The entire visit had been awkward and stilted for Alice and the children but Josiah was oblivious to that and euphorically repeated his praises of Mistress Hollis.

"Stop," Alice begged. "I don't want to hear anymore about how wonderful she is."

Josiah seemed stunned at her request. After all, he was only trying to help Alice improve herself, he said.

The days passed as the family prepared for winter. She pushed the subject of Mistress Hollis to the back of her mind.

Each morning Horace piled wood in the box by the fireplace then left to walk with the girls to the tutor's house. He in particular loved his studies, spending as much time as possible with any books he could borrow, often reciting unusual bits of information during the supper meal. Alice was so proud of the scholar and fine character he was becoming. Proud also of the girls for each one worked hard in the house and Midge spent her extra time tending the cow and pig. Alice encouraged the girls to get as much education as they could at the tutor's house. Certainly they needed it if only to raise intelligent children of their own.

. . .

Eight weeks later Agatha Hollis surprised Alice with another visit. Since the dinner at the Hollis house they had spoken politely to each other as they met at church, but that was all.

The two women again engaged in idle chit chat as they sipped warm cider. Agatha's eyes continually roved about the room, thankfully neat and tidy this time, often returning again and again to the table. As she rose to leave she walked over to the polished table and touched it with her gloved hand. "This will be mine someday when Josiah and I are married," she spoke softly, yet audibly enough for Alice to hear. "Goodbye," and she was out the door.

Alice began to laugh, harder and harder till tears poured down her cheeks. Had she heard correctly? Of course she had! If that brazen woman wanted Josiah that much she could have him, but not the table! How ludicrous! The laughter began again. She was still erupting in bouts of laughter when the children returned from their lessons. She would not explain the reason for her hilarity as they looked at her quizzically. Shrugging their shoulders they went on with their usual chores and studies.

When Josiah returned to the house at supper time, Alice looked at him as if seeing him after a long separation. His flabbiness had gone and his physique had turned more muscular from the hard work he was doing. His face was tanned and taut from exposure to fresh air. His moods varied from bursts of energy and abundant enthusiasm, to the old criticisms of earlier years, to restlessness, anger and discontent. He was obviously not happy here in St. Ann, now renamed Osnaburg. Nor was he happy with Alice or his role as father to his children anymore. They lived together as husband and wife, yet the affection developing between them had disappeared. Her hopes for a fulfilling, loving marriage were dying.

"What do you want here and now?" Alice asked him as she wiped the table. He sat gazing into the fire, smoking his pipe. She was reluctant to ask but she wanted an answer.

"What do you mean?" he asked her.

"You do not seem happy or content here. What do you want?"

He looked away, not answering.

"Do you want to go back to London?" Alice finally asked, standing before him.

"Maybe," he replied evasively.

"Do you want us as a family to move there?"

"No." He stood up and walked to the door, putting on his coat and hat. "I am going for a walk," he explained abruptly and left, returning long after Alice and the children were in bed. Alice had tried to stay awake as she waited for him but sleep had overtaken her.

In the morning Josiah left for work at the usual time. Alice stood at the door watching as he paused at the end of the walk and looked back at their home, an action she had never seen him do before. A premonition of a change settled over her as she went about her daily chores.

Supper time came and went without his appearance. As the evening wore on Alice sat waiting by the fire for his footsteps, knitting four needles around and around on a pair of socks. Still sitting and knitting as dawn crept through a crack in the shutters she did not want to acknowledge what she had feared. Was he hurt and alone along the road or had he left her and the family to fend for themselves again? She was not totally surprised if he had left for he did not like her or the responsibility of the family anymore, but she could not believe he would leave them stranded in this foreign place with no explanation, not even an excuse.

It was still early in the morning, soon after the children left for classes, when Mr. Hollis stopped his carriage in front of the house, dismounted and strode purposefully up the path to the door and knocked.

Alice was startled to see him.

"Please come in," she urged.

He stepped just inside the threshold, holding his hat in his hands. A cold, icy wind blew around him.

"Is your husband here?" he asked sternly.

"No," Alice replied.

"Did he come home yesterday or last night?"

"No."

"Then they have left together," he said harshly. "My wife (he spat the word as if it was poison) left the house yesterday at noon with a valise and did not return. Your husband left work at the noon whistle and did not return. I shall take steps to clear this up," he said, turning to walk out the door.

"Maybe it was just coincidence," Alice said weakly, grasping the edge of the door for support and trying to make herself believe it.

"I doubt it," Mr. Hollis said bitterly, stomping back to his carriage.

Alice shivered and shut the door behind him. Josiah had left them! This time there were no false reasons nor empty promises nor even goodbyes. She turned to face the room lit only by the flames in the fireplace. Rejection overwhelmed her, rejection as a wife and as a woman. A chill made her shiver again. Feelings of anger and resentment flooded her soul. "This house will shelter us as long as I'm able to care for us," she spoke fiercely to the silence. This time there was neither weeping nor paralyzing panic. She closed her eyes and breathed a prayer for strength and courage. A feeling of resolution and strength filled her soul. She had managed before and she could do it again. Somehow!

Spring

If on a Spring night I went by
And God were standing there,
What is the prayer that I would cry
To Him? This is the prayer:
O God of Courage grave,
O Master of this night of Spring!
Make firm in me a heart too brave
To ask Thee anything.

— *The Prayer,* JOHN GALSWORTHY

9

OUTSIDE THE CABIN soft, silent, steady snowflakes fell through the dark gray skies. Inside Alice fluctuated between periods of intense energy and quiet times sitting at the table staring into space, uttering prayers for guidance. Her thoughts raced helter-skelter through her mind. She spoke out loud to the empty room, "I must stop and think logically," but that was easier said than done. "Do I say anything to the children? I have to before they hear rumors from other children."

The children's exuberance of anticipated fun in the season's first snow fall was dampened by Alice's subdued demeanor as she asked them to sit on the bench by the fireplace. Her voice quavered as she began to speak. "Dear ones, it appears your Father has left on a trip. I don't know how long he will be gone. He did not say. Perhaps he went to St. John to find another job." She paused to catch her breath. The children sat wide-eyed, watching her intensely in the silence. "You will surely hear rumors that he went with Mistress Hollis. I do not know if that is true. In the meantime we must take care of each other. I am planning to cook again to earn money so that we can stay in this house as long as possible or until we need to make other plans," Alice concluded.

"I'll help with the cooking like I did before," Penny assured her Mother.

"I'm old enough to get a job," Horace added solemnly.

"I can help." Susie and Midge each added their willingness.

"I'm so proud of you all," Alice said kissing each one in turn. "Horace, girls, you must keep on with lessons at least through the end of the month. They have been paid for. We will find a way. Now, how about some hot, milk coffee?"

Nods of agreement responded to this rare treat.

The resolute words of her children reassured Alice that they would survive. Much as she wanted to sound confident to them she had qualms. "How long can I keep us in this house, one I don't even own? How long can I feed and clothe my children?" The thought of the future when they would be apprenticed or farmed out and separated to work for other people chilled her soul as she sat at the table peeling potatoes for supper. She knew it was a common practice but she needed them with her for her own sake as long as possible.

Horace threw a log into the firebox with extra vigor and left the house, slamming the door with a bang.

"Horace! Don't slam the door," Alice instinctively called after him.

Penny and Alice sat at the table discussing ideas to earn money. They concluded the best way would be for Alice to go around town inquiring for someone wanting a full-time cook or soliciting orders for home-baked pastries. She would begin the next day. With some paid work, milk and cheese from the cow, eggs from the chickens, preserved pork and hams and garden produce from summer's meager harvest stored in the root cellar, they could subsist on their own for a little while. Hopefully, Josiah would return soon to take care of his family. Though their marriage was unfulfilling it was vital he come home, for Alice had no legal rights over her family or this house.

Supper came and went without Horace. The lone candle on the table lighting the girls' studies had burned down halfway when a knock on the door interrupted the quietness. Alice's heart skipped a beat as she went to lift the latch. Maybe there was word of Josiah. Dr. Morris stood on the stone slab. In the shadows Horace stood behind him.

"What happened? Is Horace all right? Come in. Come in." Alice reached out to pull Horace into the light, checking him quickly for any cuts or bruises.

"I'm fine, Mama," he said, grinning with contained excitement.

"Mistress Marsh, please let me explain," Dr. Morris said as he took off his coat and settled on the bench at the table, leaning on his elbows with his fingers interlocked. "Horace came to me this afternoon wanting me to hire him to work full time caring for the horses and other jobs. He said he is interested in becoming a doctor some day. I have talked it over with him, and to be a doctor he certainly needs to continue with his lessons. What I propose is that he come to my home every day after class, on Saturdays and at any time lessons are canceled. He would work at chores or whatever is necessary until supper time, when it would be necessary for him to go home to study for the next day. I expect he will have chores to do at home as well. Since I would not need to put out money for his board, I will pay him a pound a month toward his lessons. If it is all right with Mr. Marsh we will try it for one month, and if I am satisfied with his work, then we will consider him hired. As he learns he can assist me in surgery sometimes to see what is truly involved in being a doctor." Dr. Morris glanced over at Horace who sat anxiously watching Alice's face for her confirmation.

"Horace, do you really want to be a doctor?" she asked. When he was six and declared he was going to be a doctor one day, candy was the influencing reason.

"Yes, Mama."

"It will be a heavy load with lessons, chopping wood and other chores," she persisted.

"I know, but I really want to do this," he pleaded.

Alice was quiet, pondering if she should give her consent. Usually the father made the decision. If not to this doctor Horace would have to be apprenticed sooner than later to someone else to learn a trade. She watched her son's eyes pleading with her. "Dr. Morris, though Mr. Marsh is not here at the present moment, I give my permission," she said at last, rising to escort him to the door. She shook his hand in gratitude adding a heart-felt "thank you."

Questions and congratulations besieged Horace before he escaped out the door to chop wood for the fire. The chattering sisters followed after him to bring in armloads of wood, dropping the pieces in the wood box by the fireplace.

"Off to bed you go," Alice commanded the girls. She reached over to give Horace a hug. "I am proud of you," she whispered in his ear. He grinned as he raced up the stairs two at a time.

As she watched, the wavering light of the single candle guiding the children to bed mounted along the stair wall till it disappeared from sight, leaving her alone in the darkness among the furniture. Once in awhile a dim redness flared up amidst the gray ashes in the fireplace, giving life to that part of the room. The darkness of the room became one with the darkness outside. Walls disappeared. Outlines faded. Definitions vanished. Alice felt her bodily restraints loosening as she melted into the darkness. The overwhelming concerns of daylight vanished from her mind and she floated freely in and out, seeing clearly the placement of every snow-covered tree, stump, rock, table, chair, book, sleeping child, spider web and dust curl. She had no concept of how long she was suspended in time and space and she was surprised to find herself waking at dawn in her bed. She turned over to look at Josiah but he was gone. No impression was left on the pillow to show where his head had lain. The reality of the last two days jolted her upright. Yet, somehow, the peaceful voyage in the darkness of the night returned to her memory, for she had seen her world more clearly than she had ever noticed it in daylight. No matter if the snow melted or the dust curls were swept away, she would try to remain steadfast even when she experienced periods of doubt. "Thank you, God," she whispered. Purposefully she rose from the comfort of bed to begin a new day, a new chapter in the story of her life.

Early in the morning, after the children left for their lessons and just as Alice had put on her cloak prepared to leave the house, Mary stopped by. She put her arms around Alice holding her close before she loosened her cloak and sat down awkwardly at the table. Hesitantly, she said the rumor was already circulating around town that Josiah and Mistress Hollis had run off together.

"Did Josiah say anything to John before he left at noon two days ago?" Alice questioned her friend.

"No, nothing. John said he just walked out the door at the noon hour as usual."

Alice confided to Mary that Josiah and Agatha had known each other in London before she married Mr. Hollis. Maybe they did leave together or maybe it was just coincidence. "I have to expect that he is gone, perhaps forever," she added with a sigh, trying to suppress tears of despair and anger. "Mr. Hollis is going to search for Agatha and Josiah, if he is with her. We cannot go back to Massachusetts, at least not now. We will need money. I am hoping to get a position as a cook with someone, or if need be, do some kind of cooking or baking to sell. Maybe you will hear of someone needing a cook. I have done it before. If you have any suggestions please let me know."

"I have not heard of anyone, but you do make delicious scones. Perhaps you could sell them," Mary said. "I will pass on the word about orders. But now I have got to leave." She buttoned her cloak and gave Alice a kiss on the cheek. "By the way, have you seen the new family that moved into the cabin just up the road from you?" she asked as she opened the door.

"No, I have not."

Alice accompanied Mary toward town, looking curiously at the newly occupied cabin as they passed. She spent the day going from house to house, store to store, soliciting any kind of baking or cooking positions that might be needed. Some people welcomed her into their homes in sympathy or curiosity. Some quickly shut their doors when they saw her. Word had spread quickly. The attitude of the latter seemed to be that surely it was Alice's fault Josiah had left. One store owner brazenly suggested that she "look for a man to take her to wife[5]." Even the pastor of the church offered little encouragement that she could manage without Josiah.

"But I have to manage if he does not come back," Alice protested fiercely.

On Saturday John Collum stopped by in the morning to deliver the last pay Josiah had earned. As he sipped two cups of precious coffee, Alice queried him about Josiah's last days at the mill. Had he indicated anything?

"No," John reiterated. "We seldom spoke after I became foreman. He became withdrawn from all of us."

"I truly appreciate your bringing me the money," Alice said gratefully, as she escorted him to the door.

"By the way, Mary isn't feeling well. I think the baby is coming. Will you please come by?" he asked as an after-thought.

"Yes, of course."

It was late in the afternoon before she took time to walk to the Collum house, only to find the local midwife cleaning teary-eyed Mary after a difficult still birth of a boy.

Mary broke into more tears of grief at losing another baby. "John wanted a boy so badly and now I have failed again," she sobbed.

Alice's attempts at comforting her friend did little to assuage the distress. She breathed a thankful prayer remembering her own miscarried pregnancy nearly a year ago. How could she have persisted with another baby in this present situation?

. . .

Slowly, steadily the clientele of people ordering pastries increased. Even the general store on Waterloo Row stocked fresh pastries from her every day. The soldiers living in the barracks in town were some of the best customers. With the additional work, Alice felt it was necessary to keep the girls at home. Much as she wished they could get more schooling she could not afford the cost. Penny quickly developed into a fine baker. In addition, she took upon herself the task of delivering the pastries and collecting the money, trudging the distance to and from town through snow and storms. She was adamant about payment upon delivery or at prior arrangements and every night she kept an accurate, detailed account of the cost and profit for the day. Each month she added in Horace's earnings if he had received any extra money from Dr. Morris. So far, with judicious spending, they managed to pay the bills and put enough money for next week's ingredients in the black tin box on the top shelf, though there was never any extra. High on the dream list was window glass. Maybe next month there would be some extra.

Susie took charge of any indoor chores in addition to her spinning the flax and wool yarn into thread for knitting. Midge assumed responsibility of caring for the cow, chickens, pig and now a sheep. This extra help by the girls allowed Alice to bake more pastries. She was thankful she had found an old bake kettle used for breads and rolls that could be set amidst the coals of the fireplace with more coals piled on the convex cover. It gave her an extra utensil for baking in addition to the fireplace oven. She forced herself to put her anger at Josiah aside. She did not have time for that. When she did think about it she had to acknowledge that she had a lot to do with Josiah's unhappiness. Maybe if she had been more loving, thoughtful or caring he would have stayed. Maybe. Much as she chastised herself she was not ready to completely let go of the anger and forgive him.

On a brilliant, sunny afternoon Alice and the girls trooped across the snow to greet the new neighbors. A knock on the door brought a quick response.

"Well, imagine this, we have company," a penetrating voice called out. "Come in. Come in."

"Thank you," Alice responded, handing over a napkin-wrapped bundle of scones as they stepped into the cabin's darkness. After their eyes adjusted from bright sunlight to the cabin's dimness they saw an elderly lady with tight white curls escaping the white cap on her head and a pinched face, skinny younger woman surrounded by half a dozen young children clinging to her skirt.

"Well, set down," the elder woman commanded, leading the way to a bench along the wall. "My name's Matilda, though every one calls me Mattie. This here's Bridget, my son's wife, with the little ones." She waved toward the others.

"How do you do. My name is Alice Marsh and these are my daughters Penny, Susie and Midge. We live across the road over there. You can just see our house from here. Welcome to our town."

"Well, imagine that. Bridget, put water on for tea then wipe the table." What followed was a lengthy list of do this and do that as she ordered Bridget to do one thing after another. Mattie leaned toward Alice and spoke sotto voce. "Well, Bridget's a little slow. I keep telling her over and over again how to do something but she just does not get it right!"

Alice looked at Bridget to see if she had heard the derogatory comment and saw the poor woman half roll her eyes at Alice then lower them in despair and shame. Alice recognized her chastised self of former days in that look.

Meanwhile the unwrapped scones sat on the edge of the table enticing the tiny hand of a wide-eyed three-year-old to reach up to take one. A sharp slap by Mattie stopped the action in mid air. "These are not for you," she said sternly, as she took one herself and began to eat in front of the children. "Well, pretty good!" she said, licking the last crumbs off her fingers between continuous questions. Since she did not wait for answers it was soon obviously unnecessary to formulate any.

Interrupting another question, Alice said, "We must be on our way," rising and signaling the girls, who had been silently standing the entire time. "Welcome again," she reiterated, slipping out the door, appalled by what she had witnessed.

From then on Mattie made a point of stopping daily at the Marsh house to relate the latest tidbits of gossip or news about everything and everyone always prefaced by "Well." The more dramatic the news the more dramatic the utterance of that word.

"It is a shame the dunking stool for gossips is not in use any-more," Midge spoke up one day after Mattie had left another tidbit of gossip.

"Midge!" Alice scolded her outspoken daughter.

. . .

It was a cold morning in January when a forceful knock inter-rupted the baking. Alice unlatched the door to see three stern-looking members of the town council standing in the doorway.

"Mistress Marsh, may we come in?" George Miltimore, spokes-man for the council, politely asked.

"Of course." Alice stepped aside for the men to enter.

"Thank you," each man said as he filed past her and sat stiffly on one of the benches. Their somber presence overspread the small room of the cabin.

"May I offer you some tea?" Alice asked. The fear of what they might have to say made her voice quaver.

"No, thank you," each replied in turn.

After a moment of awkward silence, Mr. Miltimore cleared his throat noisily and pronounced the reason for their visit. "Mistress Marsh, we are here to explain that you are no longer allowed to live here in this house. Your husband has left his obligation to farm and improve this property thus negating any title to the property."

Alice felt her old flee-and-hide emotion rising within. She forced it down. "We do not know for sure if Mr. Marsh has gone for good. He might be stranded somewhere by the snow and ice," she said.

"Mistress Marsh, surely you know there is suspicion he left with Mistress Hollis."

"At this point it is still a rumor. You do not know for sure so you cannot really say he abandoned the property."

"Mistress, you are not able to manage without him. Instead you will become wards of the town, putting a burden on everyone else. Nor do you have anyone here to put up bond money for your keep." The non-speaking men kept nodding their heads in agreement.

"With my baking and Horace working for Dr. Morris we prom-ise not to become wards of the town. We will pay any bills necessary. By the spring thaws maybe Mr. Marsh will return to fulfill his obligation. We cannot go anywhere now. Please, I beg you, let us live here through the winter at least."

The three men looked at each other. Slowly they nodded an unspoken assent to each other.

Mr. Miltimore cleared his throat again. "Um. Ah. Mistress Marsh, we agree to let you remain through till spring, unless you become a burden upon the town, in which case we will..." He left the sentence unfinished. "You will be responsible for any bills relating to the property," he concluded sternly. "Good day to you." The three men rose, tipped their hats and left.

Alice shut and latched the door. Her heart was beating fast and she felt weak in the knees. She saw Midge and Susie holding hands watching her with fear. She swallowed, moved to the baking table and began vigorously kneading dough. "Come, back to work we go." The girls gave a collective sigh of relief and turned to their chores.

Alice felt she had to do more, but what more could she do? Though she tried to estimate the correct demand of baked goods it was not always predictable. Thus it was even more frustrating when Penny returned with unsold pastries. Each piece represented money expended but not received. They could only eat so much themselves and she disliked the idea of giving it all to the pig. When she thought beyond her own interests however, she realized there were many families whose husbands and fathers were away cutting wood all winter, struggling like themselves to make ends meet, who would surely appreciate a few extra morsels of food for their children. If there were any leftovers she instructed Penny to leave portions with these families.

. . .

One early winter morning before dawn had broken Alice was awakened by the sound of Horace retching into the chamber pot. She slipped on her wrapper and hurried up the stairs with water and a damp cloth. As she held and wiped his head he threw up again and again. When he stopped she tucked him in bed, cleaned up the vomit and put water on to brew dried pennyroyal for a stomach remedy. He only protested a little when she insisted he stay home and not even think of chopping wood.

After Penny left with the day's deliveries, accompanied by Susie and Midge to help carry the extra baskets, Alice prepared to mix the pastry for the next day's orders. A knock on the door did not startle her, for she often had people stop to give or pick up orders. She was very surprised, however, to see John Collum on the doorstep on a work day.

"I just passed your girls on their way to town. May I come in?" he asked.

"Yes, of course. Come in." Alice stood aside for him to pass. She waited expectantly for him to tell her the reason for this unusual visit. "Have you heard from Josiah?" Alice finally asked, thinking that must be the reason.

"No," he answered. He purposefully advanced toward her putting his big hands on her shoulders, pushing her back against the door and pressing his body against hers. "It's been a while since Josiah left, so I know you must want it and I'm here to give it to you," he spoke against her ear, pushing against her harder as he began kissing her neck, the bushy beard rubbing her skin.

"John, stop that," Alice panted as he squeezed even harder against her.

"There's no one to hear you," he said.

She tried to push him away.

"I know you want me," he said, his voice rising with his passion. He moved his big hands down her chest to squeeze her breasts.

"Horace," Alice squeaked.

"He is not here," John said with glee.

"Horace!" Alice managed to call loudly.

"What do you want, Mama?" Horace sleepily answered back.

John quickly backed away from Alice.

"Will you please come down here? Now!" Alice called loudly.

"All right, I'm coming." They could hear Horace's feet land on the floor above and cross the room toward the stairs.

John pushed Alice aside, opened the door and stepped out just as Horace started down the stairs.

"What do you want?" Horace asked, rubbing the sleep from his eyes.

"I needed your help but it is all taken care of now," she replied breathlessly. "Thank you anyway. Just go back to bed."

He mumbled something unintelligible and went back up the stairs.

When she heard him fall into his bed she sat down heavily onto the table bench, putting her hands to her face, shaking all over. What if Horace had not been home today? "Thank you, Lord," she whispered. "How am I ever going to face that man again? How can I look at Mary the same way? What a dilemma he has put me in! What have I ever done to make him think I lusted for him?"

Thereafter Alice felt awkward each time she met Mary or the Collum girls, mumbling some weak excuse when Mary asked her and the children over for dinner. She felt badly for John's behavior was not Mary's fault, yet how could she sit there with John across the table? She kept praying.

As she walked out of the general store one day, she passed Mary walking in.

Alice managed a weak, "Hello."

Mary walked past without acknowledging the greeting. A few steps further Mary turned around and shouted at Alice, "How could you."

Alice turned and looked at her puzzled. "What?"

"Do not look so innocent! You know what I mean!"

"No."

Mary walked up to Alice and hissed in her face, "Of course you do! John told me all about it. How you lured him to your house with some trumped-up excuse that you needed his help. When he got there you tried to seduce him into taking you to bed. How could you," she furiously asked again.

"It is not true," Alice protested.

"Of course it is. John would not lie to me," Mary defended him.

"Just keep away from us," she declared, shaking a knarled fist at Alice. Luckily there were no passersby to hear the exchange.

Alice stood stunned by the encounter. She felt heartsick and so alone. A cold, biting rain of early spring pelted her face. It did little to cool her red cheeks. She walked home in a daze ready to crawl into bed and pull the covers over her head. "But I did not lure him. I did no such thing." She tried to recall every instance when they had been together, what remarks he might have misconstrued, but she could not think of anything she had done to encourage him. She even began to doubt her own memories. To add to her distress there had been no direct word from Josiah on his whereabouts. Mr. Hollis found out they had both left on the same afternoon boat for St. John. He was unable to trace them from there, though he suspected they went back to England together.

Back at home Alice's mood was suppressed yet fierce. The girls felt the difference in her but could not figure what was wrong and Alice would not explain. She worked harder than ever to produce more and more pastries to sell. Every night Horace spent hours chopping wood to feed the fire that heated the oven beside the fireplace for the extra output. The girls spun, knit, sewed, altered clothes, carried in wood, tended animals, anything to help their Mother. With the exceptions of Sundays, every waking minute was utilized productively to keep them fed and together. If they earned a lot of money maybe they could move away from this place come summer.

. . .

On a warm spring day Penny returned after deliveries excitedly telling Alice of the unusual figure she had seen in town. "There was a man walking round about who looked just like a skeleton; skin and bones with no flesh color and raggedy clothes just barely hanging on. He was frightful." She shivered from the memory of it.

"That is interesting," Alice said absent-mindedly as she counted out cups of flour into a bowl.

Nothing more was said about it as Alice and Penny continued to work in unison preparing pastries for the next day's orders.

"Penny, answer the door, please," Alice ordered when she heard a faint knock on the door later in the afternoon.

When Penny opened the door she backed up and whispered loudly to her mother, "'Tis him!"

"Who?"

"The skeleton man!" Penny now stood behind Alice for protection.

Alice walked to the door with Penny clinging to her skirt like a tiny child. Truly the figure on the slab step did look like a skeleton: eyes sunk in, bald head, long beard, no fat, flabby skin, shaky hands and a shivering white body clothed in tattered apparel.

"Alice, it is me, Franklin Fremont." Faint hints of the old familiar booming voice were the only recognizable thing about him

"Franklin!" Alice gasped in dismay and disbelief. "Come in and sit," she commanded, taking his shaking arm and leading him to the fireplace bench. She poured a jigger of rum into cider, stuck a poker into the flames, then into the liquids. "Take it," she ordered, putting the warm drink into his hands.

Before Franklin finished the drink his eyes began to droop. Alice took the cup from his hands, propped pillows around him and let him sleep.

Alice and Penny returned to their baking and Susie and Midge tiptoed back to their chores, frequently glancing at the frightful shape on the bench. This strange creature in their house could be dangerous. Yet their mother seemed to know him.

As they sat together quietly eating chicken soup and bread for supper, Franklin awoke. Alice took him some bread soaked in the chicken broth, spooning it slowly into his mouth. He began to talk in a whisper as they gathered around him in front of the fire.

"It seems so many, many years ago that we enjoyed Christmas dinner with you at the farm," he began.

"I remember that day. You had candy in your pockets," Penny exclaimed

"That is right." His face cracked a hint of a smile. "We left for New York City the next night, always traveling after dark. By the new laws, as British supporters, we were not supposed to travel outside of town."

Alice nodded, remembering the fear of capture she had the night they fled their home.

"We stayed with fellow sympathizers during the day and hid like common hoodlums." He shuddered at the memory of this bruise to his dignity. "It took us weeks to make the trip to New York where we rented a third floor bedroom from an acquaintance. The city was crowded with people like ourselves as well as British troops. There were numerous activities occurring all the time, night and day, just as if there was no war. Everyone thought the British would win, for they were better trained, but having seen the resistance in Massachusetts I had my doubts. When the war ended we were put aboard British ships and transported here to St. John, probably the same time you were." Worn out by the exertion of speaking, he closed his eyes, appearing to fall asleep.

Midge leaned over and whispered to her Mother, "Did we have to sneak away from home at night like that?"

"Yes," Alice whispered back.

"I do not remember that!" Midge looked shocked.

"That was nine years ago. You were just a baby."

"Oh."

Franklin roused himself to continue the story. Though Alice told him to wait until another day, he felt compelled to continue. "The British created a tent city called Parrtown near St. John where we were housed with thousands of other people. We were also issued food and other necessities. Isabella held up better than I, but she always was the stronger one. Just by chance she met one of her cousins there who owned property, including buildings, in Canada toward Montreal. He was excessively crippled with arthritis, especially during that cold winter in a tent, and needed our help. Though I had been promised a position with a barrister in St. John, Isabella and I decided we had to help her cousin get to his property. Then we would return some day. We stored our few belongings and sailed up the St. Lawrence River toward Montreal. There, we hired a wagon for a day-long trip to his holdings south east of the city, only to find that squatters had taken over the land and cabin and were not about to leave. Her cousin also refused to leave and we could not persuade him to wait in a nearby town for the authorities to come eject them. We did not want to leave him alone so we holed up in a tent on the property. Those squatters harassed us so continuously with foul words and threatening gestures that we felt like prisoners closed up in that tent. I insisted we get the local authorities, but before I could walk to the nearest town someone threw a burning stick at the tent when we were asleep. I dashed out and tried to pull it down. I could hear Isabella trying to wake her cousin, urging him to try and move. When I tried to enter and help Isabella something hit me and that is all I remember. When I woke up later it was still dark. Only the flicker of a single flame lit the darkness. I called and called for Isabella and her cousin but there was no answer. I saw that the center pole had fallen on the cot where her cousin had slept, crushing them both before they could get out." He stopped again. Tears slid down his cheeks. "I did not save them! They burned in the fire! I lost everything: Isabella, my reason for living, money, clothes, papers." He covered his face with shaking hands.

Alice leaned forward and took his burn-scarred trembling hands in her own, "Shush, shush. Go to sleep now," she said, tenderly moving him with Horace's help to a bed of quilts by the fire.

She dozed on the bench during the evening, waking to add more precious logs to the fire. Sometime during the long night Horace helped her to bed, promising to watch Franklin.

In the morning, as dawn seeped through the cracks in the shutters, Alice groggily walked in to see logs still glowing in the fireplace and Horace curled up on the bench sound asleep. A grimace of pain flickered across Franklin's face as he stirred, throwing the quilts off. She bent down and touched his brow with her cool hand. A fever was burning within him. She stoked the fire, putting water on to boil for an herb concoction to lessen his fever. As it heated she uncorked the plug from her crock of spring syrup, ladled out a tablespoonful and raised Franklin's head to slide the spoon into his mouth. He shook his head in a shudder of distaste.

"What did you put in that?" he whispered hoarsely.

"'Tis to lessen the spring fevers." Ticking off on her fingers, she recounted the ingredients. "I boiled dock root, thoroughwort, yarrow, mullein, sarsaparilla, coltsfoot, spearmint, May weed, dandelion root and brandy."

"Line up," Alice ordered Horace and the girls as they came into the room. She went from one to the other ladling out a generous spoonful for each. The agonized looks on their faces made Franklin chuckle in sympathy. She turned away and took a less generous spoonful herself, making a grimace and involuntary shudder. "I do not like it anymore than they do," she thought to herself, "but I am going to keep us healthy."

"When you finish deliveries, please stop at the doctor's. I want him to come check Franklin," Alice charged Penny as she was leaving.

Late in the afternoon Dr. Morris descended from his gig, looped the reins of his patient horse over a tree branch and strode to the house. "I heard about your being in our fair town," he said as he checked Franklin's temperature, eyes, mouth and abdomen. When he removed Franklin's shoes (if they could be said to have any resemblance to shoes) he let out a low whistle. Black toes were prominent in the dirt encrusted feet.

Patiently, tenderly, Dr. Morris washed the dirt away as Alice held the basin or refilled it frequently with clean warm water. She had to grit her teeth to keep from being sick at the sight, for it looked bad. Franklin lay with his eyes shut, clenching his teeth to hold back a moan of pain.

"It looks like at least half your toes will have to come off," the doctor said at last. "But you are not in very good condition for an operation. However, if we wait it will worsen." He sat back on his heels as his right hand rechecked Franklin's pulse.

Franklin stared at his feet. "Take them off," he declared emphatically.

"If you insist," Dr. Morris said. "I am going back to the house for more bandages and tools. I will bring Horace back with me to help. In the meantime just give him weak broth," he advised Alice. "And keep him warm," he called back as he hurried from the house.

Within the hour the doctor and Horace were ready. Franklin lay on the table gripping the edge with his hands. Alice sent Susie and Midge upstairs to keep out of the way while she and Penny set about preparing water and clean rags. This was her first opportunity to watch her son assisting in a medical manner. She was impressed with his cool, deliberate focus. A grownup boy worked before her determined to succeed as a doctor. She remembered the hours he spent teaching himself to make the wooden puppet dance and the nights he sat up late studying to achieve a goal he set for himself.

Her reverie was interrupted by Dr. Morris saying, "It is over and he is all right. For now." He wiped the scalpel on a towel. "Horace can change the dressings. I will stop by tomorrow to check on him." Horace helped him move Franklin to his bed of quilts by the fire. As Alice escorted the doctor to the door he turned and spoke loudly enough for Horace to hear. "I must tell you that Horace will make a fine doctor some day. He keeps his wits about him and even anticipates what I am going to do." The doctor-to-be blushed at the compliment as he moved about the room cleaning up the remnants of surgery.

"Thank you." Alice was pleased that this reticent man spoke so glowingly of her son.

"Good night."

Alice stepped outside with him, taking time to relish the balmy spring air. Stars twinkled in the clear sky. How glorious! How thankful she was for Franklin's outcome, for this old friend to be in their life again, for her family and home and for God's continuing loving care.

Horace joined her, tired yet exhilarated. Alice squeezed his arm and reached up to kiss his cheek. She was so proud of her son and the praise Dr. Morris had bestowed upon him. Life had not gone as she dreamed it would when she was sixteen. It had certainly been more challenging by its twists and turns than she could ever have imagined.

10

PENNY AND HORACE created a bed by the front wall of the house where Franklin could look out the nearby window to see the greening of the trees. Horace rigged a line to hold a quilt separating the bed from the rest of the room's activities.

Under the tender care of the Marsh family, Grandpapa Franklin, as the children now called him, regained strength and flesh on his bones. Susie and Midge took on the role of his caregivers, plying him with fresh wild strawberries, urging him to eat seconds at mealtime, often eating less themselves so that he would have plenty. This was a particularly hard sacrifice for Susie, who truly loved to eat. After the baking and cleanup were completed for the day, Alice took time to sit and have a quiet cup of shrub with Franklin while she knitted. She tried to keep the conversation light, only confiding her longing to see Jeremy, her parents and sister. Franklin listened patiently as a surrogate father, quiet yet observant. Walking was difficult with six toes missing but he persevered with canes and the girls' constant encouragement. Slowly, yet perceptively, his stamina increased a bit each day.

Meanwhile Mattie's daily visits ceased after her initial encounter with Franklin. Something in his demeanor intimidated her and she kept her distance.

. . .

One day, clear-eyed and obviously feeling stronger, Franklin walked to the table to sit, watching Alice cut scones."Do you know where Josiah is?" he asked quietly so Susie would not hear. Alice looked at him and wondered how much she should tell him."I am not sure,"she said."He left last fall. It is possible he went to London but I have had no word. We are hoping the spring thaw will bring word from him. Truthfully, I don't know if he is even alive." She turned back to her cutting, leaving out any reference to Agatha.

After a pause Franklin said,"I must tell you I saw Josiah in Montreal last fall."

Her hands shook as she lifted the scone to the griddle."How? Where?"

"We were most surprised to see each other as we entered the boat ticket office at the same time. I was there to find out the cost of passage back to St. John. After Josiah bought two tickets for London he urged me to join him for a drink at the coffee house. He wanted advice about regaining his property in Massachusetts. The treaty between Britain and America pledged that Congress would 'earnestly recommend to the states that they restore rights and property taken from the Loyalists.' We were just finishing discussing the possibilities when a lady appeared who boldly introduced herself as Agatha Marsh, Josiah's wife. He did not contradict her, but simply introduced me as an acquaintance he chanced to meet in the office. That caused me to believe you were dead. Then, when I saw you here with the children, I thought perhaps he had divorced you. Initially I did not want to sadden you by bringing up such a difficult subject, particularly since I was feeling rather ill myself,"he said, looking down at his feet. He glanced up at Alice to gauge her reaction."Perhaps he will return on a spring boat and everything will be explained,"he said kindly.

"Perhaps,"Alice said doubtfully, and changed the subject.

As the family leisurely ended their supper one balmy spring evening, Midge spoke up. "Excuse me, Grandpapa Franklin, but you never did tell us how you got here from Canada. You certainly looked like a walking skeleton that day."

"Midge!" Alice exclaimed at this bold, outspoken utterance.

"Yes, you are right. I must have looked a fright," Franklin grinned. "Where did I leave off?"

"You woke up after the fire."

Franklin was silent, remembering that traumatic scene. Then he resumed his story. "There was nothing to do but walk to town and tell the constable after I buried them the best I could. I could not swear who set the fire or even if someone knocked me unconscious. But I knew I did not want to stay in the area. There was no reason to remain." He closed his eyes as he remembered burying his beloved Isabella and her cousin. Coming back to the present, he continued,. "I was fortunate to meet a peddler who dropped me off on St. Catherine Street in Montreal. I could hardly believe my eyes, for I nearly bumped into your father."

"You saw papa?" Penny asked eagerly.

"Yes. He was purchasing passage to London. When I asked if you were all going with him he said you were staying in a town named Osnaburg in New Brunswick."

At this statement Horace snorted. Alice gave him a warning glance. Franklin did not add anything about Agatha but noticed the tightening of Alice's hands on the needles perpetually knitting another item of clothing.

He resumed his story. "I had lost my money in the fire and did not have any for passage then but I planned to get some kind of work in order to buy it later. After a few months of doing odds and ends I had saved enough money to pay to join a party of trappers who would sail down the St. Lawrence River, continue over to meet the St. John River and on down to St. John. By then I just wanted to get to St. John to pick up my belongings and start over again, though I planned to stop and look you up in this Osnaburg if possible.

"It was late fall when we left. The leader said it was the last boat of the season before ice closed the river. We made good progress during the day, docking up at night on shore. But the night before we were to start the lake passage someone must have given me something in my drink to make me sleep, for when I woke late the next morning the crew and the boat were gone with all my few possessions and money. I was so angered that I thought if I kept walking along the bank I could meet them at some point and get my goods back. I managed to keep going but I never saw them. Their craft was much faster on the lake so I had to decide whether to keep going or to turn back. Winter was coming on and I was set on getting back to St. John to put this entire part of my life behind me, so I kept walking. Eventually I was fortunate enough to have a native Micmac help me by keeping me alive during part of the winter. I was half out of my mind with sickness and merely wanted to keep going, so I took off again on foot. I was foolish to walk off during the winter," he said looking at his feet. "It took me a long time to walk this far." He stopped his reminiscence, looking out the open door at the past.

He continued. "When I stopped here at St. Ann's Point to find this Osnaburg I learned it was all the same place only now it is called Frederick's Town after His Royal Highness, the second son of King George III. I finally found someone who knew you children and where to find you. I was so relieved and delighted to see you." He smiled at this family who had nursed and adopted him.

"Splendid! What a story!" Horace exclaimed, looking with admiration at Grandpapa Franklin. The girls and Alice looked at him with wonder before she shooed the children on to their evening chores.

Alice felt as if a millstone was pressing on her chest ever since hearing the news that Josiah was married and likely in London. With the spring opening of the river she had held out hope, half expecting Josiah to return to continue developing the property and care for the family. However, boats had resumed their journeys up river and he had not appeared. The possible enforcement of their removal from this house that had been constantly on her mind now became a likely reality. She finally explained the entire situation regarding Agatha and Josiah to Franklin, expressing her concerns about having to leave the house and the area. "I did not want to tell you before. I just wanted you to get well and not have to worry about us."

They looked at each other, recognizing that friendship should have been honest from the beginning.

"I think you should prepare as if Josiah will not return. You have done amazingly well all winter taking care of your children and me and all the bills," he praised her. "Let me inquire whether there is a place you can rent in the meantime."

"I want us to stay together as a family," Alice said fiercely. She wondered if she wanted and needed her children around more than anything for her own courage and reason to live. "Wherever we are I need to be able to bake or cook or sew to earn the money we need."

"I know," Franklin said sympathetically. "If I was able I would marry you and adopt the children as my own family," he continued with a smile.

"Thank you," Alice affectionately smiled back. Each knew it was not a serious possibility at this time.

The next day Franklin walked to town, spending most of the day there. When he returned just before supper he asked to say grace, though it was Midge's turn. "Dear Lord, we gratefully thank You for this food set lovingly before us. I especially thank You for the outcome of this day. A day exceedingly good for me. You provided me with strength to walk to town and back and You provided me with a job. For this I am particularly grateful. Thank you also for a solution to this family's housing problem. Bless each one of us as we partake of your bounty." He kept his eyes closed through a grin slowly turned up at the corners of his mouth, anticipating the effect of this announcement.

"What? Where? How?"

"I begin tomorrow at the barrister's office! Remember the barrister I was going to work with before I left for Quebec? Well, believe it or not, it is Mr. Brown right here in Frederick's Town. I am to work as much as I can while I recuperate." Franklin smiled broadly. "If it works well I will find quarters in town. I am thankful for all your care but I know it put an extra burden on you all."

"But you are family," the children and Alice reassured him. "We want you to stay with us."

"I know and appreciate that, but it would be easier for me to walk if I were closer," he responded. "Also, knowing Mr. Brown and your family will make me less suspicious as a newcomer to town," he said with a smile.

"What about the house?" Alice asked, the thought foremost on her mind.

"You may stay here for the present. You have paid the bills and not become a burden on the town. It is possible Josiah will return to continue developing the property. In addition, I gave my promise to take care of you if the need ever arose and they accepted that," he explained.

"Oh, thank you!" they exclaimed as a chorus. The girls rushed over to hug and kiss this loving man. Alice reached across the table and squeezed his scarred hands in thanks.

Within a fortnight Franklin pleased Mr. Brown with his expertise and became a permanent member of the barrister's roster. In addition he secured a room at Mistress Thompson's boarding house that was much closer to the law office.

Still no communication came from Josiah.

. . .

One Indian-summer morning in early October Alice looked up from her baking to notice shadows moving outside. Through a half-opened shutter she caught a glimpse of Franklin and a group of men walking around the house. Curious, she walked outside to see what they were doing.

"Alice, I have taken the liberty of ordering windows for the house and these men are here to install them," Franklin beamed at her puzzlement.

"But the size?" Alice finally asked, flabbergasted by this welcome gift.

"I measured them one day when you were out." He laughed at her expression. "Susie and Midge shared the secret." That explained their recent whispers and giggles.

All day the hammering and setting of windows continued. By late afternoon the house gleamed and sparkled inside with a glorious fall sunset casting its glow through the glass. Alice walked from one precious sash window to the next, moving each up and down, rubbing a speck of lint off one pane of glass, admiring the fall colors outside from another. How grand they made this home look. How she had missed sunlight in the house.

"What can I do to ever thank you enough?" Alice asked Franklin as they sat at the table that gleamed even more in the sunset light.

"It is I who can never repay you," Franklin replied with deeply felt sincerity. "I hope you know you are as dear as a daughter to me and that your family is my family now," he continued, reaching over to squeeze her hands.

"Thank you," Alice replied misty eyed. They sat in companionable silence.

"Seriously, Alice, will you consider marrying me? I know Isabella would approve," Franklin spoke at last.

She looked away. Her emotions were in turmoil. Sometimes, she felt utterly alone when she was around married couples. It was even obvious that some of the other women shunned her, afraid she would take their husbands from them. Was that how Mary felt? Had she truly believed Alice would do that? Even if she had admired or fantasized about someone it certainly would not have been John Collum. She longed to have the relationship of a husband and wife that was mutually loving and caring. Could she have that with Franklin? They were friends. Would it always be a relationship of appreciation for one another? Could she relate to him as a wife? She thought of him more as a father than a lover. And he still pined for Isabel who would always be foremost in his heart. Yet, the children loved him and he returned their affection. Anyway, she could not even initiate divorce since she was legally Josiah's property. Were there any other options? Franklin was so thoughtful and helpful, and being taken to wife by him would solve a lot of her problems. But . . . neither one would accept living together as husband and wife when they were not legally married.

She turned back to him and spoke tenderly, "Oh, Franklin, even if Josiah divorced me, that status is so frowned upon. It would affect both your position in town and the children. How could I do that to all of you?" she answered.

Franklin resigned himself to her answer, perhaps even slightly relieved that he would not have to divide his heart with Isabel and Alice. "I understand, but please let me continue to consider you as my family."

"Of course!"

The daily sunshine invigorated all the Marshes. Life took on a new glory. Seen through the new windows even cloudy, rainy days were beautiful to them all. How many years had it been since they could look out their own windows to see God's creative, evolving world? During the last years at their home in Massachusetts the windows had been broken and boarded. They had grown accustomed again to the sunlight through windows while at Joan's home and with John and Martha but when they came here and lost the daily light inside, a dreariness had come over them all. For years.

. . .

Christmas was going to be a celebration of this new joy of life. Alice and the girls planned a Saturday afternoon for having all their acquaintances, customers and Grandpapa Franklin come by for pastries and hot drinks. It was a way to thank them for their support. Though the year had been difficult and a severe test to their fortitude, the Marshes had so much to be thankful for in their lives. They were together and still in their light-filled house.

Saturday dawned crisp and cold. A light snow covered the trees and bushes. Horace brushed snow off the path and filled the wood box. All morning Alice and the girls did last-minute baking and cleaning to prepare for the event. She bustled around the rooms, issued orders, sometimes telling two girls to do the same thing, and scurried around right up to the arrival of the first guests, flustered and anxious that the tea party be perfect since this was the first one in their home.

The table was hidden by trays of marchpane, lemon suckets, spiced nuts, candied rose petals, nut pies, varieties of fruit scones and tea cakes. Kettles of hard cider sat by the fire, as well as whipped sylabub, raisin wine, dandelion wine and spruce beer. All was ready. She inspected the girls in their prettiest dresses and Horace and Franklin looking handsome in clean shirts before she turned to open the door to their first guests. The Collums did not come, though Alice had debated long and hard within herself before finally issuing the invitation. People were busy and lived far apart, making it difficult to form deep friendships, so she was sad to have lost the friendship of even one person. Mattie, Bridget, her husband and all the children came by. It was rather comical watching Mattie try to rein in her gossiping tongue each time Franklin looked her way. Surprisingly Mr. Hollis came along with Will, who kept watching Penny as she served the hot punch, appearing to notice her for the first time. Alice followed his glance to her daughter and noticed with pride how lovely and mature Penny appeared.

Each visitor came and lingered, enjoying the warm glow of shared conversation. With dusk closing in, the guests reluctantly left. As the last of them were shaking Alice's hand in thanks at the doorway a middle-aged man and two younger men in British sailor uniforms turned in at the walk. She casually noticed their approach in the gloaming but did not recognize them.

Franklin joined her at the door. He had seemed fidgety as the afternoon wore on, frequently glancing out the window as if expecting someone. The new arrivals were obviously the ones, for he stepped out to greet them on the path.

As they got closer to the door Alice stared at the young men, one in particular.

"Jeremy!" she exclaimed, running on the trampled, snowy path to embrace him. "Oh, Jeremy!" She looked at her handsome older son and then squeezed him tightly again. He was alive! "And Robby!" Alice clasped her nephew in an enveloping hug. Linking her hands through their arms she almost dragged them into the house, calling, "Horace, girls, see who is here!"

Squeals of delight and surprise filled the room as the siblings embraced each other and their cousin.

Franklin followed with the older man and Alice turned to see them standing in the doorway. Embarrassed by her rude manners she went over to them and shook the gentleman's hand, "I apologize, sir, for neglecting my manners. Please, welcome to our home. My name is Alice Marsh."

"Mistress Marsh, I am Captain MacTavish of his majesty's naval service," he responded in strong Scottish brogue.

"Please, Captain MacTavish, help yourself to some cider or rum and pastry." Alice directed him to the table still amply supplied with delicious pastries.

She turned to Franklin who stood by the door beaming with delight at the scene before him. "Franklin," Alice spoke softly, moving close to stand beside him, tucking her arm in his. "I know you had something to do with this reunion. Please tell me."

Franklin looked at her then told a simple story. "I contacted your father who learned from Joan's husband that the boys had been captured by the British. I know Captain MacTavish from years ago. I wrote to him and he found where they were and had the boys transferred to his ship. I knew that he was a good, fair man and would treat them well. He indicated that the ship would dock in St. John around this time. It did not take much persuasion to get him to bring the boys here. That is all there is to it."

"I do not expect it was that simple," Alice said, stretching up to give him an affectionate kiss on the cheek. She left him to return to the boys, plying them with food and drink. Her cheeks were still flushed red from the excitement as she left the boys to speak briefly with the Captain, thanking him for the kindness he was according her son and nephew. He responded courteously but with reticence.

It was well after dark when Franklin and the Captain came over to Alice to say good night. "The Captain will be staying at the boarding house with me. The boys can sleep here until Monday when they need to return to the ship," Franklin explained.

"So soon?" Alice gasped.

"Good night and thank you for the refreshments, Mistress Marsh," the Captain said as he shook her hand formally and acknowledged the salutes of Jeremy and Rob.

"Captain, will you be able to come for supper Sunday afternoon? Franklin always makes it a routine to come then. We would be happy to have you as well," Alice said invitingly.

"Thank you, I will, if Mr. Fremont is planning to do so." He stepped out into the cold air.

The family sat around the fire reliving the day, enjoying being together again. The girls and Horace begged the boys to tell them all their adventures.

Taking turns, the two boys shared their story. Jeremy began. "Our boat was being repaired so we were helping Old Joe on his boat sail out to the banks for cod. A heavy fog settled over us so we set anchor to wait it out. In the morning after the fog lifted, lo and behold, we were approached by a British ship."

Rob chimed in. "We had no choice but to let ourselves be boarded. They searched the boat, only finding fish, then they took me and Jeremy on board to take us to a prison in England, claiming we were surely privateers. Papa and old Joe were left to go alone. We heard the canon fire and we thought old Joe's boat was blown up killing my father and Joe. Luckily my brother Tom had stayed home this trip with a broken arm.

Jeremy picked up the story. "Mr. Fremont heard from Grandpapa that they got home injured but safely. Uncle is a good sailor. Anyhow, the British kept us below deck for some days. Not much there in the way of food. We were whispering how we could escape when they hauled us up to the next deck to work during a gun fight. Some of their men had been shot and all hands were needed. I thought about trying to get topside, jump overboard and swim to one of the other ships but my chances of making it in the fighting were fairly slim."

"So did I," Rob added. "But in the meantime they made me haul water to the surgeon."

Jeremy shuddered as he remembered his part. "I had to help hold the men down while the ship's doctor cut off their legs or arms. At first I wanted the men to live, being pro British and all, but then I wanted them to die because they were fighting Americans. I was confused for I did not know whose side I was on. The poor lads my own age were suffering so and I remembered your words, Mama, that all people were children of God. Therefore we were brothers and all alike no matter where we lived. If that was so then I could not wish my brother to die. I pictured Horace lying on that table and it shook me."

Rob carried on. "We never had a good chance to escape, for they kept us down below most of the time and gave us the worst chores to do. They were harsh task masters on that ship," he said fiercely.

Jeremy continued. "A couple of months ago while we were imprisoned in England we were ordered to Captain MacTavish's ship. He has allowed us to be on deck and has taught us a lot about being sailors since we signed on. He is fair but tough. We were surprised when he brought us here, not even telling us why we were coming. I knew from your old letter that you were coming to Nova Scotia but I never dreamed I would really see you for I didn't know where you lived. What a wonderful sight you were standing in the doorway, Mama." He turned his face away to hide the tears filling his eyes. The emotion of being with his family again choked his words.

Alice reached over and patted his shoulder. "Oh, my son, my dear, dear son," she whispered.

Silence filled the room as each family member thought of the words the boys had spoken.

"I think 'tis time we all went to bed," Alice finally broke the silence, rising to set the fire for the night. "It has been an exciting day."

"Can the boys sleep in with me?" Horace asked.

"Fine," his mother agreed. "That is the best arrangement."

Reluctantly the children complied and went to bed. Alice locked the door, snuffed the candles and sat before the banked fireplace embers deep in thought and prayers of thanksgiving.

Presently Jeremy joined her. "I cannot sleep," he said, sitting beside her.

"Neither can I," Alice replied. The two sat quietly for some time.

"Mama, where is papa?" Jeremy asked. "Your letter said you were all coming to Nova Scotia. Is he dead?"

"The last I heard, he was going to London," Alice answered.

"When will he be back?"

"I do not expect he will come back," Alice said resignedly. "The rumor is he went with a Mistress Hollis. Perhaps some day we will know the whole story."

Jeremy clenched his fists in anger, began to utter a sailor's epithet, then closed his mouth tightly.

Again silence as they became absorbed in their own thoughts.

"Do you like the sea, Jeremy?" Alice eventually asked.

"Noooo," he replied slowly. "Mama, I am confused," he finally blurted out. "Papa wanted us to be loyal to the British, saying the rebels were wrong, and they did do some awful things to us, but when I listened to the other sailors berate the Americans I wanted to speak up and defend them for I really am an American too. The more I think about it the more I want to go back to Massachusetts or some place else around there. Rob feels the same way I do. He is homesick and wants to see his family. I would like to get some land and become a farmer," he added shyly.

"I understand," Alice said. She left unspoken the turmoil she felt within herself about choosing to stay here or return to her native country. Sometimes she felt so isolated and alone in this place. Was she grieving for the family left behind? Maybe she would still feel lonely if she returned. This unsettled feeling must be a symptom of unrest within herself.

"How long are you required to stay with the Captain?" Alice asked.

"I do not know. It has been almost three years since we were seized but we did sign on as British sailors," Jeremy sighed.

"Perhaps Grandpapa Franklin can speak to the captain. Just keep praying about it, all the while planning for the time you are free," Alice said. "Maybe you will not have much time left."

"Every trip lasts such a long time. But maybe I can convince Captain MacTavish to relieve me sooner since we were initially impressed against our will. Then I could come help you and the girls and Horace," Jeremy said hopefully.

"That would be wonderful. Thus far, we are doing all right," Alice said, making light of their day-to-day struggle as she patted his knee. "I'll keep praying you will be given an answer soon. Now we really must get some sleep. We have a church service early in the morning." She stood up, leaning over to kiss Jeremy on the top of his head. "Good night, sweet boy."

Sunday afternoon, after the church services, they all gathered around the cherry table for a meal of thanksgiving. The late afternoon hours passed with tales of the sea and lands far from Alice's knowledge. In the relaxed atmosphere even the captain seemed to unbend.

Next morning Alice was in the midst of mixing oats for breakfast when a knock interrupted her concentration. She automatically wiped her hands on her apron as she walked to open the door.

Captain MacTavish stood as if at attention on the doorstep. " I have come to escort the boys to the ship," he said formally.

"Step in, please. I think they are still sleeping." She stood aside for him to enter, ordering Penny to go upstairs to waken them.

"It will be a few minutes, sir," Penny explained shyly when she came back down stairs.

"Would you like a cup of coffee and breakfast while you are waiting?" Alice asked the captain who was still standing stiffly by the door.

"No breakfast nor coffee, thank you. I just ate with Mr. Fremont" he answered formally. He did take a seat by the fire, fingering his hat in his hands and looking quite uncomfortable.

"I hope you do not mind, but I must stir the oats," Alice said, bending before the pot hanging above the fire and trying to keep her mind on the task before her, yet conscious of the captain's eyes watching her.

The captain rose when the boys rushed down the stairs. "We must be off," he ordered.

Alice put some leftover pastries from the party in a sack insisting they take them for the journey. She hugged and kissed her nephew and shook the captain's firm hand. After the teary-eyed girls and Horace had said goodbye, Alice gave Jeremy a long embrace and kiss one last time. "Goodbye. God speed," Alice whispered, watching them disappear from sight.

11

*H*OW *THE DAYS TUMBLED PAST,* blowing off the new calendar like chaff in the wind. Another new year and
another new spring were upon the land and upon the family.

Alice lifted her head to smell the balmy fresh air ruffling her
skirts as she gathered an armload of wood from the dwindling pile.
Snowdrops peeked up through the last vestiges of snow around
the logs. The light of a new day was flushing the eastern sky. She
spied a robin flitting through the trees. The sound of an ax wielded
by Horace reverberated through the air. Where had the months
gone? Had she kept her head down all winter hibernating like a
bear, absorbed in baking and worries about money and the house?
Where was the courage to carry on joyfully that she had prayed for?
Surely she had much to be grateful for just knowing Jeremy was
alive.

"Mama, may I ask you something?" Penny inquired as she
loaded her own arms with firewood.

"Of course," Alice replied absently, still lost in thought.

"Can we finish baking early enough to get the house cleaned up before Will Hollis comes to call tonight? He is coming is he not?" She blushed at the thought of the evening's potential.

Alice smiled at her lovely eldest daughter. "He asked me if it could be tonight and we will certainly try to be ready."

"Thank you." Penny would have skipped to the house if her arms had not been weighed down with wood.

They dropped the split logs into the wood box, removed their capes, brushed off their aprons and proceeded to set the day's baking ingredients onto the table. They had done this routine so often no words of instruction nor questions needed to pass between them.

Alice paused to look at her maturing daughters as if seeing them after a long absence. Had she been that absorbed not to be conscious of her children's lives? Susie had already begun the day's rhythmic dance, spinning flax fibers into thread in the second room corner by the front window. She was an excellent, fast spinner. Curly, red-haired Midge sang a ditty as she passed the window on her round of daily outdoor chores: milking the cow and feeding the chickens, pigs and sheep. She always seemed to be humming or singing, and in general, enjoying life. After their few years of learning reading, writing and spelling, the girls obediently stayed home to help their mother. In the evening they did handwork or separated flax for the fibers. On Sundays they ceased most chores to attend church and relax, entertaining themselves by playing the recorders, reading or watching Horace and the dancing man.

Horace was seldom around during the day. He filled the waking hours studying, working with Dr. Morris and splitting wood for the fireplace. He was sturdy but so tired that he collapsed into bed each night to rise before dawn to begin the routine over again.

Alice realized that tiredness afflicted them all. Each of them had worked constantly to survive another severe winter in this developing area.

They had received no communication from Jeremy since his brief visit around Christmas time. There had been one letter, held at the General Post Office for a month until Alice could accumulate money for the postage, from her sister Joan detailing the last days of their mother's illness and her death. She wrote that their father was despondent now, shuffling dazedly through the tiny house. He could not concentrate enough to continue teaching the children, and when he did speak to them, the words were sharply uttered or mumbled in an incoherent whisper. She was relieved to have received a letter from Rob and thankful that Alice had been able to see him.

After reading her sister's letter Alice let tears seep from her eyes with longing to see her family again. Sometimes she felt very alone even in her children's presence. She had often yearned to be with her parents or sister just to lean on them for support. Now her mother was dead and her father was beyond helping her. She grieved that she had not been there to help care for them. Perhaps, if she had disobeyed Josiah's demands and stayed she could have helped. But what would have happened to the children? Sadness filled her soul. Why had she not taken more time to learn about her parents and their dreams and delights? At times, this feeling of loneliness here in the wilds of New Brunswick made the pressure to keep going more than she could bear. When these dark emotions came over her she tried to recall the sense of courage evoked by the love and companionship of her Lord that she had dreamt of when she had been ill. That remembrance gave her the nudge from behind to sustain her and help her move on hour after hour, day after day.

Shortly after Penny left with the day's deliveries, Grandpapa Franklin interrupted their daytime routine. After enthusiastic hugs from Susie and Midge, he settled on the bench by the work table, watching Alice roll and cut dough for scones and place them on the griddle over the tall-legged trivet standing amidst the coals.

"I am afraid I have bad news," he stated quietly. "The money has already been paid out to Josiah for the lost property in Massachusetts. Since it belonged to him you are not entitled to any compensation, not even for your lost furniture or goods."

Alice nodded, as if already expecting that answer. "We tried." Last fall, when she read in the New Brunswick *Advertiser* about money allocated through a lottery in England to be paid to Loyalists as compensation for losses of property, she had asked Franklin to put in a request for her. She knew it was unlikely because she had not owned the property but if Josiah was dead perhaps she, or Jeremy as older son, would receive some settlement.

"At least we know Josiah is still alive," she said resignedly. "Am I pleased with that news? Yes and no. I don't really know," she confessed to this loyal friend.

"I am concerned about this property, however," Franklin continued. "I know it has been a hard struggle for you to keep up with the bills, to say nothing of all the other expenses you have. But since it does not meet the original stipulations required it will eventually revert back to the town. You recall so many acres had to be cleared, a house erected and farming begun, all by the end of three years. The house is here but the acreage is not cleared and time has run out. I will only be able to delay the decision of the authorities for so long. If you give me your permission I will try to contact Josiah through an office in London and get him to return to finish clearing the property or dispose of it." He patted her shoulder as he stood and put on his coat and hat. "Somehow we will find an answer," he added, trying to sound encouraging.

"Please do what you can to find Josiah and thank you for coming by to tell me," Alice said softly. She touched his arm affectionately. He was a staunch friend.

Alice escorted him to the door with a call of "goodbye" from Susie in the background. When she turned back to the room she felt energized. The lethargy of the winter dropped away from her shoulders. She had decisions to make. She had not told the children about trying to get compensation money because it was unlikely to happen. Sometime, she would have to tell them that their time in this place might soon run out but not yet. "Tonight is Penny's night to shine," she told herself as she tidied up the room and wiped flour off the long center table. She lovingly touched a gleam of sunlight reflecting off the polished wood.

Penny rushed into the house, eager to make sure everything was in perfect order for the expected visitor. Poor Susie could not get the scattered flax fibers off the floor fast enough to suit her sister. Alice intervened in the argument. "Calm yourselves!" she ordered. They ate a quick, light supper, cleared the table and washed and dried the dishes all accompanied by considerable teasing of Penny, who could hardly contain her excitement.

A light knock announced the arrival of Will Hollis. Alice, Susie and Midge welcomed him in but his eyes only looked past them to find Penny. The two young people looked shyly at each other as they took seats on the bench by the hearth, oblivious of anyone else's presence. A quick word by Alice sent Susie and Midge up to their room.

Alice settled into the rocker in the far corner of the room and gathered her knitting from the box, automatically making her fingers move the needles in and out of the yarn. She had so much to consider. Thoughts about Josiah raced to the forefront of her mind. For weeks on end she was able to forget him, yet here he was again dictating the march of her days.

She had asked Franklin to determine whether Josiah had divorced her and married again. He could not find any record of it. Accordingly, she was still married and subject to her husband's dictates. She considered what she could do to force Josiah to tend to his obligation about the property and their marital status. "Perhaps I could write him a letter urging him to settle our lives one way or another," she thought. "Maybe he could transfer the land to the boys' names so that we could continue to live here. It might work. Horace would not be able to finish clearing the land and still continue studying to be a doctor, a dream he should fulfill, but Jeremy yearns to be a farmer. Franklin can add the letter to his other request. Oh dear. Perhaps it is time for us to move into town or back to be near Joan and Father. I have got to know where we stand."

Alice found some paper, a pen, ink and pounce in the sideboard drawer. She set a candle on the table, pausing to think of the wording. Should she sound bitter or chatty? At last she began to write, conscious that Penny and Will were quietly whispering on the bench.

> Josiah, I hope this letter finds you happy.

"No, I don't mean that," and she crossed that line out, starting again on another sheet.

> Josiah, you would be proud of your children — how they have matured and grown. Jeremy is enlisted in the British naval service, Horace is well on his way in studies to becoming a doctor and Penny, Susie and Midge are helpful, beautiful young women.

"Maybe this reminder of his children will tweak his conscience."

> Our old friend and lawyer, Franklin Fremont, has informed me you are still alive and that you received compensation for the Massachusetts property. He is requesting that you proceed to settle the question of this Fredericton (now the shortened form of Frederick's Town) property as time has run out on the original mandate. I have paid the expenses and maintained it since you left, though we have not been able to clear the required number of acres. If you have no interest in the property would you transfer it to Jeremy or Horace's name?
>
> I am urging you to respond hastily about this property and whether your family will continue living here. Of great importance to me is the status of our marriage. I must also know that!
>
> Awaiting your prompt reply, I remain hopeful that these questions can be resolved in a timely manner.
>
> Your wife, Alice

By the time she finished the letter and sealed it, tucking it in her pocket, the late hour indicated that it was time for Will to leave.

"Good night, Will," Alice and Penny chorused from the doorway. Penny automatically kissed Alice good night and dreamily climbed up to bed, failing to ask Alice about the letter, perhaps not even realizing her mother had been writing one.

The next afternoon, Saturday, when the baking was finished for the day, Alice walked to the law office to see Franklin.

"Will you please forward this letter to Josiah along with your letter? I have requested that he fulfill his obligations regarding this property and enlighten me of the status of our marriage. I must know!" she uttered. "I don't know if he will respond but I have got to try," she explained, handing it across the desk.

"Of course." Franklin took the letter without any comment about Alice's request. He looked weary and in pain.

"Are you feeling ill?" Alice looked at him worriedly. She had failed to notice before how frail he looked.

"I am fine," he answered with a wan smile. "My legs are bothering me some today. I apologize for not rising. Please do not worry about me."

"You are family so of course I will worry," Alice replied vigorously. "Please take care of yourself," she begged.

"I will." Politely he made an automatic half motion to rise from his chair.

"Don't get up. I can let myself out," Alice said, backing out of the room. "Goodbye and thank you. Will we see you tomorrow?"

"As usual."

She reminded herself to be more aware and solicitous of Franklin as she walked out the door. "I must have been in a heavy fog these past few months," she berated herself again, keeping her eyes downcast to avoid the muddy puddles.

"Good day, Mistress Marsh," a voice hailed her.

Alice looked up, recognizing the figure of Captain MacTavish walking toward her.

"Good day, Captain," she said. "How nice to see you again. Is my son Jeremy with you?" she asked hopefully.

"No, Mistress. He and his cousin failed to return to the ship at the stop in St. John. I am hoping you have heard from them," he answered gravely.

Alice looked at him, surprised and worried by his gravity. "No, I have not heard from him since your visit at Christmas time," she replied shakily. "Please, tell me what happened."

"Let me walk you to your home and I will tell you all I know," the Captain said, taking hold of her elbow with a firm grip.

They walked in silence along the street. As they passed the church, he finally spoke. "When we docked in St. John, Jeremy and Rob, along with other sailors, had shore leave until the next day. Yet, the two failed to appear on time. The report from the other men was that the boys were going to do an errand before meeting at the local tavern. However, they never came. The sailors assumed the boys had changed their minds so did not go looking for them. No one saw them since the time they parted on Water Street. The authorities cannot find them and I came here hoping you knew where they were." He looked at her face to read the answer in her eyes.

"I have not heard anything," Alice said gravely, thankful for the strength of the Captain's hand holding her. "What can I do to help?" Her thoughts were on the predicament that Jeremy was in, not even realizing how adeptly the Captain guided her around puddles of melting, dirty snow.

"Thank you for walking me home," Alice said, standing on the granite step. For an instant she was hesitant about opening the door, fearing Jeremy might be in the house and wanting to shield him from any possible punishment. "But if I don't invite him in," she thought to herself, "he might think Jeremy is here. Of course my son would have to face the Captain's wrath if he has done anything wrong." The Captain stood waiting for an invitation. "We are not cleaned up from baking but will you come in for some refreshment?" Alice apologized, unlatching the door.

"Thank you, I will," he replied, stepping over the threshold after her. Holding his hat in his hand he formally greeted each girl and took a seat on the bench by the fireplace, letting his gray eyes rove around the room as he looked for signs of Jeremy's presence.

A quick glance told Alice that nothing had changed since she left earlier. She furtively watched the Captain as she moved about gathering cider and pewter mugs. She thought he looked relieved when he did not see any evidence of her son, but the gravity of his face soon returned. She was angry he could think Jeremy had jumped ship or that he believed she could be hiding him. However, she was grateful he came in person to check. She worried something terrible may have happened to the boys. Surely Jeremy would not have left of his own accord. There had to be some other explanation.

Trying to keep her voice calm before the girls she politely inquired, "How long are you planning to stay in Fredericton?"

"Until tomorrow," he replied. "Or the next day," he added as an after thought. "I was on my way to see Mr. Fremont when I saw you."

"I was just in to see him. I am concerned about his health," Alice spoke.

"Is he ill?" the Captain asked.

"He is tired and I think the damp weather has made his legs ache," Alice explained. "He still plans to come to dinner tomorrow, however. Captain, will you please join us for dinner also?" She hoped he could be reassured that Jeremy was not here. Or, better, perhaps he would have received good news by then.

"Thank you. I will be sure to come. Now I must be on my way. Thank you for the cider," he said, rising and walking to the door. "Good day, Mistress and young ladies," he said, half bowing in their direction.

Alice closed the door quietly behind him, and then quickly busied herself with preparations for supper and mixing the Indian pudding for Sunday's meal. Questions about Jeremy swirled in her head. "Have you heard anything from Jeremy?" she asked the girls even knowing if they had received a letter she would have been told.

"No, Mother. Why?"

Alice explained the reason for the Captain's visit.

"Mama, you put in too much molasses!" Penny exclaimed, watching her mother.

"Oh, dear, I miscounted," Alice said. "I will have to add more cornmeal and double the recipe. My mind is not on my work I'm afraid," she explained with a sigh. The letter to Josiah, Franklin's health and now Jeremy. "Is it any wonder I cannot think clearly?" she mused, stirring the batter. She stuck her finger in the mix then to her mouth to taste for the right balance of flavors. "I must stop tasting all the time. My dresses are getting tighter," she chastised herself.

"Mama, I heard you tell Captain MacTavish that Grandpapa Franklin is not feeling well. Is he really sick?" Penny worriedly asked.

"No, I don't think so. I imagine the weather is bothering his legs," Alice reassured her. "You can be his nurse when he comes tomorrow."

Alice slept fitfully during the night, half anticipating a tap on the door by Jeremy. Where could he be? What could have happened to him? Had he really left the ship to go back to America? During supper they had informed Horace about Jeremy's absence without leave from the ship, but he had not heard from him either. They were all worried, imagining all sorts of scenarios.

After church services the following rainy day, Franklin, the Captain and Alice rode in Franklin's shay as Will Hollis and the Marsh children walked home to a simple dinner of rabbit stew with dumplings and varieties of pickles, ending with the Indian pudding. The Captain looked solemn at not seeing any evidence of Jeremy in the house. Was he worried? His look puzzled Alice. For the first time she really looked at this guest in their house. He was slightly taller than she but because of his erect stance he appeared even taller. He was solidly built, well tanned from exposure to all kinds of weather.

His beard was neatly trimmed and streaked with gray, as were the thinning hairs on his head that at one time must have been red. Lines of wrinkles extended from the outer edges of his eyes, which always seemed alert and inquisitive. In all a pleasant face.

Sunday afternoons, after the second church service of the day, were treated as a time to rest and relax. It was Alice's favorite time of the week as the one day she could stop baking pastries and the one day she was sure Mattie would not stop by unannounced. Often she sat knitting by the fire or outside under a tree tatting a piece of lace for a collar with Penny. Susie and Franklin were usually in deep conversation about a book while Horace practiced with his dancing man, the rat-a-tat beat echoing through the house. Midge could often be found with the farm animals. Each had their own way of relaxing.

Today, in an effort to take their minds off the imagined predicament of Jeremy and Rob, the girls and boys kept the Captain busy relating adventure stories of his travels around the world. Many of the tales were humorous and Alice wiped tears of laughter off her face. She giggled again.

"Oh, Captain, that story was so amusing. I don't remember the last time I laughed so hard." She smiled at him, relaxed and comfortable in the fellowship of her family and these friends.

"Will you play us some tunes?" Franklin suggested to the family during a lull in the conversation.

"Certainly," the girls said, rushing to set up the music stands in the center of the table. Penny retrieved recorders from their box, handing them to Alice, Horace and each girl. As merry tunes filled the cabin, Franklin tapped his foot to the rhythms.

"Do you play?" Alice politely asked the Captain at the end of one melody.

"Some," he replied.

"Please join us."

Horace handed him a tenor recorder. The Captain wiped the mouthpiece, settled his fingers over the holes and began to play a haunting, plaintive highland melody as his audience sat transfixed.

"How beautiful!" Alice whispered. She saw a strong, disciplined man before her, with a gentle sensitivity he was reluctant for anyone to see. "Please play more."

"If you will join me," he said, pointing to one of the songs in the book.

During the next hour music and laughter filled the cabin. As dusk began to settle over the room, Alice lit more candles. Their soft light cast a flickering golden glow over this happy yet worried gathering. For a time she had managed to suppress the questions that had occupied her mind over the past two days.

"We really must leave now," Franklin said, rousing himself from dozing on the bench by the fire. He shuffled his canes from hand to hand as Alice helped him on with his coat. "Will, you may ride home with us," he instructed. Will looked to Penny for a request to stay but reluctantly he put on his coat as well. The Captain expertly slid into his coat and then stood before Alice. Taking her hand in his he said, "Thank you for the wonderful meal and afternoon. Do not worry. I am sure there will be a reasonable explanation and everything will be all right," He continued to hold her hand.

"Please let me know if you hear anything," Alice said.

"I will. Be of good cheer," the Captain replied. The warm pressure of his hand on hers made her feel a friend was looking after her.

"Please, Captain, what is your first name?" Alice asked. "I feel I should call you something other than Captain."

"Ian."

"Thank you, Ian," she replied softly, finally extricating her hand from his. She turned to say goodbye to Will and Franklin.

As Alice closed the door on their guests, she turned to Penny. "Now, come sit beside me and let me hear about your prospects with Will."

"I know he loves me and I love him," Penny stoutly declared. "He wants to marry me but he thinks he must be given more responsibility and more pay at the mill before he can marry, and his father will not let him have it yet. It is entirely unfair! After all,

Will is twenty and smart and I am nearly an old maid." She pulled out a handkerchief and dabbed away tears beginning to slide down her face.

Alice took Penny's hands in her own. What could she say? "Is your heart set on Will? I have seen other young men interested in you."

"I only love Will," Penny sniffled.

"Wait until the end of summer and see what happens. Just continue to be your sweet self and add items to your hope chest," Alice encouraged her, but felt the words were not received.

Susie and Midge added their words of encouragement too. Everyone liked quiet Will, though it was difficult to really know him, for he rarely spoke more than one or two words to anyone but Penny.

When Franklin came to dinner the following Sunday afternoon, he explained that the Captain had left on a sailing ship down river to St. John and back to his own ship which was returning to England. He had looked around Fredericton without seeing the boys and was disturbed and disappointed that they had possibly jumped ship. He did not relish the idea of having to mete out punishment when he found them, especially since he had come to know Alice and the rest of the family. The boys' possible defection had upset him as a personal betrayal of his efforts to help them.

. . .

On Friday, before the family rose for the day, a repeated cane tap sounded at the door waking them all. Alice pulled on her wrapper and tiptoed to stand by the door.

The insistent tap tap sounded again.

"Alice," Franklin called from outside.

"Franklin?" Alice responded in surprise.

"Yes. It is I."

Alice unbolted and opened the door, seeing the form of Franklin silhouetted against the moonlight.

He stepped across the threshold as Alice quickly shut the door. She lit a candle and stood before him, the girls and Horace crowding behind her. In the wavering light he looked serious as he sat down heavily on the bench. "Jeremy and Rob have been found."

Alice's heart stood still.

"They are alive but in the infirmary in St. John. I have few details, but I am going down there to see what happened and what I can do to help."

"I will go with you." Alice breathed out.

"It would be better if you stayed here."

"But I have got to go."

"I think it would be better for Horace to come with me. We will be gone at least 10 days and his medical training would be more useful." His arguments finally persuaded her.

"Of course I'll go," Horace spoke firmly. In a flurry of activity he was ready.

Alice lifted the black tin box down off the shelf, pulled out some money and handed it to Horace.

After shoving it in his pocket he bent down to give her a kiss. "I will stop by Dr. Morris's on my way to let him know." With a hasty goodbye they were off.

. . .

Hour by hour, day by day her mind battled between her apprehensive emotions and her reasoning. Each day seemed twice as long as normal. She was glad for the work that occupied her waking hours, yet in the night's quiet worry rose up like a storm. She prayed to keep the imagined outcomes at bay and tried to concentrate on the boys' recovery instead.

On the twelfth day joy erupted as the young men were helped into the house, plied with food and drink and questions. Their faces were still swollen and yellow green from severe beatings. Jeremy had a bandage covering a gash across one cheek and an obvious broken nose. Both of Rob's arms were in casts. The swelling and discoloration made the boys almost unrecognizable.

Alice tentatively closed her arms around Jeremy.

He winced slightly, looking at her with love and relief in his eyes. "Hello, Mama," he whispered hoarsely.

She let him go and reached over to kiss her nephew who was trying to smile through swollen lips.

Interrupting the girls' barrage of questions Franklin spoke gently yet firmly, "Let the boys rest before you pressure them to tell you what happened."

"All right, Grandpapa Franklin," Susie said, but their curiosity could only last until the afternoon meal the following day when the questions began again.

Jeremy related the story. "When Rob and I left the ship on leave in St. John we parted with the rest of the men and went to deliver a letter to the family of a sailor we met in the islands. We were going up King Street when we asked a man standing on the corner outside a tavern for directions. He told us to go a certain way. In fact, he would show us the way himself. We didn't pay much attention to two men who came out of the tavern and began to follow us. We should have been suspicious because the street he took us on didn't seem to have houses on it. As we were about to turn back all three men charged us, dragged us into an alley and then into a building, some kind of old warehouse I would guess." He grinned. "It was a grand fight but we were knocked unconscious, tied up, shoved into a basement room with no windows and robbed of all our pay. It turns out the man we were with was their leader. I don't know how many days we were there. I think they were going to try and sell us to some renegade ship but we were not put on a ship right off. Every once in a while, we could hear them arguing about what to do with us. We heard them say they had waited too long and there was a big effort being put by Captain MacTavish to find us. I think they were afraid they would get caught and jailed. One night we could hear a lot of arguing and movement up stairs before two of them came down and started to beat us pretty badly with black jacks. I'm sure they were trying to kill us. They would have too except the leader hollered down something and they rushed out. I don't know how long we were there before the authorities found us. It seems some young boys had heard our yelling and gone for help. I don't remember yelling, nor does Rob, but it appears we did." He closed his eyes from the exertion.

"Oh my dears, how horrible. I am so thankful you are alive and safe," Alice murmured, overcome with relief. "Thanks be to God," she uttered a prayer of thanksgiving.

"Captain MacTavish even came here looking for you," Midge said.

"Mr. Fremont got word off to Captain MacTavish," Rob stated.

Jeremy added. "After the authorities got all the information they could, and the doctor said we could come here to recuperate, Horace and Grandpapa Franklin brought us home on the next boat."

Slowly the excitement subsided and everyone began to relax, settling into the regular routines of the day.

"Mama, I don't really want to go back on that ship or any other ever again," Jeremy said resolutely as they sat together drinking cups of tea one afternoon. "I worry about you."

"I know you do and I love you for it," she replied with a smile. "You are home now so just relax and rest."

"I want to help you and perhaps even take the family back to America some day," he persisted.

"Have you told the Captain these thoughts?" Alice asked.

"No, not yet."

"I think you should. There might be some way you can be released. For now just rest and get better," she said bending over to pat his leg. She breathed a silent prayer of thanks that he was home with her once again and that Rob was safe as well.

12

WITHIN DAYS NOTICEABLE IMPROVEMENT was seen in the boys' health and coloring. The girls vied with each other for the duty of feeding Rob and it was a sad day for them when Dr. Morris removed the casts and he could feed himself. As soon as he was able, Jeremy assumed the role of wood supplier, spending hour after hour sawing, chopping, splitting and stacking. There was much outdoor work for the entire family to do, as it was already mid June.

Late one warm afternoon, Alice and the girls were squatting among rows of early peas, picking the full pods and obstinate weeds. Alice pushed her bonnet back to feel the warmth of the welcome sunshine.

Midge saw a visitor come walking around the corner of the house and called out, "Good afternoon, Captain,"

"Good afternoon," he answered back.

Alice sat back on her heels and waved a dirt encrusted hand to him. "Good afternoon," she called out to him. Her cheeks glowed red from the warm sun — or was it excitement at the Captain's

arrival? Since their last meeting she often thought of him, recalling the warmth of his hand when he said goodbye. Over and over
again she reminded herself not to think of him in any way but as
Jeremy's commander. She was a married woman. Besides, she still
recalled the shame and hurt she had experienced with Dr. Hill.
Though that incident was so many, many years ago, she did not
want to replicate it. Alice pulled her bonnet forward to hide the
blush settling in her face and rose to greet the Captain.

"When did you arrive in town Captain ... Ian?"

"I docked this morning and stopped by to see Mr. Fremont. The
authorities in St. John explained what happened and he provided
more details of the boys' mishap. Two of the culprits were caught
but the lads are needed to identify them. Where are Jeremy and
Rob now?" he asked.

"In the woods sawing some trees that fell in an ice storm," Alice
replied, waving her hand toward the dense woods behind the house.
"They have been able to cut quite a few in the time they have been
here, which has helped fill the wood pile. It takes so much wood to
keep the fires going all year," she chattered on. There was constant
apprehension about the wood supply. It required ten cords each winter just to keep warmth in the cabin, but with all the extra baking
Alice did, much more was required. It was necessary to burn at least
two bushels in the oven each day to get enough hard wood coals
to heat it for baking. With trees ten to twelve feet in diameter, the
manpower necessary to fell the trees and then cut them into usable
pieces was daunting. Before Jeremy's help Horace and Alice had been
sawing branches from trees already downed by storms or ones Josiah
cut before he left, which Horace then split into burnable sized pieces.

The Captain walked past the garden plots still interspersed with
tree stumps, following the sounds of a two-man crosscut saw. He
reappeared a short time later. "The boys want to finish the tree they
are working on. I told them we would talk later," he said, coming to
stand by Alice who was again squatting in the garden patch.

"Dears, let us stop and rest for a little while," Alice suggested to her
daughters. "Susie, will you please go in the house to get some shrub?"

Alice pulled a dipper of water from the rain barrel to rinse the dirt from her hands and passed the dipper on to Penny before splashing some cool water on her face.

The girls led the way over to sit in the shade of a maple tree. Alice and the Captain were ready to follow as Susie emerged carrying a wooden tray with cups, a pitcher of raspberry shrub and ginger cookies.

"Let me help you," the Captain said, reaching to carry the pitcher.

"Thank you," Susie murmured quietly, blinking in astonishment as he took the pitcher from her hands.

Everyone sat, relaxed and quiet, nibbling cookies and drinking, watching the chickens peck for bugs in the weeded garden patches. Alice and the Captain continued to sit under the tree after the girls returned to their picking. Alice drew a basket of newly-picked peas beside her and began shelling them. Ian reached over, gathering handfuls into his lap, expertly zipping the pods open and sliding the green treasures into the brass pot. A companionable silence settled over them, broken only by the gentle plop plop of new peas dropping from their shells. When that was finished Ian gathered the empty shells into the basket and carried them over to the pig trough. He returned, stretching out lazily beside Alice.

She looked at him. "Thank you but I am surprised and puzzled that you are so helpful."

"What do you mean?"

"Why, carrying the pitcher for Susie and now helping with pea shelling. Every other man I know would consider these things women's work and not lift a finger to make their work a little easier. It is deeply appreciated."

Ian remained quiet as he looked into space. "When one is at sea there is much time for reflection," he began. "I remembered growing up at home watching my mother struggle day in and day out to fulfill every whim my father demanded of her, in addition to raising me and my brothers and one sister. Spinning, gardening, baking, sewing, cleaning, candle dipping, soap making and on and on the list went. It wore her down to an early grave. I am ashamed to admit that when I married I expected the same type of servitude from my wife each time I returned from a voyage. I never even considered the extra burden imposed on her while I was at sea. When I returned from a voyage to find out she had died, I was devastated." He paused, remembering the past. "As I said, there is a great deal of time for reflection while watching the waves. I realized how demanding and ungrateful and often thoughtless I had been. Carrying a pitcher or shelling peas is just a little way to help share the burden," he said, smiling at Alice.

"I am sorry you lost your wife," Alice replied sympathetically. This was the first time she had heard him speak of anything about his life other than travels on the sea.

He nodded to her in appreciation. "Thank you," he murmured.

Alice pulled a tatting shuttle from her pocket. She noticed the Captain watch her fingers nimbly pass it in and out of the thread stored in her skirt pocket.

"I am making pillow edgings for Penny's hope chest," she explained.

The Captain nodded again then began to tell her about his latest trip on the ocean and the ports he had docked at. His humorous descriptions of the people he met brought a smile and chuckle to Alice.

"Do you have family back home?" Alice asked after a quiet interlude.

"I have a daughter who was raised by one of my brothers after my wife died and two wee grandsons in Aberdeen," he answered. "And no, I do not have a family in every port I visit," he said with a twinkle in his eyes.

Alice felt flustered to realize he had read her thoughts. Her embarrassment was covered by the appearance of Jeremy and Rob from the wood lot. Darkness had already closed in around the dense trees. The Captain rose to meet them, turning to help Alice to her feet.

"I must fix supper. You will stay, won't you?" she asked, looking at the Captain.

"Yes," he replied with a smile and she hurried off to the house past the lush growth of climbing hollyhocks and herbs by the back door.

They sat around the shiny table enjoying fresh peas and cod fish cakes for supper.

"I will take the boys back with me tomorrow," the Captain explained as the meal was finished.

Alice looked at her older son, catching the look of despair on his face. "How much longer do they have to serve with you?" she asked. "The boys had been captured and put in prison. I know they signed on with you later but is there any way they can be released early?" She was trying to sound out the Captain, realizing both boys' desire to be free.

"Do you want to be released?" he asked, looking at the boys intently.

Jeremy and Rob looked at the Captain directly and nodded their heads in assent.

"I will do what I can," the Captain promised.

"Thank you," she gratefully responded, believing him. In the few times she had met him, and from Franklin's report, she felt he was sincere, fair and of good character.

The Captain rose from the bench. "I am going to stay with Mr. Fremont tonight and I will be back early in the morning," he said, looking at Jeremy and Rob.

Alice walked to the door with him.

"Good night, Alice . . . Alicia," he said softly as he took her hand in his own, raised it to his lips and kissed it gently.

Alicia? How lovely the change of her name sounded. How soft the kiss.

"Good night, Ian," Alice responded, closing the door as he walked toward the road, glad the low candlelight hid the blush rising to her cheeks.

She busied herself gathering the boys' few belongings together as well as a package of pastries and dried soup for their journey.

The children lingered around the table, unwilling to break their companionship. When would they be together again?

"I am sorry to break up this lovely time together, but there is work tomorrow. Off to bed you go," Alice said, shooing them with her hand toward their rooms.

Jeremy lingered behind. "Mama, I simply can't go and leave you with all this work," he said with conviction.

"Jeremy, you have done so much to help me while you have been here. I am deeply grateful. Much as your help is needed and very welcome, I will not encourage you to be dishonorable by staying here. You must go with the Captain, identify those murderous fiends and fulfill whatever obligations you have left. I am sure he will try to get you released. Then you can come back to us free and clear," she said, giving him an affectionate hug. "You know I am very proud of you," she added.

"All right, Mama," Jeremy slowly responded, closing his arms around her and giving her a kiss on the top of her head.

Dawn came all too soon as sad goodbyes and sisterly tears moistened the faces of Jeremy and Rob. The girls walked arm in arm with the boys to the borrowed shay as Ian walked slowly behind with Alice, tucking her arm in his. "May I write to you?" he asked Alice.

"Of course. I would like that. And I will write back," she promised.

The men rode out of their lives one more time.

"Back to work, girls," Alice ordered, brushing tears from her eyes. Life certainly was not easy. They were willing to work hard, but it seemed they were frantically treading water just to exist. Alice clung to the remembrance of God's support and loving care, rejecting from her mind the pastor's fiery preachment that her past sins had brought on the result of their poor economic condition. The God she leaned on was a loving, supportive God, not a sadistic, vindictive one.

"Alice. Well! Did you hear the dreadful news?" Out-of-breath Mattie rushed in the door later in the morning.

"What news?" Alice asked, sliding the bench out from under the table with her foot.

"Well, John Collum was pushed into one of the saws at the mill and killed this morning!" Mattie said breathlessly, yet relishing the gory tale. "It seems he had had an illicit relationship with the wife of one of the men. Wicked! Wicked!" She paused to take a big breath. "Well, when her husband found out about it, he was so angry that he confronted John, and without waiting for a response, he pushed him into the saw. The doctor and your son could do nothing to save him." She paused dramatically. "Well — they took the man to a cell down by the guard house," she added, watching for the reaction of her listeners.

Alice and the girls looked shocked.

"Oh dear. Poor Mary." Alice murmured, her hands suspended in air over the dough.

"Well, there had been rumors that he had been having relationships outside his marriage," Mattie continued, reaching over to take a warm scone off the cooling rack.

Alice turned her face away from Mattie and resumed kneading vigorously. "I never heard about that," she murmured, remembering the day John tried to seduce her. She had never told anyone about that episode. Obviously there must have been others if this story was true.

"Well, I heard about it off and on," Mattie spoke knowingly, waving a sticky finger to emphasize the veracity of her story. "You used to be friends with the Collums, did you not? Did you ever hear or see anything like that?" she asked, waiting for more tidbits to add to her gossip.

"We never saw anything like that," Penny chimed in. Alice was relieved not to have to lie to this gossipy neighbor.

"Well, I must be off," Mattie said, rising to rush out the door. She lifted her skirt to avoid the morning dew as she cut across the lot to the next neighbor's house to repeat the story.

"How horrible!" sympathetic Susie exclaimed, wiping tears from her eyes with her apron. "I remember he always made shadow figures on the wall for us. I wondered why we had not been to their house or they here for a long time. Perhaps because of what Father had done," she spoke sadly, having received some nasty, thoughtless remarks and been shunned by some of the girls in the community. "I suppose we were all just too busy," she answered her own question.

"Most likely," Alice murmured. "We only saw them at church." Their meetings at church had been efforts at avoidance on the part of Mary, John and Alice. The girls had continued to talk with each other but seldom socialized outside the nooning hour.

Alice took a deep breath, measured out more ingredients and baked an additional batch of currant scones, asking Penny to take them to the Collum house on her rounds. She decided that she should not go herself and cause Mary more grief by her presence that would remind Mary of their confrontation at the store. Truthfully, she was afraid to encounter that anger again.

"Did you see Mistress Collum when you delivered the scones?" Alice asked her daughter when she returned. She had to admit she was curious.

"No, Maryann answered the door and I gave them to her. There certainly were a lot of people there, including soldiers and officers," Penny explained. "The story is all over town. Everywhere I went there were different versions of what happened. It must have been awful!" She shivered, imagining the scene.

Three days later the funeral service was conducted at the church. Alice, Horace and the girls attended sitting in the back of the large crowd. Most of the attendees were there to support Mary, though there were curious thrill seekers as well. As the service progressed Mary wailed and left her seat, clinging and sobbing over the closed casket until she was helped back to her seat by Mr. Hollis and the deacon. The entire proceeding was unsettling to everyone. Alice had such mixed emotions she decided to forego the cemetery interment service. She tucked her hand in Horace's elbow as they walked home, sobered by the fragility of life.

. . .

It was a hot August day when Midge and Susie returned from blueberry picking, laughing uproariously as they recounted their antics trying to shoo a bear out of a blueberry patch by Midge flapping her apron, dancing and squawking like a chicken while Susie whistled and stamped her feet. The bear just looked at these strange creatures as it continued to pluck berries. The girls decided the prudent thing to do was to let the bear have that patch that day.

"That was a dangerous thing to do," Alice said. "If it was a mother bear with cubs nearby, you could have been injured."

The girls' faces sobered but often hilarity erupted to break the tenor of the days as they recalled the incident and another bout of giggling would commence.

. . .

As summer had progressed, Will Hollis and Penny had spent many nights sitting and talking quietly on the bench under the maple tree after chores were finished. Their romance blossomed alongside the flowers under Alice's watchful eyes. Walks up and down the road were permissible when accompanied by Susie or Midge.

One late August evening Mr. Hollis accompanied Will to the Marsh home. After welcoming generalities, Alice and Penny sat on one side of the table, Will and Mr. Hollis on the other. Alice saw Mr. Hollis regularly at church but had little contact with him otherwise. She sat watching and waiting for him to speak.

He sat up straighter and brought his eyes to rest upon her. "Hm. Um." His voice took on the tone of a man who always got his way. "Mistress Marsh, my son William wishes to marry your daughter Penelope. I have strong reservations against this marriage. First, because I do not feel either one is old enough. Second, because your daughter has no dowry to bring to this union. Third, because I think she desires William for his money and position and fourth, because of the scandal of her father," he enumerated, half rising from the bench to leave.

"Please sit, Mr. Hollis," Alice ordered, surprised at her stern tone of voice, but angry at his statements. "Let me tell you how I feel about this marriage. First, I feel they are old enough for marriage for they have both assumed responsibilities showing they are able to perform as adults. Second, Penny has a hope chest full of linens and other goods she has created or acquired to bring to a home. There is certainly no money but she has excellent skills in management of a house as well as with money. Third, she has been acquainted with Will since you moved here, having plenty of time to know him and Will to know her, as well as for you to know she is neither a flirtatious nor frivolous girl. Furthermore, her character is exemplary and is not tied to the actions of her father anymore than Will is to the actions of his stepmother."

Mr. Hollis turned red in the face at this last reference. He had divorced Agatha and put her out of his mind. As far as he was concerned she had never existed in his life.

The two adults glared at each other.

"All right, I consent," Mr. Hollis finally stated. He relaxed in his posture and reached for a cup of shrub.

"Thank you! Thank you!" came a joyful chorus from Penny and Will who both reached across the table to hold hands.

"As do I. And I thank you also," said Alice with a big smile.

The families then decided that a late fall or early new year date would be best for the wedding in order to avoid the rush of saw mill work during the late winter when spring thaws allowed the logs to float down the river to the mill. The two parents then parted amicably at the door, Mr. Hollis having accepted the reality of the situation.

. . .

In the remaining days and weeks of summer Alice and the girls feverishly gathered berries and herbs for drying, stored vegetables from the garden in the root cellar for the coming winter, boiled bayberries for candles, salted pork and hams and made sausages, all in addition to their regular chores and baking. Far into the night by moonlight Alice or the girls and Horace often sawed logs that Jeremy had cut. The following day Horace would split them and the girls would stack. The winter stockpile increased by slow increments. Would it be enough? Alice worried. There were no extra minutes for visiting or any forms of frivolity.

The monotony of continual work was broken by letters from Ian, bright spots of interest and humor, that she read over and over relating his latest travels. In one of his first letters he had verified the boys' story. The third thief had not been caught yet. From the two that were in jail the authorities learned there had been a number of other similar instances, unfortunately not all with such good outcomes.

. . .

It was a warm Indian-summer day in mid October when a gentle knock on the jamb by the open door caused Alice to look up from her baking table and call, "Come in." The dim light inside and the bright light outside showed the figure of a woman silhouetted in the doorway.

"Alice?" the figure spoke as it moved into the room.

"Why, Mary, come in please," Alice said warily, trying to keep the shock out of her voice. She moved the bench out for Mary to sit. "Can I serve you a cool drink?" Alice asked to cover her surprise.

"No, I really cannot stay long," Mary said, looking around the room as if seeing it for the first time. "I left my girls by the garden talking to Midge. She is so grown up!" For some time she sat stiffly upright, appearing uncomfortable. Alice kept cutting scones and putting them on the cooking griddle, glancing on and off at her guest.

"I came to apologize," Mary finally blurted out.

"Apologize? For what?" Alice asked, surprised.

"For the things I said that day, in front of the store. I did not believe you because I wanted you to be guilty, not John. But, since his death . . ." She caught a sob, bolstered her courage and continued. "Since then I have learned that he tried and succeeded with a number of women. I did so want to believe him when I asked him about his 'visits,' the ones he told me about." She paused then took a big breath before continuing. "I just came to say that I am sorry and goodbye. The girls and I are leaving for St. John. We will be living with Uncle John and Aunt Martha. They are getting older and need our help," she said. With that Mary rose to leave.

"Oh, Mary, thank you for coming by," Alice said gratefully, moving around the table to give Mary a hug. "I hope you have a happier life with Uncle John and Aunt Martha. Please give them my regards."

The two women walked arm in arm out to the garden patch, no longer lush and green but scraggy and brown, and exchanged good-byes. Alice watched the Collum family walk out of sight up the road and marveled how people moved in and out of each other's lives, all the while changing and growing. She turned to pick up a squash from the pile the girls had gathered earlier before she headed toward the back door.. She paused to cup a lone bright red hollyhock blossom in her hand, remembering again her mother and Elizabeth.

. . .

The winter chill forced the family to put on extra clothes as the light of November days shortened. Ice began to cover the rain barrel overnight, signaling the onset of another winter.

Late one afternoon Alice answered a knock at the door to find Ian standing there.

"Why, Ian, how nice to see you! Is Jeremy with you?" she asked, looking behind him. Flustered yet delighted to see this unexpected visitor she stepped aside for him to enter.

"No, he is back on the ship in St. John. I made a quick visit up here to see you and Mr. Fremont," he added. "Will you come for a walk with me?"

Alice glanced at the baking table.

"Go ahead, Mama, I'll finish up," Penny said.

Ian helped Alice with her cape. She fastened the hood over her head and tucked her hands in the rabbit muff. The two left the house and walked companionably up the street toward the hill. Ian pulled her elbow close to his side.

"Alice. Alicia," he repeated her name. "I heard the name Alicia spoken in Spain and it sounded soft and sweet. More like you," he said, smiling at her.

"I like the sound of it, too," she replied, responding to the smile in his eyes. They walked on, keeping step rhythmically together, as Alice chatted about the latest happenings, particularly the upcoming wedding.

At the rock outcropping above the town they stopped to look back at smoke rising from fireplace chimneys scattered around the valley below, the dark river with its last-minute shipping activity and the thickening clouds of a winter storm gathering in the western sky.

Ian pulled her tighter to his side to shield her from the brisk wind. Alice liked his protectiveness and moved even closer, totally at ease in his presence.

"Alicia, I have been considering leaving the sea and settling down," he said. His face began to flush as he looked at her, "but I want to settle down with you, here or wherever you want. I know you do not know me too well yet, but I love you and I want to marry you." He looked at her anxiously for a welcoming response. "I want to be with you and care for you all the rest of our days," he continued. He removed her muff and held her hands tightly in is own. "Alicia, will you marry me? Please?" his voice and eyes pleaded.

"Oh, Ian!" Alice began to cry, overwhelmed by the emotion of honor and love that he had just bestowed upon her. "I am beginning to love you, too, but I cannot marry you. I am already married!" she said between sobs as she looked at his loving face. She bent her face into his greatcoat to brush away the tears.

"He may very well be dead," Ian spoke vehemently.

"Perhaps, but I could not marry until I knew for sure," she answered, her voice muffled by the fabric of his greatcoat. There had never been any response to the letters from Franklin or Alice.

He lifted her face up towards his own.

They looked at each other sorrowfully, the longing for the love of one another evident on their faces.

Ian bent his face toward Alice, kissing the tears from her cheeks. "I will keep asking until you know for sure," he spoke between kisses. He pulled her closer to his chest.."I love you. I love you."he whispered. Pushing her back far enough to see her face, he looked at her for a long moment, memorizing the features, then bent down and kissed her with a warm, lingering kiss. She responded to his kiss, returning the passion she felt for his love, then reluctantly pulled herself away.

Snowflakes began to float softly down melting with the tears on Alice's face. Ian tucked her arm in his as they slowly walked in a sorrowful silence, emphasized by gathering darkness, down the hill toward home. At her doorstep Ian's face showed conflicting emotions of disappointment, sadness and anger at Josiah as he looked at Alice. He gave her arm a squeeze and turned away.

"Will you not come in for a moment?"Alice pleaded.

"No. I must get on the ship to St. John" he replied brusquely, turning to walk quickly down the road.

Through blurred eyes Alice watched him go.

"Damn. Damn you, Josiah!"she cried angrily, swearing out loud for the first time in her life.

Summer

It is too rash, too unadvis'd, too sudden;
Too like the lightning, which doth cease to be
Ere one can say it lightens. Sweet, good-night!
This bud of love, by summer's ripening breath,
May prove a beauteous flower when next we meet.

— *Romeo and Juliet,* WILLIAM SHAKESPEARE

13

"*HOLD STILL*," Susie ordered Penny. The girls stood in their bedroom applying the finishing touches to the simple yellow brocade wedding gown. The ceremony was about to begin downstairs.

"Ouch!" Penny squealed, as Midge poked a crown of dried flowers around her sister's brown curls. All the preparations were completed; the banns[6] had been properly read for three weeks in church, the house cleaned and decorated, the table laden with fruit and nut-filled cakes, assorted pastries and sweets. They could hear the hum of conversation as guests arrived.

Alice knocked and entered the room carrying a box still wrapped in shipping paper. She unwound the wrapping and removed the cover as her three daughters gathered around. Inside lay three necklaces with varying colored gemstones. Alice lovingly fastened one around each girl's neck. "These were kept for you by your grandmother. Aunt Joan sent them to me when I wrote her of the wedding. Grandpapa Franklin kept the box so you would not see them until today. Now is the right time to give them to you." She stood admiring the happy, healthful glow on the faces of her three daughters and silently said a prayer of thanks for each one of them.

"I remember playing with these stones when Grandmama wore them," Penny said, caressing them with her hands.

"You all look so beautiful," Alice said with pride. She kissed each daughter, giving Penny an extra squeeze around the shoulders.

"May I come in?" A male voice accompanied the tapping on the door.

"Jeremy! Come in," they chorused. "When did you come? How? Is Rob with you? Is the Captain with you?" All the questions besieged him at once.

"Whoa! I'll explain later." He grinned, coming over to put his hands on Penny's arms and said admiringly, "You look radiant, sister dear. Much too nice for Will Hollis. He's a lucky fellow. I'll see you downstairs." He bent down and kissed Alice on the top of her head as he passed her.

Alice followed, joyful for having all her children together and at the thought of maybe seeing Ian again. Her eyes scanned the room downstairs but he was not there. Momentary disappointment flooded her emotions.

Penny followed Susie and Midge as they slowly descended the stairs. Horace and Jeremy joined the sisters to stand behind Penny and Will, whose eyes were only on each other. The happy couple joined hands and stood solemnly facing the pastor. How appropriate to begin their lives together on this first day of the new year.

Alice slipped her hand onto Franklin's thin arm, remembering images of days past as Penny developed from a baby to this mature, lovely woman promising to leave her old life and start anew. Alice dismissed thoughts of possible challenges that might arise in the baking and delivery. The plan was for Penny and Will to live with Mr. Hollis at his house where Penny would become the hostess and manager. For now, Penny would come back to her old home each morning to help finish the baking and make deliveries. She had shown Susie how to keep the accounting records each evening. With these arrangements Alice felt they would manage.

After the marriage service the smiling, blushing couple was toasted with rum, cider and punch before the guests began filling up on all the food spread across the table. Even Mr. Hollis smiled and exchanged pleasantries with everyone. Franklin declared that Penny was as precious as a granddaughter to him as he kissed her on the forehead and presented the couple with a gift of a mantle clock. The newly-wed couple sat on their favorite bench by the fire to examine their other gifts. Among them were three 'lucky' bread peels[7] from customers and a silver tea pot made in England, sent by the Captain and delivered by Jeremy.

"How thoughtful," Alice said softly, silently thanking this dear man.

"Captain MacTavish offloaded me in St. John but wasn't stopping long enough to come here," Jeremy explained.

"Where is Cousin Rob?" Horace asked.

"The Captain's taking him home to Massachusetts. By the way, the Captain asked me to give you this letter," Jeremy said, handing it to Alice with the Captain's wax seal on the closure.

"Thank you." She tucked the letter in her skirt pocket to read later in the privacy of her room. Off and on during the festivities she reached in to touch the letter, excited to have it yet fearful the Captain might end any association with her since she could not marry him.

To a loud chorus of cheers, Mr. Hollis helped the couple into his flower-bedecked sleigh pulled by a bell-laden horse to drive them around town before depositing them at his home, now Penny's home as well.

The rum flowed freely as the afternoon wore on. Horace entertained the guests by dancing the wooden man expertly on the board. Franklin dozed by the fire. Reluctant to end the festivities the guests gradually left as darkness closed around the cabin. Jeremy and Horace woke Franklin, helped him to his feet and, supporting his arms, assisted him into his sleigh.

Susie, Midge and Alice cleared the table, putting leftovers into the pie chest and packing the wedding gifts into a corner for later retrieval.

"It was such a lovely wedding," Susie said dreamily.

"Maybe we'll have another one before the year is out," Midge added slyly.

"You mean it?" Susie asked surprised. "Has George or Jeb asked you?"

"Not yet but it won't be long now!" she answered smugly.

"They both paid a lot of attention to you today. It's not fair for you to tease both of them at the same time," Susie pouted. Midge's joyous spirit attracted young men to her, while quiet, shy Susie seldom elicited any attention from boys.

"Why not? I'm testing which one works the hardest to win me. Whoever it is will get a good bargain," Midge declared, proud of her skills with animal husbandry.

"They certainly will," Alice joined in. Midge's energy and bartering powers had kept this family satisfactorily supplied with extra produce, fruits, spices and other products. In addition, the innumerable hours Susie contributed of dancing to and fro at the spinning wheel were just as valuable to the welfare of the family. If they had not managed so well, life would have been much harder.

Jeremy and Horace walked back into the house, cheeks glowing from the cold winter air. The family sat around the table as Jeremy explained his timely appearance.

"I'm free to work with you here, Mama," he began. "Captain MacTavish arranged all the details for me and Rob to go home permanently. He's taking a load of goods to Massachusetts and New York, then on to the Islands, Africa and back to England. He even ordered the sails up to make a fast crossing so he could get me to St. John in time for the wedding. It was a rush but I made it." He smiled, satisfied and happy.

"And what a joyous surprise it was," Alice smiled back, patting his hand.

Jeremy hesitated. "I want you to know that someday I would like to return to America and buy a farm."

"I know," Alice acknowledged.

The tired family finally dispersed to their rooms. Alice shut her bedroom door but, before undressing or brushing her long hair, she removed Ian's letter from her pocket. Sitting on the edge of the bed close by the candle she read:

Dear Alicia,

I must admit I was sorry you did not make me the happiest man in the world when we were last together. However, I have not given up hope that someday you will become my wife. I will continue to woo you until the day that the door of hope is forever closed to me. I was hoping to deliver Jeremy to you in person, but there is just a brief moment for me to write this note before the sails are up and I must be on my way to America. This moment gives me one more opportunity to tell you how much I admire you and love you. Please remember that.

My best wishes to Penelope and Will for a long, happy marriage.

Please continue to write to me. I cherish your letters.

Until we meet again, my love flows to you every day as the wind blows me around the sea and back to you.

Yours, Ian

Alice clasped the letter to her heart, delighted to be loved. Little by little tears formed in her eyes and slid down her cheeks. A feeling of hopelessness that this developing love would ever be fulfilled crowded out the joy she had felt a moment ago. Would she go through the rest of her life without the fulfillment of this man's true love? She carried the candle to the cherry table, wiped the tears from her eyes and sat in thought about the reply she would write. The words came at last, spilling out the love she felt for this thoughtful, wonderful, loving man.

My Dearest One,

The snow has been falling silently all day and accumulating with steady softness. There is a quietness in the air — almost the same as lying fully under the covers as I did as a child. This soft blanket of snow reminds me of you and the quiet warmth of the love you declared to me on the hillside. It brings back one of my dreams of lying close to you with your arms around me — your wife — under the covers in the quietness of night. Such a lovely dream.

So many things remind me of you since I saw you last. External things, like Midge humming the melody of the Scottish air you played, the shape of someone walking on the street, or the love of Penny and Will as they recited their marriage vows today. But frequently it is the internal feelings that bubble to the surface — memories of feelings and closeness brought on by something as soft as the snow.

I have found it particularly difficult putting you out of my mind since we last met. It had been increasingly hard as time went on in the past, but now? I know the difference this time is your asking me to marry you. What an honor! And what a commitment of your love!

Part of me wants to think about you constantly, reminiscing and dreaming, while the other part of me tries to relegate you to the closet shelf of broken hearts. It is causing me much turmoil, almost creating two realities.

Anyhow, dearest heart, sweet dreams to you tonight. I love you! I love you! I love you! Tuck my loving thoughts into the box on your closet shelf and peek at it each day. Just remember in the back recesses of your mind that someone loves you dearly. That thought alone can fill your heart with joy and warmth when a day does not go particularly well. Just knowing you love me has made some difficult days much more tolerable for me.

Lovingly, Alicia

She reread the letter, but could not bring herself to ready it for mailing. It seemed much too personal and loving to trust it to the mail. Besides, she was married and must not even entertain the thought of loving him. She tucked it away in the back of one of her dresser drawers to hand to Ian in person, if she was ever free to become his wife. Tears of anguish filled her eyes as she gradually dropped off to sleep.

The next day the family and Franklin gaily trooped to the Hollis house to visit the coming-out bride and groom. The spirits flowed freely in the left parlor where Will held court with the men while the ladies drank tea more sedately in the right parlor.

The daily routine of the new year settled into place. Jeremy found a job in one of the warehouses on the docks. Horace assisted the doctor full time now. Penny glowed with happiness, coming by each morning in a sleigh to help Alice. Susie kept the spinning wheel going and Midge hummed and sang her way through chores. Alice, in turn, baked even more as orders increased. She realized she was trying to hurry the days along. Maybe that way Ian would arrive sooner on a visit.

The overriding concern of the family was Franklin's deteriorating health. Each week they noticed perceptible changes as he sat at the dinner table after church. Looks of anxiety passed among them as they gazed at him. Susie and Midge continued to act as his nurses, urging him to eat just one more bite. He assured them all that he was fine, just a little tired.

· · ·

On a bitter cold morning in mid-February Horace hurried into the house. "Mama, you must come. Franklin is very sick and he is asking for you. Dr. Morris is with him, but it doesn't appear as if there is much time," he said, taking Alice's cloak off the hook by the door.

"Susie, please take the bread out of the oven soon," Alice ordered, wiping flour off her hands.

"Of course," Susie replied. "Give Grandpapa Franklin our love."

"I will," Alice called back, already halfway out the door. Horace helped her into the doctor's sleigh, urging the horse to trot quickly on their way to Mistress Thompson's boarding house.

Alice had never been in Franklin's room. It was a moderate-sized room lined with shelves of books. Books were stacked on tables and chairs and even in the corner on the floor. Now, whatever space was left was crowded with people. She brushed past the pastor and George Miltimore to the bed and bent down to take Franklin's hand in hers. This small frame before her bore no resemblance to the large man of pre-war days. "Franklin, 'tis me, Alice. I am here."

He slowly opened his eyes. "Alice...I wanted to thank you for being a family to me. It was my reason for living after Isabella died." He struggled to get the words out as a cough choked off his breathing. "You. You. Isabella...." His weak voice trailed off. He looked beyond Alice intently, gave her hands a weak squeeze and breathed his last.

"Franklin, we love you," Alice whispered as tears crowded her eyes. She lifted his hand and kissed it goodbye.

Dr. Morris checked the pulse, nodded, closed Franklin's eyes and covered the head.

Horace put his arms around Alice in a comforting hold. Numbed by her grief she let him escort her to the door of the room.

Mr. Brown, Franklin's business partner in the law firm, followed them into the hall. Alice had not even realized he had been in the room.

"Mistress Marsh, as Mr. Freemont's friend and lawyer I handled his business affairs and I will make the funeral arrangements. I know how much he appreciated your family, just as if you were his own," he said, shaking her hand.

"Thank you," Alice whispered, turning to hold Horace's arm as they proceeded down the stairs to the sleigh waiting to go back home.

"I have to get the sleigh back to Dr. Morris," Horace said, helping Alice alight. "I'll be back tonight."

Alice slowly walked the snowy path to the house she called home, opened the door and hung her cloak on the peg. She nodded "yes" to the girls as she took a seat on the bench that Franklin always occupied. Susie brought Alice some hot cider and sat before her. Midge hovered by them as Alice told the details of the morning. They sat quietly as each remembered this man who had become a dear family member, mentor and friend to them all. They would miss him. Alice in particular felt that the supporting underpinning of her life had just broken away, leaving her unsteady and vulnerable. She realized how much she had relied upon Franklin to answer her questions, support her, advise her and, in general, act the part of a father to her and grandfather to her children.

In the afternoon Mistress Thompson came by the house. She cried loudly into her handkerchief. "He was such a kind man to me and everyone at the house. I know he thought of you as family, but would you let me hold the wake and reception at the boarding house? We all loved him too and he felt at home there. Besides, it is closer for everyone in town," she requested between sniffles.

"Yes," Alice agreed. "What can we do to help?"

Mistress Thompson hesitated. "Pastries would be nice," she requested at last.

"We will bring some over for both the wake and reception," Alice said, wondering how she could manage the extra work. With Midge and Susie's help she would make it work even if it meant baking through the evening.

Mistress Thompson lingered over a warm drink, periodically sobbing while repeatedly explaining what a good man Franklin had been. Alice fidgeted. She wanted to begin baking because she had to finish for deliveries the next day as well as for the boarding house. She did not want to be rude but she finally instructed Susie to stoke the fire. She hoped the guest would take the cue to leave. When that did not work Alice stood up saying, "Mistress Thompson, I am actually quite harried and want to begin making pastries for your house. Will you excuse me while I start?" She then proceeded to set ingredients from the shelf by the dry sink onto the table.

"Of course," Mistress Thompson said, rising and coming over to envelop Alice in a bosomy embrace. "Thank you. Thank you," she repeated over and over until Alice extricated herself and rushed the woman out the door.

No sooner had Alice got her hands in the dough than chatty Mattie walked in without knocking.

"Well, did you hear Franklin Fremont died this morning?" she asked.

"Yes" Alice replied.

"Well, I wonder how much money he had? You know that Mistress Thompson was putting her grasping fingers out to catch him as a husband. Did you ever hear the like? I believe she will take as much as she can get or steal."

"No!" Alice looked shocked. She had never imagined that Mistress Thompson might stoop to stealing Franklin's possessions. Should she ask Mr. Brown to keep watch over them? Surely that was not necessary. Besides, what did Franklin have that was so valuable?

"Well, I imagine his will might leave her something. Do you know if he had a will?" she asked.

"No, we never discussed his personal affairs," Alice replied. "You'll excuse me, for I've got a great many pastries to bake for tomorrow's delivery," she said, edging the neighbor toward the door.

"Well, I will keep my ears open and let you know what I find out," Mattie said, leaving to pass the word on to the next house. Though she did not live in town nor close to any neighbor, there was very little that transpired that she did not know or imagine to be happening. She used to watch and report to Alice if she had heard an inappropriate word or saw unseemly behavior from the girls. They, in return, mouthed a secret name for her, "Wicked witch," knowing Alice would threaten to wash their mouths out with soap if they uttered it out loud. Calling a woman a witch was simply not done anymore and their mother would not tolerate it.

With Midge and Susie's help Alice kept busy far into the night preparing extra pastries while Horace and Jeremy split and stacked more wood by the fireplace.

Two days later Franklin's casket was interred in the mausoleum to await spring burial. There were so many attendees after the service who gathered for the reception at the boarding house that Mistress Thompson could not accommodate everyone in the parlor and dining room. Some had to stand on the stairs and even out on the cold front porch. She fluttered about, alternately sobbing ("crocodile tears," Horace whispered) or ordering people to "stand here" or "move over there" in a piercing voice. It was quite a scene, likely not at all what Franklin would have chosen.

As the crowd dispersed from the boarding house Mr. Brown took Alice's arm. "Franklin left a will, and you and your family are mentioned in it. Please, can you come by the office now for me to read it?" he asked.

"We can," Alice replied, indicating the change of plans to all the children.

The family sat in Mr. Brown's office, next door to the one Franklin had occupied. Mistress Thompson entered with a flurry, bright eyed and no longer sobbing. "See, I told you so. Crocodile tears," Horace whispered.

Alice shot him a warning look to hush.

Mr. Brown produced a paper and proceeded to read from it. "To Mistress Thompson I give the extra bedding I had purchased with my own funds. I thank her for her constant concern. To Jeremy and Horace Marsh I leave my horse, shay and sleigh. To Jeremy Marsh I leave my telescope. To Horace Marsh I leave my Hepplewhite desk and chair for his future office. To Penelope and Martha Marsh I leave each a brooch, one jade and one onyx, that had belonged to my wife Isabella. To Susannah Marsh I leave my literature books and bookcases. To Alice Marsh I leave the chased silver tray we bought from her many years ago." Mr. Brown looked up at her quizzically then resumed his reading. "In addition, after any expenses regarding my funeral or other obligations that might have arisen are satisfied, the remainder of my money is to go to Alice Marsh in a trust fund that will be paid to her yearly. At her death any remaining is to be divided among her children or their descendants." Mr. Brown looked up from his reading and interjected, "It is a modest amount, for Franklin gave away much of his money in charitable gifts." He returned to his reading. "I stipulate that should Josiah Marsh return he cannot claim the funds for his own use. If that should occur the money is to revert to the children of Alice." He concluded by saying, "There are one or two more items pertaining to other people not here at this time."

Mistress Thompson stood up protesting, "Franklin owed me money and he promised me the extra furniture and books."

Mr. Brown listened to her with a frown on his face. "Do you have anything in writing to substantiate that?" he asked politely.

"Ahhh. No, but he made a verbal agreement," she claimed loudly. However, Mr. Brown's steady gaze caused her to lower her eyes and sink back on the chair in silence.

"If you have a claim, submit it to me in writing with proof and it will be processed. I have gone through Mr. Fremont's ledgers and found all his bills have been paid in full to date," Mr. Brown spoke courteously and evenly. "Mistress Marsh, I will make arrangements for his items to be delivered to you as soon as possible," he added, rising. "Until then, Mistress Thompson, please do not allow anything to be disturbed in the room Mr. Fremont occupied," he warned as he escorted everyone from his office. As they left the room, Mr. Brown spoke quietly to Alice. "Mistress Marsh, I would appreciate it if you would please give me an address for Captain MacTavish. Franklin left a letter and gift for him that I am obligated to deliver."

"Of course and thank you for all your help and concern for Franklin."

"He was a noble man," Mr. Brown said thoughtfully.

The added work, the funeral and the reading depleted their energy, and the family walked to their homes in silence.

Wearily, Alice sat at the table composing a letter to Ian.

Dear Ian,

It is with deep sadness that I write to tell you that Franklin died this week. The reception after the funeral was held today at Mistress Thompson's boarding house. He would have been honored yet humbled by the great number of people who attended to pay their respects. So many spoke of the quiet charity he had given them during his years here. Franklin seemed to know instinctively the number of coins needed and quietly slipped them into their hands at the right moment. This generosity explains a mystery at our house that sometimes puzzled me. There always seemed to be enough coins in my strong box for ingredients and bills when some weeks I thought more money went out than came in. Neither the girls, who did the collecting, nor I could fully explain the discrepancy. I believe it was Franklin's way of helping us without destroying our need to be independent. It reminds me of the story in 1st Kings of Elisha and the widow with the flour and oil that never ran out until the drought was over. Surely God was working through Franklin. Our family will truly miss him as I am sure you will as well.

Jeremy's presence has alleviated the constant pressure on Horace to keep the wood pile ahead of the fireplace demands. The two boys work well together. Again, I thank you for your help in allowing him to return home to us.

I received your letter from Spain last week. From your description it must be a beautiful place.

Please keep writing. I miss your visits and look forward to seeing you again. Soon.

Yours truly,
Alicia

She reread the letter, wanting to add 'I love you' but was afraid to commit herself on paper should Josiah ever return and her heart break yet again.

14

*W*INTER WAS RELUCTANT to release its grip on the land. Cold and periodic snow storms from the northwest swept over the hill and down into the valley. Days of sleet and freezing rain challenged anyone intrepid enough to venture forth. Ice clogged the river. Leaden-gray skies dominated the horizon. The prolonged winter frustrated everyone, producing shortened tempers or depression that affected the behavior of all. Longing for the sun's cherished warmth in spring became intense.

Alice was no exception. Some days she just wanted to stay in bed with the covers pulled over her head. Other times she sat by the fire cradling a cup of hot tea in her hands, not even considering the work that needed to be done. This lethargic attitude depleted her energy and she found it took much longer than usual to finish her tasks. Where was her courage and confidence and energy? Where was the cheerful spirit she tried to put forth each day? What was going to happen to them if they had to leave the house soon as Mr. Miltimore intimated one afternoon after church service? She missed Franklin's reassuring presence every week. She dreamt of laying her head on Ian's shoulder and feeling his strong arms around her. "I am deluding myself, for it can never be," she argued with herself, feeling even more depressed and lonely at the thought.

To add to the depression Mattie came by one morning after several days absence. Her usual gossipy chatter was missing as she took a seat by the table.

Alice eyed her somber neighbor as she pushed the tray of scones across the table.

"Well." Mattie took a deep breath and began again. "Well, two of my grandbabies died of whooping cough last night." She automatically took a bite and swallowed. "Three-year-old Lucy and four-year-old Paul. Poor, poor wee ones." With her apron she dabbed at tears beginning to run down her wrinkled cheeks.

"Oh, my dear," Alice sympathized as she laid aside her spoon and sat beside Mattie, drawing her close. This was the first time she had ever heard or seen Mattie express any loving emotion regarding her grandchildren.

Mattie wept. Between sobs she spoke about her grief at the loss.

"Please let me walk home with you," Alice asked as Mattie rose to leave.

"Well, if you would."

"I shan't be long," Alice called out to Susie in the next room as she gathered a napkin full of warm scones and supported Mattie's arm as they crossed the icy ground.

Red-eyed Bridget looked up from the hearth as the two women walked in the door. Alice went over and knelt beside the younger woman, putting her hand on Bridget's arm. At this simple act of sympathy tears began to form again in Bridget's eyes. She rubbed them away, stood up and began to chop a cabbage. "It happens," she said resignedly.

"Well, it was the Lord's will," Mattie pontificated.

Still kneeling by the hearth Alice looked up at Mattie, appalled by her statement. She protested vehemently, "No, it was not." Turning to Bridget, she asked, "Is there anything I can do?"

"No, thank you," Bridget replied dully.

Alice rose, set the scones on the table and moved to open the door. "I am so sorry," she said softly before she stepped out into the gray day. She did not want to linger in that house watching Bridget shut her pain away or debating the Lord's will with Mattie.

She mouthed a swift prayer of gratitude for never having had to experience the same loss of her own dear children. This thankfulness warred with the depression and loneliness she was feeling this bitter winter. She wondered when she would ever move beyond this point in her life. Her sadness and questioning about life carried over to the interment of Lucy and Paul. She watched helplessly as Bridget drew a hard shell of grief and pain tighter about herself.

Alice anxiously watched Penny each morning when she came to help with the baking and delivery, having to drive the horse-drawn sleigh over the snow-covered roads or struggle to keep upright on icy ground as she walked to the customers' houses. She looked wan, tired and kept losing weight. Some days she arrived late complaining of nausea. Alice thought she was likely pregnant but Penny would not confirm it yet.

On a particularly gray, foggy morning Penny opened the door, walked in and sat immediately on the bench by the fire. She shivered, pulling her cloak tighter around her shoulders. Icy tears rolled down her cheeks.

"Penny, dear, we must get the doctor to see you," Alice said, filling a cup with hot tea and handing it to her daughter.

"Yes, Mama," Penny whispered, at last willing to be examined.

Alice helped Penny to the downstairs bed, covering her with extra quilts. "Penny, may Susie use the sleigh to do the deliveries?" she asked.

Penny nodded.

"Susie, you do the deliveries this morning. Stop at the mill and tell Will that Penny is here then stop at the doctor's to ask him to come here," she ordered.

Within the hour Will was sitting anxiously by Penny wiping away her tears and trying to comfort her spirits. Thankfully, Dr.

Morris was at his house and free to come look at Penny later in the morning.

"It is true, Will and Mistress Marsh, that Penny is going to have a child. I advise that she stay in bed until she becomes stronger and the baby is growing well," Dr. Morris stated as he returned to the main room, relaxing for a few minutes with a cup of hot cider from Alice. "I must tell you again how much I appreciate the work that Horace is doing. He is proving to be a good doctor." Dr. Morris could not help but extol Horace's abilities every time he saw Alice.

"Thank you," Alice said, graciously accepting the compliment of her son.

"I must get Penny home," Will declared as he stopped his troubled pacing in front of them.

"Of course."

Alice went into the bedroom to help Penny.

"Mama, I will be all right. The housekeeper, Mistress Joseph, will take good care of me." Penny reached over to grasp her mother's hand. "Please come by as often as you can to see me," she implored as fear and bravery played against each other in her face and voice.

"Dear One, of course I will. You will be fine. Just rest and do as the doctor says," Alice reassured her.

"Let me help you," Dr. Morris said. With the two men supporting Penny between them they walked slowly over the dirty snow to Will's sleigh as Alice stood outside the door waving goodbye. She hoped Penny would have as much success carrying a baby to term as she had had.

When Susie returned to the house after deliveries of the pastries she said, "Mama, I've been thinking. If I do the deliveries each morning, that will still give me time in the afternoon and evening to spin the flax and wool."

Alice nodded in grateful assent. She had not thought about this change to her business yet.

"How wonderful that we are going to have a baby in the family!" Susie exclaimed excitedly. She was delighted for her sister. "Imagine, you are going to be a grandmama," she said teasingly to Alice.

215

"So I am. 'Tis exciting, isn't it?" She beamed at the thought.

In the evening Alice sat at the table writing a letter to Ian. She felt that sharing her thoughts brought her closer to him. It was a way to feel his support even if he was not by her side. She kept the letter chatty, full of news about Penny, the family and questions about the lands he was sailing to. His letters to her were the bright lights in the dreary, sunless days.

. . .

Spring finally burst the bonds of winter. It appeared to happen overnight. as ice broke in the river and moved swiftly downstream, carrying cut logs to the sawmills. Flooding covered the low lands and miniature lakes appeared in fields and yards. Shipping began to move up river to unload at the warehouses situated along the banks. Even the slippery, muddy roads were not too big a nuisance to dampen the people's jubilant spirits.

The Marsh family life was full of routine and good spirits. Penny gained strength and the baby grew steadily within her. When George and Jeb came to visit Midge, Jeb's interest now began to turn more often toward Susie and the two frequently spent their evenings discussing books together, history in particular. Jeremy had become infatuated with the chandler's daughter, visiting her more than one night a week if her mother allowed it. Horace spent many evenings assisting Dr. Morris. Alice's own spirits lifted with the sunshine of spring and the budding of the trees. She marveled at the sight of so many shades of green. Although the work load had increased with more orders and less help, Alice deliberately found opportunities for spare time of her own. She delighted in having many more books in the house. For so long a time, it seemed, she had restricted her reading. Though she could have borrowed books from Franklin in the past, she had refused to allow herself the leisure of moments of relaxation. Now, she was inspired to read about the lands Ian touched on his travels. It opened fresh new ideas and interests to her. She reflected that she was the same woman who had loved reading many years ago, but in the years between, she had closed herself to that world of thoughts.

Late on a warm May afternoon Alice stood on a kitchen chair engrossed in washing the winter dirt off the outside windows in the front of the house. She hummed a lilting ditty as she washed and polished, sometimes leaning back to admire the bright reflection. Although conscious of the grind of wagon wheels on the road, she paid little attention until a familiar voice from the past spoke behind her.

"Good afternoon. Alice?"

Her arm held the wet rag poised in mid air. Could it be? Slowly she turned to observe the man standing below her.

"Josiah?" she asked, surprised and momentarily believing this man standing before her was an illusion. She looked at a portly, colorfully dressed man in out-dated English-style clothes wearing a high-crowned black felt hat on his head. His orange riding coat had double collars and tight-fitting sleeves with the coattails reaching below his knees. Loops and button closures were prominent on the front and sleeves. His yellow breeches reached just below his knees with ribbon loops. Dusty black jockey boots reached up to the breeches. The costume looked ludicrous on this old man trying to appear young, so different from the man she used to know.

"It is me." He turned, haughtily signaling with a glass-topped black walking stick for the drayman to unload a trunk from the wagon and carry it to the door.

Alice watched the action hardly believing it was happening, "Let me finish this window," she said, deliberately turning her back on him as she proceeded to slowly wipe the last residue of water off the glass. When she turned he was still there. She stepped off the chair without holding out her hand for assistance, emptied the pail of water in the flowerbed and carried the pail and chair to the back door, followed by Josiah. She kept silent for there was so much she wanted to say and ask but she needed time to collect her thoughts for this totally unexpected arrival.

After spreading the wet rag over a bush to dry and bleach she turned to face Josiah. "Why did you come back?" she asked forthrightly.

"To be with my family, of course," he replied with a note of feigned hurt in his voice. "And to see to the property," he added.

Could it be he really intended to live here again? Alice was doubtful. "Then let me show it to you," she said.

More than three-quarters of the lot was still heavily wooded with maples, oaks, birch, ash and fir trees. Alice turned and walked ahead of him pointing out the vegetables and herbs planted amidst the decaying stumps and the two young, blooming apple trees close by the west side of the house. She led him past the closed in lean-to to the penned area along the east side near the back door.

"Midge, your father is here," Alice said, leaning over the slat fence. Midge was sitting in the corner bottle feeding a newborn lamb in her lap.

"Good afternoon." Midge said politely as she looked up warily at this man who was her father. She was uncertain how to react, having only lived a few years with him.. "The ewe had three lambs and will only feed two. This wee one was rejected, but it will not die if I can help it," she vigorously exclaimed while remaining seated.

Alice resumed the tour showing Josiah the pig pen with its sow and nine hungry piglets, the tethered cow grazing on the edge of the woods and the fallen tree partially cut for firewood. She led him along the path toward the house, shooing chickens out of the way, past the flower bed with hollyhocks beginning their climb toward the sun and around to the front and finally into the house.

"I wonder what he sees this time," she mused. The late afternoon sun cast a burnished bronze glow across the wide plank floor. The scoured baking and eating table sat prominently in the center of the room on the right. A book lay open on a chair and two pictures of mythological scenes hung on the wall between the windows with Franklin's desk and chair placed underneath. Full bookcases reached floor to ceiling in the front corner. Narrow stairs curved around the chimney that divided the house. The open doorway to the bedroom on the left showed a room filled with afternoon light. A quilted curtain divided this room in two. In the front Susie moved to and fro spinning wool into yarn. In the back section a chest of drawers and the corner of the built-in bed were visible. Pegs on the wall held Alice's two extra dresses. Over time Alice had been able to plaster the walls in the main room but not the bedroom. To her eyes it was an amiable, cozy home full of work and the chatter of an active, healthy family. Altogether a place of harmony and contented living.

"Susie, your father is here," Alice spoke from the bedroom doorway, stepping aside for Josiah to move forward.

Susie stopped the wheel and stood to one side. "Good afternoon, Papa," she said politely.

"Good afternoon, Susie," he replied, looking at her closely.

"Let me fix some tea." Alice moved away from them toward the water kettle keeping warm close by the low coals. She filled the tea pot and set three cups on the table. Opening the pie chest she removed a plate of cold, maple-sugar filled biscuits and set it on the table, then called Susie and Josiah to sit as he continued to regale his daughter with the wonderful life he had been living in England.

As she slowly drank her cup of tea, Alice looked at Josiah more closely. His face was flushed and there was puffiness around his eyes and in his hands, which shook slightly as he lifted his cup. She noticed some fraying on the cuffs of his jacket and around the collar. "He is not so well off," she conjectured to herself. Often she had fantasized what she would say if he returned, but now she felt numb listening to him talk on and on about the wonders of London.

The usual chatter among the young Marshes was absent during the evening meal as they ate. They occasionally glanced surreptitiously at their father but Alice kept her eyes focused on her plate.

"What are your plans? How long will you be staying? Are you here for good now?" All at once these questions from his children besieged him as he was finishing his meal.

"Of course, I promise to stay here with you from now on," he assured them. "I will need a little while to settle in, though," he added.

The boys looked at him skeptically. They excused themselves, kissed their mother and left the house. The sound of sawing and chopping of firewood could be heard until dark when it suddenly quieted and the boys went to their evening visits or study.

Susie and Midge were overjoyed to introduce this father who really existed to their beaux, Jeb and George, when they came by to visit the girls. Excusing themselves they went out to sit on the bench under the tree.

Alice and Josiah continued to sit opposite each other at the table.

"Where have you been all this time?" Alice asked, eventually breaking the uneasy silence.

"In London, mostly."

"Mistress Hollis? ... Is she still? ... What I mean is ... are you still living with her?"

He looked down at his hands, finally looking up discomfited. "We did for awhile, but — she moved on. Believe me, Alice, I am persuaded it is you I want to be with," he said, reaching over to enclose her hands.

She tugged them back to grasp the teacup.

"Are you sure?"

"Oh, yes."

"When did you part ways with each other?" she asked, looking at him directly.

"Oh, during the year," was the vague answer.

"Why did you wait so long to come back?"

He dropped his eyes. "I needed to gather money to make the trip."

"Then why did you never write? Did you ever receive the letters Franklin Fremont and I wrote?"

No reply. Just a slight shrug.

"By the way, Franklin died this past February," she informed him.

"That is unfortunate," Josiah replied unemotionally

Alice weighed the responses he had given. During the past years she thought she had forgiven him, but with his surprise appearance and vague explanations, she became unsettled as frustration and anger began to resurface and replace the detachment she had felt earlier. Anger concerning their children and the loss of a loving, supportive father in their lives. Anger that she had been left alone to support and keep the family together. Again! Anger at his failure to respond to Franklin's letter or even her own. She was not ready to break down the wall she had created around her emotions towards him. Not yet.

"Excuse me," she said, rising. "I earn money by baking. I have to prepare for tomorrow's orders," she explained, going to the door and reminding the girls to come in. "You can sleep in the front bedroom. I will go upstairs with the girls," she told Josiah.

"Sleep with me, Alice," he begged.

"No, not tonight," she replied firmly, moving into the bedroom. She was not ready to share her bed with this man, her husband yet a stranger. She turned to the dresser, reaching into one of the drawers to remove undergarments. Feeling the letter to Ian, she slipped it among the folds of her chemise and shut the drawer with finality. Brushing past him she said, "Good night, Josiah," trying to keep multiple emotions in check.

Far into the night she lay awake confused and worried. Could she believe Josiah would really embrace life here in Fredericton? Her own life was being turned upside down again. Another change! Over and over she mouthed prayers for insight. At this moment it was too hard for her to utter prayers of gratitude for the many blessings she had already received this day. She just could not find the words.

Long before daylight, she slipped out of bed, tiptoeing downstairs to stoke the fire for baking and to heat water for tea. She sat at the table cradling the warm cup in her hands, staring into the firelight, her mind suspended somewhere between dreams and grief. The methodical ticktock of the wall clock entered her consciousness, returning her to reality. She came to a decision. With tears streaming down her cheeks she removed the letter to Ian from her pocket. Passionately she held it to her lips for a moment, kissed it then dropped it into the flames, watching the words disappear as the paper flared until it turned to ash. "Goodbye Ian, my love, my dream," she whispered. Convention, duty and legal ties dictated her decision. The choice had been made for her. Josiah, her husband, was back. "Courage, courage," she whispered to herself. Resolutely, she turned and busied herself with the day's orders of scones, doughnuts and pastries.

"Well! Well!" Mattie uttered, walking in the house earlier than usual without knocking. "I saw you had a gentleman visitor with a trunk yesterday," she said, openly glancing at the closed bedroom door, obviously disappointed it was shut.

"Why yes," Alice replied. There was no use trying to deny the arrival from this all-seeing neighbor.

"Well, is it a relative?" The neighbor boldly pursued her curiosity.

"Uh huh," Alice continued nonchalantly, smiling mischievously to herself. She was not going to divulge too much too soon.

"Well, is he staying long?"

"Likely."

"Well, I guess I will be on my way," Mattie spoke slowly, frustrated that she had not learned the identity of this visitor.

"Thank you for stopping by," Alice said, walking to the door with the inquisitive neighbor. "I will tell my husband you were inquiring about him," she said sweetly, starting to giggle as she shut the door on the surprised look crossing her neighbor's face. Susie and Alice periodically erupted into hushed laughter at the remembrance of the open-mouthed look on Mattie's face.

It was nearly mid morning when Josiah arose and walked into the main room wearing a paisley robe. Susie had left with the deliveries, the boys were off to work and Midge was attending to her outside chores. Alice was kneading dough for bread.

"Good morning," Josiah said exuberantly, coming over to plant a kiss on her cheek. She neither responded nor turned away from the motion. Her thoughts were in conflict.

"May I have some tea?" he asked.

With floury hands Alice motioned to a mug, the tea caddy and tea kettle and then pushed over a plate of fresh doughnuts.

"Sit for a while," he requested.

"I cannot," she answered, continuing to knead.

"By the way, where is Penny?"

"She was married January 1st this year but is confined to bed during her pregnancy," Alice informed him.

"I would like to see her."

"I know she would like to see you but it might be rather awkward. She married Will Hollis and lives in the same house with Mr. Hollis, Sr."

Josiah blushed slightly, not pursuing the subject. He stood up. "I think I will take a walk around town," he said to cover his embarrassment, leaving the house after dressing and returning just before the evening meal.

This routine continued for two weeks. The old Josiah surfaced once in awhile, questioning or critical of Alice's decisions. Other times he gushed with protestations of affection or feigned interest, asking questions of the boys yet barely listening to their answers, frequently demanding the use of the horse and shay, ignoring the girls except to ask them to fill his tea cup. His presence put a damper on the entire family.

"Josiah, are you planning to help Jeremy finish developing this property into a working farm?" Alice asked one day.

"I never liked farming. You know that. And I have not done any for a long time. Besides, my back hurts."

"I never knew you disliked it so much," she replied in surprise. "Time has run out and you have to do something with the property or the town will take it back. With Franklin's influence we managed to hold on to it longer than usual. We can't continue to live in this uncertainty." She pressed the point that was on her mind.

"I will sell it if I can."

. . .

For days Alice had debated within herself how to find words to write Ian about Josiah's return. "The sooner the better," she told herself one afternoon when she was alone in the house. Gathering the writing implements she wrote

223

Dear Ian,

Oh, how much she longed to tell him she loved him, his chatty letters, his humor and his smiles, but she could not put those words on the paper. What came from her were the stilted, unemotional words of farewell.

I am writing to inform you that my husband, Josiah, has returned to Fredericton. I have valued your friendship and deeply thank you for your help to Jeremy and for your presence in our lives.

Sincerely,
Alice Marsh

Before she changed her mind, she sealed it and walked out to meet the mail rider on his afternoon rounds. As he sped away with the letter, Alice symbolically turned her back upon it to return slowly to the house.

. . .

A week later Alice reached into the black-painted tin box kept on the top shelf for money to pay the miller who waited at the door. It was empty! She returned to the door where he stood. "I'm so sorry, Mr. Phelps. I don't have the money to pay you today," she said, embarrassed and perplexed. She always kept the money on hand for him.

Mr. Phelps hesitated, looking sympathetically at her obvious discomfort. "I will give you one bag of flour today and you can pay me next time. You have always paid me before," he spoke kindly, walking in and setting the bag by the table.

"Oh, thank you. I need it to bake tomorrow's orders," Alice fervently said, grasping his hands in thanks.

She escorted him to the door and shut it firmly behind him. Where had the money gone? It had never disappeared before. Had Josiah taken it as he had in Gloucester? Could she believe he had done it again?

"Josiah, did you take money out of the black box?" she confronted him as soon as he strolled into the house late in the afternoon.

He looked at her. "Why, yes," he said confidently. "I needed it."

"For what?"

"For my tobacco and some new handkerchiefs."

"Why didn't you ask me? That money pays for my baking supplies which I have to order all the way from the James Stewart store in St. John as well as from the miller here in town." Her rising anger made her want to scream at him or strike him; anything that would vent her rage.

"I did not know. Besides, what difference does it make? You can always charge them," he said, dismissing the gravity of his action, and coming over to pull her into his arms. "What is yours is mine, you know," he added, trying to make light of it, yet with an undertone of rightful possession.

Alice seethed with anger. She slipped out of his grasp, picked up the pail of slop for the pigs and headed out the back door, slamming it behind her. Must she live like this from now on? It was many days before she could speak to him with civility. His reaction in turn became one of indignation and blame. It was not her place to control the family's money, which rightfully belonged to him as her husband.

. . .

One day in late June Josiah arrived home earlier than usual and he was exuberant. "I have got a buyer for the house and property."

Alice sat down heavily on the bench. "What?"

"He is going to buy everything, including the animals, at a good price. I certainly bargained with him to get the best price and it worked." He was jubilant.

"When?" Alice asked, stunned.

"It should be completed by the end of July." He rattled on and on, pacing the floor excitedly.

"Where will we go?" she whispered, half hearing his words.

He stopped before her, momentarily puzzled by her question.

"Why, London, of course. We will buy a town house. You will have some new clothes and a maid to do your work." He leaned toward her, placing his hands on her shoulders. "It will be wonderful," he spoke reassuringly.

"But I don't want to go. We've built a home here and a business. Why must we go?"

"Because I do not want to stay in this awful wilderness."

"How will I know the same thing won't happen again? That you won't leave without a word or explanation, stranding us alone in a strange country?" Alice questioned, voicing her deepest fear.

Josiah pulled her up into his arms. "Of course it will not happen again. I promise you," he asserted.

Alice looked into his eyes for the truth. She could not help but be skeptical of this promise, words he had uttered before. She believed they were like the vapors rising over a pond on a fall morning that disappeared in the sunlight of day.

As the children came in one by one, Josiah related the news to them. They were as stunned as Alice had been.

"You can't sell my animals," Midge cried in protest.

"But just imagine how lovely you will look in new dresses, joining in London society," he exhorted the girls, ignoring their protests. They were aghast. Tears flowed.

"Josiah, there is not enough money for all that," Alice exclaimed. "There is money due on this property, then the purchase of passage and all the other things. 'Tis not possible. Besides, I don't want to live in London," she protested.

"I can't go," Horace spoke.

"Nor will I," Jeremy joined in.

"Then the two of you can stay here." Their father promptly dismissed his sons' presence in this move regarding the family.

All evening tears and raised voices filled the house. Bedtimes were the final means of escape, though only Josiah's snores indicated sleep.

The morning light revealed the sleepless, frustrating hours each had endured.

Midge and Susie tiptoed around the big room preparing for the chores of the day, whispering to Alice their intent to live with Penny, if possible. The boys silently ate breakfast after morning chores and left the house quietly.

"I can't do this again!" Alice muttered under her breath as she slammed the bread dough down on the table. Picked up— slammed down. Picked up—slammed down. Her arms rose higher and higher with each action. The anger consumed her mind as she went through the routine by rote. Her children did not want to move across the ocean any more than she did. Maybe they could make arrangements for their lives here but what about her? It was not just a question of feasibility but also her obligation to be Josiah's wife, obedient to his desires. Could she leave her children forever? And it would be forever! Her head ached and furrows creased her brow. Surely there had to be a reasonable solution.

15

Alice walked alone along the dusty road toward Penny's home. It was late afternoon and the summer's heat caused trickles of perspiration to dampen the hair under her bonnet and stream down her neck. The sweat of her hands moistened the tatting pattern she was creating. She paused in the shade of a maple tree to shift the basket she was carrying to her other arm, wipe her face and catch her breath. She fanned herself with her wet handkerchief, took a labored breath and continued her walk.

As she approached the Hollis house she saw the housekeeper sitting on the top front step fanning herself with a folded newspaper. "Hello, Mistress Joseph. Is Mistress Hollis awake?" she asked. A profusion of hollyhock stalks was growing on each side of the steps. Alice smiled briefly, recalling the spring night when Midge and Susie conspiratorially planted the seeds to surprise Penny with this remembrance of home.

"She should be," was the short, laconic reply. The heavy-set housekeeper half turned, creating a narrow path for Alice to squeeze past to cross the porch and enter through the open door.

"Penny,'tis Mother,"Alice called up the stairs in the house.
"Come up, please."

In the shaded bedroom Alice emptied the basket she was carrying, taking out a bottle of raspberry shrub and two pastries wrapped in a tea towel and placing them on the table by the open window. She filled two glasses with the drink all the while keeping up a barrage of questions about Penny's health.

Her daughter awkwardly walked from the bed to the chair, absent-mindedly responding to the questions.

After a lull in the conversation, Alice spoke of the burden on her mind."Penny, your father has sold the property. He expects the sale to be finalized by the end of July. I must admit I'm in a quandary about what to do. He wants to take Susie, Midge and me and return to London. Your brothers want to stay here and your sisters don't want to go." She paused."Frankly, neither do I,"she added in a small voice.

"Mama, Susie stopped by this morning and told me. She and Midge want to come live here. In a way they would be a big help, especially when the baby comes. I didn't know if she had said anything to you about it yet. I mentioned it briefly to Will when he came home for dinner and he's in favor of it but we'll discuss it more tonight."

Alice was surprised, for Susie had not said anything to her about talking to Penny earlier.

"Perhaps you could live here with us too," Penny added as an afterthought. Alice realized Penny was quite adult now, no longer a youthful girl.

"I don't know."Alice sighed."Thank you anyhow,"she added.

"Mama . . . have you ever asked yourself why? Why you had to suffer so many hardships?"Penny hesitantly asked.

"Why me?"Alice laughed, remembering the same question she had asked herself years ago. "Why not me? I'm not above having trials, crises and problems like everyone else. Along with these has come strength to handle them, hopefully with some wisdom and, more importantly, empathy for everyone else."She paused, reflect-

ing on the changes in her thinking over the years. God's supportive, loving hand had held hers as she moved through the days and
the years. "There has been an overflowing cup of joy as well, full of
sweetness to dilute the sour drops of life," she added bending forward to pat her daughter's hand. "Now I must be on my way," she
said gathering the empty glasses, taking them downstairs and setting them on the edge of the dry sink. She then returned to gather
the tea towel with its crumbs into the basket.

"You know, Mama, Papa has never come by to see me," Penny
said with tears in her eyes as her mother was about to leave the
room.

"I believe he is embarrassed, afraid he might meet Mr. Hollis,
Sr.," Alice explained for him.

"He could come when Mr. Hollis is at work," Penny stated
accusingly, hurt and angry.

"I know," Alice said. She could not give any more excuses for his
behavior. "Goodbye, dear one. I'll see you again soon," she whispered, bending over to give her daughter a kiss and a pat at the
evidence of her growing grandchild.

On the return walk home she wondered how much longer she
would be able to visit Penny. "Oh, Lord, I don't want to go away
from my children. Not yet anyway. I want to be here for my first
grandchild, for the weddings and babies that will come soon
enough."

After the hot, dusty walk Alice sat on the bench in the shade
of the maple tree, fanning her flushed face with the damp handkerchief as she looked at this house she called home. She lingered
until duty prompted her to step inside the oppressively hot house.
She saw Josiah lounging by the open window with his feet propped
on the foot stool.

"Why were you just sitting outside?" Josiah questioned accusingly.

"It was too hot to come in," Alice defended her action. "Josiah,
please go by and see Penny," Alice continued. "She's unhappy that
you haven't come to visit her yet."

"You know I cannot go to that house," he replied testily, looking up from the local newspaper.

"You can, Josiah, during the day when Mr. Hollis is at the mill. Please make a point of going. Soon!" Alice begged. "She needs to see you."

Josiah shrugged. "Perhaps someday," he said unconvincingly.

Fueled by the heat of the day and full of anger and sadness, Alice stood in front of the father of her children. "You are a coward, Josiah. Just like you have always been." She said the word she had tried not to acknowledge all these years.

He looked at her with astonishment. "What? Certainly, I am not a coward," he protested. "Whatever happened to you? Indeed, I think you must be sick in the head."

"No, I have changed. Look at what I have had to face. You left us to struggle in Massachusetts and here, giving us no support while you lived in safety and comfort in England. Twice! Since your return, you have done nothing to help, yet you want the money and proceeds we earn. On top of that you did not even have the courage to tell me you were leaving, with or without that woman." She stopped, unable to find more words to express her anger and frustration.

Ignoring her last sentence he said, "You can see I am not able to handle a saw," he excused himself, pointing to his swollen legs. "And I certainly will not bake bread," he sneered.

"You're perfectly capable of tramping around town, though, standing to watch bear baiting," Alice retorted sharply.

For once in his life he was at a loss for words for Alice. He sputtered as he arose from his chair, set his tall hat on his head, picked up his walking stick and stomped out of the house, even with swollen legs.

Flushed and shaking from this uncharacteristic outburst, Alice sat down wearily at the table, resting her head on her hands. She could not believe she had confronted her husband in such a manner. "But I had to say it," she whispered to justify her action.

Susie knelt beside her Mother to hand her a cup. "Have some cold switchel, Mama," she said. "I'm glad you spoke up," she added.

"Oh, dear one," Alice exclaimed, looking up in surprise. "I forgot you were in the house. I should not have spoken like that in your presence."

"Yes, you needed to say it."

"But he is your father and deserves your respect."

"No! Respect is earned and he has done little to earn my respect," thoughtful Susie proclaimed.

After moments of silence, Alice whispered, "Thank you for the drink," leaning over to give her daughter a kiss on the head. She was comforted by her presence and support.

Supper time came and went without Josiah's presence. Alice imagined and hoped he had finally gone to see Penny.

It was well after their usual bedtime before Josiah walked in, quietly closing the open door behind him.

"Josiah," Alice whispered his name. She was sitting in the dark by the open window fanning herself to create any kind of coolness possible in the smothering humidity.

He stopped his movement toward the bedroom.

"Did you visit Penny?"

He hesitated. "No."

"Where have you been?"

"About." He turned to leave the room, then turned back to approach Alice. "You have changed." he said, standing before her and looking at her intently.

"Yes, I know I have changed some," Alice replied thoughtfully. "So much has happened in our lives since we married. I wonder if I would have stayed the same person if we had continued to live along the pike, watching the days and years pass, with no war to disrupt our lives," she continued. "It seemed a simpler time."

Each silently remembered the past.

"I believe it was," Josiah said after a long moment "When I came back I thought you would be the same person I married, responsive to me and my interests, and that we would begin again where we left off. I see now the separation has changed all that. You are not the same." He pondered his next statement. "However, I expect you to be my wife. Perhaps we can find affectionate feelings for each other again. After the property is sold we will move to England. I am much happier there. With the sale of this property and your yearly income from Franklin we will do very well. Remember, as my wife ..."He left the sentence unfinished."You will fit in, I expect,"he said, looking her over with doubtful eyes. The old Josiah emerged, belittling Alice and dictating the direction of their lives to suit his own desires. Having ended the conversation, he turned to go to the downstairs bedroom.

Alice spoke up."There will be no money from Franklin."

Josiah turned,"I know what the will says, but I intend to have it changed. You are still my wife and I am your husband. Any money you have belongs to me." He shut the door with finality. The door reopened."Speaking of Franklin, how often did you sleep with him?"

"I never did! How can you even think that I did?"

"Why else would he leave you any money?"

"Because we were family to him and him to us."

"I do not believe that,"he declared, shutting the door again.

Why did he care? How could he judge her if she had?

Furious and afraid she would take a poker to his head if she stayed inside, Alice went out and walked around and around the stumped yard in the pale moonlight."Husband and wife! Wife and husband!" she muttered. "In name only." Perspiration beaded on her upper lip. Could she believe his words that they could be affectionate again? Not any more. He had said those same words before they left America. Multiple emotions raced through her: anger, distress, despair, depression, pleading prayers. "Franklin, how I wish you were still here. I need you. I need your wisdom,"she spoke to the trees. She recalled the distant memory of Ian and his professed love for her. Somehow, it made her feel better yet overwhelmingly sad. She pushed the longing for him back into the recesses of her mind. It was not to be.

The half moon slipped behind dark clouds. She finally felt very tired yet calm enough to tiptoe into the house. She took a pillow off a chair and laid down on the floor. She could not sleep with

Josiah in that oppressively hot bedroom. Not tonight. When she had rejoined him in the downstairs bed, Josiah did as usual, satisfying his own physical desires then turning away from her. Though he had said it was her he had always wanted, it was quite apparent that this was not so. He cared nothing for her!

. . .

In the steamy days that followed, there were long hours of baking on the griddle over the open fire, of opening and closing the oven door, of weeding and of gathering ripened berries and vegetables to feed the family and fill pastry orders. Alice tried to shut her mind to the impending finality of the move from this house, yet its presence nagged at her constantly. She could not reconcile it within herself nor summon the effort to sort and pack for a move. Day following day brought the inevitable closer as she prayed for an answer that would give her peace.

Josiah was often euphoric as he anticipated the move to London and the grand life he expected to live. In this mood he was excessively sweet to Alice, constantly interrupting her to stop her chores and be attentive to him. On other days he was irritable and angry, snappish and moody. His behavior was unpredictable, causing each one in the house to tip-toe in his presence. How could she reconcile to that moodiness?

Truthfully Alice wanted Josiah out of the house on his jaunts to town. When he was in the house she resented his presence, his disturbance of the ordered life she had created while he was gone.

. . .

Midge spoke up as supper was finishing one evening. "Papa, Mama? George and Jeb would like to speak with you tonight." Susie nodded in agreement.

The parents waited, seating themselves on a damp wooden bench outside in the cooling evening breeze. Thankfully, a quick thunderstorm had alleviated the heat and humidity. Alice suppressed a laugh as the young men arrived, dressed in their Sunday best, obviously nervous.

Jeb spoke first, standing before Alice and Josiah. "Mr. and Mistress Marsh, I am requesting the hand of your daughter Susie — Susanna — in marriage. I have a certain future in my father's store. I love your daughter and will care for her properly all the days of her life." He paused, nervously turning his tall beaver hat around and around in his hands. Susie stepped close to him and looked at him with pride, then to her parents expectantly.

George stepped beside Jeb, proclaiming his love and affection for Midge and asking permission to marry her. "She will be an excellent helpmate to our family on the farm," he added, turning beet red with embarrassment.

Midge stepped beside him, taking his hand and smiling broadly at him. "We want to be married together as soon as possible," she stated forthrightly.

Alice protested. "You're too young, especially you Midge. I can't let you do this."

"I am but yet 16, the same age you were when you married father," Midge argued.

Josiah stood up. "It is my decision and I say of course they can be married," he proclaimed, effusively pumping each young man's hand.

Alice started to continue her protest but stopped, rose and solemnly gave each young person a kiss. She was still upset. "They are too young," she thought, "though perhaps I am being selfish and don't want to lose them from my everyday life."

Relief, laughter and excitement competed for attention with the blazing sunset as discussion of plans flowed from lip to lip. Darkness settled around them and fireflies danced and blinked among the grasses and trees, seeming to catch the wedding fever.

As the two young couples strolled off to the parson's house, seeking his blessings and commitment to perform the double ceremony, Alice and Josiah sat quietly together.

"The weddings solve your problem, do they not?" Josiah asked, sucking on his pipe. "Now you do not have to fret about their future." He beamed with satisfaction as if he had personally solved her problem.

Alice nodded, heavy-hearted at the rapid changes occurring in such a short time. "I know they are old enough but I will miss having my daughters about me," she said. Suddenly, she felt very tired and old. "I'm tired and I'm going to bed. Good night," she said, rising to walk slowly into the house to the too-small bed.

The next morning Alice asked each girl if she really truly loved the boy she became engaged to the night before or was she marrying only to avoid having to move to England. Susie and Midge assured her they really loved Jeb and George and Alice accepted their explanations though still with some reservations.

Wedding excitement and details pushed thoughts of moving to the back of Alice's mind. The double ceremony would be held in the yard, weather permitting.

"Mama," this, and "Mama," that, added to the demands of each day. Friends and future relations frequently stopped by with gifts for the brides to be, accompanied by squeals of delight at each offering. The hope chests spilled over.

"I'm glad 'tis summertime and the windows can be open. Otherwise, we'd be deaf with all this squealing," remarked Horace one afternoon.

"You're home early," Alice commented, handing him a fresh doughnut.

"I just got back from a trip down country to Fredericton Junction. I have been offered a position as assistant to the doctor there. He's frail and needs someone to help him. Dr. Morris encouraged me to take it and I accepted. I didn't want to tell you about it until I had a chance to see what the situation would be. I think I will like it. After the girls' weddings I'll settle there in the doctor's house where there is plenty of room for me."

Alice experienced a moment of despair. Stalwart, supportive Horace leaving! She wrapped her arms around him, congratulating him with tears in her eyes.

The news heightened the excitement around the polished table during supper as questions and answers flew back and forth among the siblings. Alice's heart beat with mingled pride and sadness. Soon her family would be dispersed to homes of their own and she would be the one farthest away when she went to London with Josiah.

Josiah walked in the open door just as supper was over. A slap of silence settled over the family as each one looked at him to gauge his mood.

"Did you eat yet?" Alice asked reservedly.

"No. What is all the noise about that I heard coming up the walk?"

"I was telling about a position I accepted in the next town down country," Horace said politely.

"Well, congratulations. I hope it pays you well."

"I expect it will be adequate. Now, excuse me, but I have to go help Dr. Morris." Horace rose, removed his plate, gave Alice a kiss on the cheek and walked out the door.

Jeremy, Susie and Midge each excused themselves, cleared their dishes off the table and left the room.

Alice set a bountiful plate of garden vegetables and fresh bread before Josiah. The early evening sun cast a satiny glow across the long table. Many years of sharing food and work had added to the glow since she had first seen it in the tent.

"What are you thinking about?" Josiah asked, breaking off a piece of bread and soaking it in the vegetable juices.

"I was just remembering this table when I first saw it in the tent."

"We are a lot better off now. With the property sale and your money from Franklin we will live a high life."

"I told you there won't be any money from Franklin," Alice reminded him.

"I will contest that decision. Why did Franklin put such a clause in to begin with?" Josiah would never understand Franklin's reasoning. He began expounding on the many items he planned to purchase once they arrived in London.

"Why?" Alice interrupted his dialogue.

"Why, what?"

"Why do you want me to go with you? You don't love me," she said quietly, looking down at her worn hands.

"Because you are my wife. Socially, a wife is very beneficial. Financially as well, of course. Besides, perhaps someday when you become more affectionate I will love you again," he explained bluntly.

Alice looked up at him with amazement and sorrow. What about him loving her first? She stood up and began to noisily clear the rest of the dishes off the table. "Please go for a walk. I want to be alone," she said abruptly.

"Fine then, if that is your attitude!" Josiah snapped, stomping out the door.

As Alice washed the dishes the debate raged within her as she pondered the options before her. If she stayed in Fredericton, continuing to bake while living with one of the children, she would be able to see them and their families grow, as well as be of help to them. It was the usual role of a widowed mother. But she was not a widow. If Josiah divorced her, the stigma and ostracism would reflect negatively upon herself as well as her children. She could not let that happen to them. Did she owe allegiance to Josiah as her husband? Why could they not just live apart as they had been doing for so many years? No. He could force her to go if he chose to do so. Could they find some kind of affection again? Never! Money, money, money! That is all she meant to him now. What would her life be like in England? Would she be utterly miserable or find a happy new life? The adventure of discovering a world beyond her immediate realm briefly sparked her imagination. She had shown courage to accept change before when circumstances forced it upon her. Would she have it again to embark on this new venture? A prayer of "help" rose with the steam of the dishwater.

. . .

The following afternoon, a cold, heavy rain halted work in the garden. The baking was done for the day and, as usual, Josiah had left for some unknown place. Alice sat staring into space with a cup of hot tea warming her hands when a thought came to her. She rose and pulled on her bonnet. "Susie, I'm going into town. I shan't be long," she stated, leaving the house with an umbrella and walking resolutely along the road to the office of the lawyer, Mr. Brown.

"Do you have a few minutes to see me?" she asked him, shaking the water off.

"Of course, Mistress Marsh," he said, rising to set a chair before his desk.

"Mr. Brown, I need your advice." Alice explained the situation to him.

He listened quietly as she told of her fears and her dilemma.

"Mistress Marsh, you have built a steady business here in Fredericton, but you do not have enough capital to buy a house, nor can you own one. You might be able to continue your business with one of the children. However, as long as you are married your income from the business is rightfully your husband's. A divorce by him is possible but you would be looked on as disreputable and perhaps lose business because of it. Also, remember that Mr. Marsh cannot access the money from Mr. Fremont's trust and it would revert to the children."

"He insists the will can get it reversed," Alice said.

"No, I do not think it is possible," he replied.

Mr. Brown sat silent for a few minutes. "I cannot tell you to stay or go. That is your decision. Either way you will be dependent upon his choices. The payment of the trust will not be until the end of the year. If at that time you are alone I will have this year's amount turned over to you. If not, I will divide it among the children. It is not very much as you recall. We can make a decision on a yearly basis."

"Thank you for listening," Alice said, rising and shaking his hand. There were no more answers to her quandary than before. However, it had helped to discuss it.

On the walk home she reviewed the conversation with Mr. Brown that had given her a chance to express her thoughts. He had not been able to solve her dilemma. But — there was one answer she had not thought of before. What if Josiah died soon? She thought about his shortness of breath, his shaking hands and his puffy face and feet. It was amazing he could walk as much as he did. That would certainly alter plans. "I wish he would!" she whispered fiercely. "No. No. I cannot wish that," she chastised herself, shaking the umbrella and her head at the same time to scatter this idea from her mind.

She did not think Josiah would ever agree to live apart as before now that money was involved. She resigned herself to move to England. Somehow, she would make the best of the situation. The God she believed in would give her the courage and insight to carry on. With head up she walked firmly toward home, where she immediately became involved in more wedding details.

. . .

Due to legal concerns regarding the property, settlement was postponed until the latter half of August which worked out well since the double wedding was scheduled to take place on the second Saturday afternoon in August. That day the weather was idyllic, not too hot nor too cool. No clouds obscured the sun. On the side yard a backdrop of white daisies, pink phlox and purple lobelia gently swayed in front of red and pink hollyhocks. A perfect setting for a wedding. Friends and family took their seats on benches laid across stumps facing the flowers, their eyes fixed on George and Jeb solemnly waiting for their brides. Before long, Midge and Susie emerged from the front door walking together to the side yard with Penny following behind, straightening the folds of Midge's dress. Each girl wore the latest fashion of a dress over lace pants, ordered and shipped up from Stanton Hazard's store in St. John.

All too soon the vows were uttered and the service was over. Everyone relaxed, their conversations flowing along with the punch. Mistress Joseph had been recruited to help serve the refreshments, which disappeared off the plates as soon as she brought them out of the house. Candies vanished from the chased silver tray into welcoming mouths. Alice wished Franklin was here to see the tray on this joyous day. Penny had insisted on directing the reception details and now, flushed and happy to be useful, she moved around the yard followed by an anxious Will who kept insisting she sit down and rest.

Once in awhile Alice looked to see what Josiah was doing. She had asked Jeremy and Horace to make sure there was no confrontation between Josiah and Mr. Hollis, Sr. should he attend. That would spoil the day for the girls. Mr. Hollis, Sr. sent his regrets, claiming a previous appointment. Josiah stayed in the background until he was sure Mr. Hollis, Sr. was not coming, and then became the charming host flitting from guest to guest and expounding on the idyllic life he expected to renew in London.

As the afternoon sunshine waned to a soft glow, Midge and George, Susie and Jeb kissed Alice goodbye and drove off in separate carriages to their new homes accompanied by loud cheers. Will finally persuaded Penny to let him take her home to rest, taking Mistress Joseph in the carriage with them. The other guests gradually dispersed. The party was over.

"'Tis just like making a pie. It takes a long time to prepare and yet 'tis gone in a matter of minutes," Alice commented with a sigh of contentment to Mattie.

"Well, it was beautiful. Beautiful. Beautiful." Further adjectives failed her for the moment. "Bridget, come over here and help Mistress Marsh clean up," she ordered.

"Thank you, Bridget. I would appreciate your help." Alice smiled in assent as the two carried borrowed punch glasses into the house.

Jeremy and Horace put away benches and picked up scattered items. "Papa, Horace and I are going into town for awhile, Mama," Jeremy said, poking his head in the door.

"All right. Goodbye." Alice continued to wash punch cups as Bridget dried them.

"Well, we are through at last. We'll be on our way," Mattie said, watching Bridget hang the towel over the rack to dry.

"Thank you, thank you," Alice said sincerely, giving Bridget a squeeze around her bony shoulders as she handed her a plate of leftover pastries.

When the door closed Alice slumped onto the familiar bench by the fireplace and looked around the room that had been home. In a week it would belong to someone else. She did not try to stop the few tears of weariness and loneliness that slid from her eyes.

16

THE FOLLOWING SATURDAY MORNING Jeremy and Horace rose well before dawn. With a cold doughnut in hand, Jeremy left, soon returning with a borrowed wagon that he braked close to the front door. He unhitched the team of horses for the animals to graze on the side grass. In the meantime, Alice warmed a pot of milk gravy over a few hot coals to pour on cold Johnnycake as the last meal served in this house. Her fingers lingered on the polished cherry wood as the boys carried the table past her and out the door to the wagon bed, followed by Franklin's old desk and chair, two side chairs, as well as Horace's trunk and medical supplies. Most of the furniture was going to Horace's new home. Susie had already moved the books, bookcases and bedding along with the spinning wheel to Jeb's house. Midge did not want any of the furniture. However, she had insisted on taking the rejected pet lamb, and her father had finally, reluctantly relented, grumbling because he would have to pay the new owner for it.

"Josiah, 'tis time to get up," Alice called, knocking on the bedroom door. "The boys need to load the dresser on the wagon."

"Yes. Yes." Gradually they could hear movement in the room. He emerged from the room disheveled and sleepy eyed. "Why must you do this so early?" he grumbled.

Jeremy explained, "By the time we drive to Fredericton Junction, unload and get back with the wagon, it will be dark. I told Mr. Hollis I'd have the wagon from the mill back tonight."

"'Tis a beautiful morning, Josiah. Come out and eat," Alice said to placate him, leading the way to the bench with a plate of food for him in her hand. She sat on the bench beside him as he ate, listening to the boys shuffle the dresser across the floor.

"Mama, we'll drop your trunks at Mistress Thompson's boarding house on the way," Jeremy explained as the last of the items were loaded and tied securely. Josiah had insisted they stay there until Tuesday. Settlement on the house was scheduled for Monday. They would leave the next day on the boat heading down river to St. John. "Horace will follow the wagon with the horse and shay. Papa, do you want to come with us?" Jeremy asked politely.

"No," Josiah replied testily. "I would not be of any help to you," he explained further.

"Then we're off," Jeremy said, swinging himself up to the seat, gathering the reins and calling "giddap" to the horses.

"Be careful," Alice called after him.

Horace came over to say goodbye. Alice rose from the bench and gripped her younger son in a long embrace. When would she ever see him again? "I love you, dear one," she whispered in his ear and kissed his cheek. "Take care."

"I will, Mama, and I have the dancing man," he assured her, smiling and returning her kiss with one on the cheek before climbing into the shay, flicking the reins on the horse's back and driving along the road until he was out of sight in the dust.

Alice's eyes followed the action. When she could no longer see him she turned to her husband. "Please, Josiah, why do you insist I go to London with you?" she asked again, hoping he would agree to let her stay here.

He looked at her. "Because you are my wife and obliged to do as I request. Besides, I need you with me," he said matter of factly without any emotion.

"Is it because you think there will be money from Franklin?"

He neither confirmed nor denied her question. "We will make it work out," he added.

Alice, unsatisfied with his answer, took his empty plate into the house and began vigorously sweeping the floors upstairs under the built-in beds, pushing the dust to fall down the stairs.

Cough. "Must you make so much dust?" Josiah coughed again from below. "I am going out. I will see you at Mistress Thompson's when you are finished," Josiah called up the stairs, his voice echoing throughout the empty rooms.

For the rest of the morning and well into the afternoon Alice swept, dusted the sills, washed the windows and removed the ashes from the fireplace into the ash pit with the turkey wing. She was not going to turn over a dirty house to someone else. They could tear it down for all she cared but it would be clean when they did it. Her pride in the work she had put in this home spurred her on.

At last, the final speck of dust was off the floor. Alice stood the broom by the back door and stepped out to take a hollyhock blossom into each hand. Out of habit, she then plucked some early seed heads and put them in her apron pocket. Was there anything more she needed to do? All the customers and suppliers had been notified of her departure and the last of the bills had been paid. She could not think of anything she might have missed. Returning for one last look at the rooms that had held tears, laughter, music, work and most of all, love, she said with finality, "'Tis done!" She walked with hollow echoes across the floor and out the front entrance, closing the door quietly behind her. She hesitated for one last look at the flowers and trees, whispered a "goodbye" before treading the path to the road without looking back.

With determined steps Alice approached Mattie's house and knocked at the open door. "Yoo hoo," she called.

"Come in!" Bridget called.

"I'm here to say goodbye," Alice said, walking across the floor to Bridget.

"Mother Mattie is in town. I'll tell her you came by," Bridget informed Alice. She stood tall and reserved as she looked unsmiling at Alice. In an uncharacteristic action she reached over and hugged Alice. "Thank you, thank you," she whispered before stepping back, embarrassed by this act.

Alice smiled and patted Bridget's arm. "Please take care of yourself and the wee ones," Alice said as she turned to leave the house.

"Another transition," she mused as she walked slowly along the dusty road, trying to fill her mind's eye with every twist and turn, every tree and bush along the familiar road. She recalled a similar moment on a spring night in Massachusetts. What would she find this time on the other side? She hurried her steps as she neared Penny's home.

Seeing Mistress Joseph inside the open door, she knocked on the jamb. "Good afternoon, Mistress Joseph. What a lovely day this is."

"Good afternoon, Mistress Marsh. It truly is lovely and what a grand day it was last Saturday for the wedding, too," the housekeeper replied with a rare smile.

"I thank you again for helping serve at the wedding. I am very grateful for all the work you did," Alice said sincerely, smiling at the housekeeper as they stood at the open door.

"You are welcome" she answered, somewhat embarrassed by the compliment. "Mistress Hollis is sitting in the back yard," she said, motioning around the edge of the house.

"Thank you." Alice walked back down the porch steps, past the blooming hollyhocks and around the corner of the house to take a seat under the tree near Penny.

"Mistress Joseph was saying what a lovely wedding we had last Saturday," Alice commented.

"It was a beautiful wedding, almost as nice as mine," Penny said, smiling in remembrance. "And we did have good times at their open houses the next day."

"Yes, we surely did," Alice smiled, remembering being served tea by Susie and Midge in their new homes. "Thank you again for all your help at the wedding," Alice said, leaning over to pat her daughter's hand.

Penny's smile faded. "Mama, Papa did not speak to me at the wedding. Why not? 'Tis as though I was not even there. I greeted him but he only looked at me, mumbled a weak response and then turned to speak with a complete stranger. He didn't even speak to Will!" She was indignant at this slight to her husband.

"I don't know, Penny. I can only think that he doesn't know how to love, and when he sees you, he is embarrassed. I suppose the best defense he has is to ignore you children However, you must remember that you are deeply loved by so many other people — especially your family — and you need not dwell on the one who cannot love you. It is sad that he is so unhappy with this life, but that is his choice. You must choose to give your love back in abundance to those who love you and you'll find over time that the hole he left in your heart is filled up."

Penny sighed. "I will try."

Mother and daughter sat in companionable silence enjoying the air and watching bees buzz in and out of the nearby flower blossoms. Finally, Alice broke the silence. "The disposition of the house will be on Monday, then we leave down river on Tuesday. I'll be by on Monday to spend the day with you. I'm nearly finished knitting an outfit for my first grandbaby and I can't wait to show it to you." She rose to bend over and hug her daughter. She did not feel as brave or happy as she had tried to sound.

. . .

Sunday Alice attended church services in the building she had called her spiritual home over the years. She breathed a gentle prayer for courage and guidance and then let the petitions go, trusting that God would give her both as had been done in the past.

Late in the afternoon Jeremy asked Alice and Josiah to walk with him, though Josiah declined.

"Mama, the wedding got me thinking that I'd like to marry Nancy soon. What do you think of her?" Jeremy said, holding Alice's hand on his arm.

"I think she's a wonderful girl. If you love each other then plan to get married. In the meantime, save as much as possible. That way, when you get married, you will have money to support her and for other things you will need. It will make life easier for you both," Alice replied. "Enough of my preaching though. Are you still thinking of going back to America as well?"

"I'd like to but Nancy wants to stay here close to her family. Her father wants me to join him at his shop but I really would like to move back to America and get a farm." He was torn.

"I understand your dilemma. However, if you truly love her it won't matter where you live," Alice said thoughtfully. "Perhaps you can get a farm here. Maybe later on the two of you will decide to move back. Trust that God will guide you. For now, let's enjoy the walk."

Monday Alice spent the day helping Penny wash and sort baby clothes while Josiah attended the house settlement. Penny and Will, Susie and Jeb, Midge and George joined Alice and Jeremy for six o'clock supper at the boarding house as Jeremy was renting a room there too. Mistress Thompson was strict about meal times and the family had to begin without Josiah. It was a strained meal after Josiah arrived late in a bad mood, finding fault with the food, the weather, everything. It added to the strain of teary goodbyes.

In the privacy of their room Alice asked, "What is the matter? Did the transfer go through?"

"Oh, yes. Your Mr. Brown was the buyer's lawyer. After the town got their share in the transaction, which I am sure they cheated me on, I told Mr. Brown that I plan to have Franklin's will overturned but he said it could not be done. Well, I will take him to high court in London if necessary." He got angrier as he recalled the loud words they had exchanged. He took the bills out of his purse, counting them over and over. "I knew it! I knew it! All those fees.

There should have been more money!" His voice was failing him as his anger increased.

"Please calm down, Josiah," Alice implored.

"I am going out," Josiah said abruptly, shoving the bills into the purse and leaving the room.

Alice looked at the closed door. Pacing back and forth across the faded carpet, she spoke out loud. "I cannot go! I simply cannot! I do not want to live the rest of my life sitting in a room alone while he goes who knows where, trying to adjust to his mood swings. I don't like him and I certainly don't love him any more!" she shouted to the room. "There, I've said it. God, please give me insight. Guide me. I can survive without him as I have done for years. I'll not go! We can live separately as before. If need be, I'll even slip back to America and live with Joan. Besides, all he wants is the money, not me. I will manage. I will not go!" she said out loud to the room once more, stamping her foot in emphasis. "When he comes in I'll tell him. If he refuses I'll move into Jeremy's room for tonight. One way or another I will make the necessary arrangements." Exhausted by the intense emotions of the evening she sat in the chair by the open window waiting for him to return. Her body slowly relaxed in thankfulness now that she felt a right decision had been made. She slipped into a sleep so sound that she never heard Josiah tiptoe into the room and get in bed without waking her.

The vociferous conversation of birds just before dawn awakened her. Her neck had a crick in it from its awkward position in the chair and her left arm tingled. She was surprised to see Josiah sitting up in bed asleep for she had not heard him come in. She remembered her decision of the night before and still felt sure it was right. He would definitely argue when she told him but she hoped she was confident enough to stand her ground.

She shivered in the cool air, stretched and quietly tiptoed over to the wash stand, splashing water over her face. She glanced at Josiah and saw he had been writing a letter, the pen hanging loosely in his fingers. She reached over to take the paper and pen from his hand. Something in his lack of movement or breathing caught her attention. She felt for a pulse but it was not there. She shook him and he rolled onto his side. He was dead!

"Oh, Josiah." All the frustrations, the anger, the disappointments, the shared lives, the past hopes came together in her utterance of his name.

She tucked the letter in her pocket, opened the door and went down the hall to Jeremy's room.

"Jeremy," she whispered, tapping on the door. After three calls of his name he sleepily looked at her from the open door.

"Is it time to take you to the boat?"

"No. Please come. Your father is dead," Alice said, pulling Jeremy down the hall to the other room.

He pushed past her to check on his father, confirming Alice's words. "I'll get Dr. Morris. You stay in my room until I get back," he said, guiding her to his room and seating her in a chair. "I'll be back soon," he said, bending over to give her shoulder a squeeze. A mauve dawn was beginning to show in the east window.

Alice felt numb. "Oh, Lord, I didn't really want him to die," she prayed guiltily, putting her face in her hands, as she recalled the wish she had made weeks before. Her jaws tightened and she began to shiver with cold, unable to stop.

"'Tis all right, Mama," Jeremy crooned over and over again, wrapping a blanket around her.

"Drink this, Mistress Marsh," Dr. Morris commanded, thrusting a glass with a cloudy liquid into her hands.

Alice did as she was told and began to calm down. Mistress Thompson, Mr. Brown, Will and Mr. Hollis crowded around her, filling the room with their concern.

"We think it best if you come home with me," Will said, helping Alice to her feet and supporting her to his carriage. Alice puzzled briefly in her mind. How did all these people get there so quickly? She suddenly realized it had been an hour or so since she had found Josiah dead. Had she fallen asleep?" She never could answer that question.

Penny insisted that Alice eat a bite of breakfast and have a cup of strong tea before shooing her to bed in the spare room. As Alice began to remove her dress she felt paper in her pocket. It was the letter Josiah had been writing. She took it out and, curious, began to read the last words he wrote before he died.

Dearest Agatha,
I am on my way back to England and your loving arms. The closer the days bring me to you the more excited I am to hold you in my arms again. It will not be long now. Alice is with me but that will not keep me . . .

Alice sat on the edge of the bed, fingering the paper. His rejection of her in the words he had written affected her ego less than she imagined it would have. Momentarily she felt angry realizing he would probably have left her in England to return to that woman again as he had done before. The decision she had made the night before had been the right one. Now there were no tears, only a deep sadness for their unfulfilled lives together. Their lives and passions had separated so many, many years before. It was hard to recall the love she had felt for him initially. Had there ever really been love, or had it been an infatuation of youth and convenience? Perhaps it was merely the expected thing to do? A lifetime ago far, far in the past. A life together and apart bound by marriage vows that disappeared long before he put the ink on this paper. Slowly she tore the sheet into tiny and tinier pieces, dropping them into the chamber pot and watching them dissolve in the yellow water. She then lay back against the pillows and fell asleep.

Alice woke with fear clutching her heart. Her clothes were soaked from the sweat of a bad dream. She began to cry from the guilt she still felt over the death wish.

"Mama, please don't cry," Jeremy said as he rushed to put his arms around her, having heard the cry as he passed the door.

"Oh, Jeremy, I feel so guilty. I caused your father's death,"

"Of course you didn't. He had a heart attack, Dr. Morris said."

"But one day I had wished he would die." Alice sobbed harder.

"Mama, look at me. Do you remember when I told you about being on the ship and wishing the enemy boys would die?"

Alice nodded.

"Do you think my thoughts were responsible for the death of some of them and not others?"

"No."

"Then believe me, your wish did not kill him. His body couldn't keep on living, that's all. Now put that thought away and come have some supper. We need you," he said, giving her a kiss on her forehead.

"Thank you," Alice whispered, allowing him to pull her up..

Her growing family gathered around her as they buried Josiah at the local cemetery in the cool morning air. Only Penny became teary eyed. She had so longed for her father's love and now it would never come. Alice watched as Will put his arm around his wife and she turned to smile at him. "Someday the hole will be filled," Alice thought to herself.

They gathered after the service at Penny and Will's house where each of Alice's children urged her to come live with them. Who needed her the most? The girls were newly married with homes already containing other relations. Jeremy would likely marry soon.

Alice finally decided. "Horace, if I can be of help to you now I'll live with you as long as you need me, providing the doctor would approve," Alice announced, holding a cup of tea in her hand.

"I would love to have you live with me. The doctor even suggested it and I know he would welcome you," he said, giving her a broad smile from his chair.

"That settles it then. I won't be too far away that I won't be able to come help you when you need me," she added, looking at each girl intently and then at Jeremy. "Mr. Brown will handle Franklin's money for me, and the money from the property sale will cover my needs for some time to come. I love you all so much."

"Goodbye, goodbye," Alice called from Horace's shay as they drove toward another chapter in her life. She was silent, wondering what the days ahead would have in store for her. How could she make a beneficial difference in this world that her forthcoming grandchildren would enter? She closed her hand over the imaginary hand of the companion she always remembered was at her side and whispered a grateful, "thank you."

. . .

Joy, tinged with a sweet sadness, filled the days following the move to a room in the doctor's home where Horace assisted. She missed the chatter of the girls' presence in the house but was happy for them in their new homes. Her hours were occupied with cooking, management of the widower's house and garden, as well as assisting the men whenever needed in their practice. She kept busy in all the waking moments.

Penny sent a note early in November asking her to come back to Fredericton. The baby was due within a week or two and she wanted her mother with her.

Alice hurried off at once to support the arrival of her first grandchild. She felt she was holding a miracle in her arms each time she picked up the robust baby girl Penny and Will named Charity. Even Mr. Hollis, Sr. insisted on holding the wee one each night when he returned from the mill.

. . .

The day before Christmas Horace drove a sleigh to Fredericton. All Alice's children and their spouses, including Jeremy's fiancée Nancy, filled Penny and Will's house with songs and laughter on Christmas day.

The next day Horace tucked a bear-skin rug over their legs as he and Alice returned to Fredericton Junction.

It was evening when they entered the house.

"I'll get the fire going in your room right away," Horace said.

"Thank you but not tonight. I'm weary and going right to bed," Alice said as she kissed him good night.

She closed the bedroom door, removed her coat, hat and gloves and looked at this room. Her room in this house. A few of her possessions lay out on the dresser. Recognizable but strange. In this cold room she realized she had kept herself constantly busy and occupied these past four months out of habit. She had not even taken time to read a book. The mental intrusion of Josiah's dictates and his denigration of her were diminishing. "'Tis done. Let it go. I am free to be who I am," she whispered as she took a deep breath, prepared for bed and dropped off to a relaxed sleep with prayers on her lips.

When she woke in the morning there was a feeling of peace in her soul. While waiting for water to boil for coffee she sat at the beloved cherry table in the large kitchen and began a letter to Ian, one she had put off writing all this time.

Dear Ian,

I hope this letter finds you and your family in good health. My family is well and happy with the recent birth of Penny and Will's daughter Charity. Susie and Midge were married this past summer and Jeremy is engaged to be married in the spring.

I am writing to inform you that Josiah died. I feel it is right to tell you. If your feelings about me remain the same I would be happy to renew our acquaintance. If you have found someone else to share your life with I will understand and be happy for you. I wish you deep joy in your life.

Again, I thank you for your help and friendship.

Cordially,
Alice Marsh

P.S. I have moved in with Horace at Fredericton Junction.

Alice sealed the letter with fond remembrance of this man in her life. She then set cereal, bread and honey on the table for the doctor, Horace and herself.

. . .

The routine of days pushed forward. Two years had quickly passed. Three more grandchildren had joined her family and added joy to her life. Just lately the old doctor had died, leaving the practice and house to Horace.

A thought occurred to Alice as she sat at the table drinking coffee with her son."Horace, remember the three orphan children you told me about? What would you think about bringing them to live here?"Alice asked as her hands circled a cup of hot coffee."I would love to be a grandmother to them; to scrub their faces, to teach them to work in the garden, to read to them and to simply love them,"she added enthusiastically.

Horace's surprised look soon changed to a grin as he too became excited about sharing his home."Let me see if it can be arranged," he said, leaving the house for his early morning rounds.

Within days the house was filled with activity as three children — a boy of four, a girl of three and a nine-month-old baby girl — entered their new home. It did not take too many months for the children to relax in their trust that Grandmama Alice and Uncle Horace would truly love and care for them.

. . .

Months whizzed off the calendar. The hope of a renewed friendship with Ian had faded as each season followed another with no reply from him. However, the longing in Alice's heart was comforted with children's laughter, joy and sibling arguments. Now nine pairs of childish legs ran up and down stairs, in and out of doors. Meanwhile, she had had no difficulty refusing a proposal from Deacon Holt last year, a self-centered, narrow-minded man who did not like snotty-nosed little monsters around. She felt no affection for him and could not choose a life she knew would crush her spirit even with his promise of great affluence.

Last spring Horace brought his lovely bride Emily, a willing participant, into the boisterous crowd that was pushing out the walls of this house, a crowd that begged many nights for the rat-a-tat tat of the dancing man.

Weather permitting, Alice concentrated her energies on the gardens, particularly the flowers, including many beloved hollyhocks, and she encouraged the children to plant, weed and harvest the bounty with her.

. . .

On a clear day in October Alice and the younger children were gathering squash from the vegetable garden and putting them in a basket. The beauty of the day drew her mind from the task before her. She sat back on her heels and looked at the wonder surrounding her; blue skies, puffy clouds, colors of autumn sprinkled across the hills like a vegetable soup pot. A tiny breeze ruffled the leaves that played tag with sunbeams, sending some dancing across the space toward earth in a universe full of glory."Thank you, God,"she whispered.

"Mother Marsh."Emily called from the corner of the house.

"Yes?"

"You have a visitor."

Alice turned to see a man follow her daughter-in-law. She gasped with surprise and delight.

"Good morning, Alicia,"the familiar voice spoke softly.

"Ian? Oh, Ian, I'm so glad to see you,"Alice blurted out while trying to rise from her squatted position.

He put his hands forth to help, keeping her secure in his grasp as he looked at her."We frequently meet in the garden, do we not?" he said with a smile.

Alice laughed then a blush colored her cheeks. She was not dressed in her best clothes and she was aware of the silver streaking her hair under the bonnet. However, even with a new scar down one cheek, Ian looked exceedingly fine and grand, tanned from days in the sun.

"How wonderful to see you again!" Alice joyfully exclaimed, leading him to a bench under an apple tree. "Please, tell me all about your life these past years. It is so good to see you again,"she reiterated.

"I was captured by the Spanish and held captive in the West Indies until exchanged."His jaw tightened at the remembrance of that humiliation. "I finally got your letter when I arrived in England last month and came here as quickly as I could."

Alice smiled. "I thought you had moved forward with your life. Perhaps finding another woman you loved and married." She stopped, unwilling to voice the sadness she had felt.

"Oh, dear Alicia, there has never been any other woman since I met you. When you wrote me that your husband had returned I was angry to think he had come back into your life but I realized I had to respect your decision," he replied. "So much wasted time has passed. Please, let me come back into your life now and marry you," he implored, cupping her face in his hand. "If you are still free?" he added with a touch of concern in his voice.

"Oh, I'm free. And yes, yes, I will marry you. I can't wait to spend the rest of our lives together."

"Neither can I," Ian said, leaning forward to give her a kiss.

Unabashedly throwing her arms around him she kissed him passionately.

"Grandmama, why are you kissing this man?" four-year-old Doris asked, tugging on Alice's apron.

"Because I love this man who will be your Grandpapa."

"And I love your Grandmama," Ian replied with a broad smile, reaching down to lift the child onto his lap.

Therefore all seasons shall be sweet to thee,
Whether the summer clothe the general earth
With greenness, or the redbreast sit and sing
Betwixt the tufts of snow on the bare branch
Of mossy apple-tree, while the nigh thatch
Smokes in the sun-thaw; whether the eve-drops fall
Heard only in the traces of the blast,
Or if the secret ministry of frost
Shall hang them up in silent icicles,
Quietly shining to the quiet moon.

— *The Good, Great Man,* SAMUEL TAYLOR COLERIDGE

Endnotes

1. **Grape ketchup.** (Chapter 2, pg. 16) Since they thought tomatoes poisonous, the colonists made their ketchup from other fruits and vegetables, including peaches, walnuts, grapes, and cucumbers. They chopped the food very fine and mixed it with sugar, salt, pepper, mustard, and whatever spices were on hand.

   — *The Colonial Cookbook* by Lucille Recht Penner

2. **Pudding or puddin' cap.** (Chapter 2, pg. 16) An old term for sausage applied to a roll of material encircling a toddler that kept them from hurting themselves when they fell. Frequently it was a thick roll or cushion that encircled the head as protection from injury when a child fell.

   — *Children's Costume in America 1607-1910* by Estelle Ansley Worrell

3. **Pounce.** (Chapter 2, pg. 24) Fine sand held in a pounce pot used to pretreat the surface of the paper and after writing to dry the ink faster.

   — *Everyday Life in Colonial America From 1607-1783* by Dale Taylor

4. **Nooning.** (Chapter 8, pg. 119) Intermission on Sabbath Day during a church service. Church sermons often lasted two to three hours, even as long as five with the prayers frequently one, two or more hours in length. The nooning was a time of intermission for the attendants to go to a neighboring house or tavern for a time of rest and a luncheon of brown bread, doughnuts, or ginger bread. In some instances the church built a noon-house or "Sabba-day House" near the church or "meeting house" for this purpose with horse-stalls at one end for the farmers' "duds and horses" and a chimney at the other end. A great fire of logs was built there each Sunday for warmth (the church building was unheated) and for foot-stoves to be filled.

Boys and girls were not permitted to indulge in idle talk nor play in the nooning house. During this time they had a sermon read to them by a deacon and sometimes they had to explain aloud the notes they had taken during the sermon in the morning.

— *Home Life in Colonial Days* by Alice Morse Earle 1898 edition

5. Take to wife. (Chapter 9, pg. 138) A phrase meaning that the couple could not legally marry because there was no proof that the former husband was dead.

— *Founding Mothers* by Cokie Roberts

6. Banns. (Chapter 13, pg. 199) Announcement read in church three weeks in a row. The intent was to inform people of the forthcoming marriage. Anyone who knew that the bride or groom were already married was to come forth with the information. In some marriage services today the pastor asks for the same reason, "if anyone knows why these two shall not be married speak now or forever hold their peace."

7. Peel. (Chapter 13, pg. 201) A long-handled shovel called a peel or slice used to place food well within the hot oven. It was sprinkled with meal, dough placed thereon, and by a dexterous twist of the wrist thrown on the cabbage or oak leaves laid far into the oven. The bread peel was a universal gift to a bride, signifying domestic utility and plenty, and considered to be luck-bearing. It is possible to see peels in use today at pizza makers' ovens.

— *Home and Child Life in Colonial Days*, ed. by Shirley Glubok

Recipes

SWITCHEL: *sometimes called* HAYMAKERS' SWITCHEL

1 gallon water   1 cup molasses
2 cups sugar   1 cup vinegar
1 tsp. ginger

Stir the ingredients together thoroughly, "put in a stone jug," says the old recipe, and "hang in the well to cool."

> — *The Yankee Cookbook* by Imogene Wolcott,
> Ives Washburn, Inc., New York 1939, 1963

SHRUB

1 pint blackberries, or   1¼ cups sugar
   berries of any kind   ¼ cup cider vinegar

Mix the berries and cider vinegar in a jar. Cover and store in the refrigerator for 24 hours. Rub the berry mixture through a strainer with the back of a spoon into a saucepan. Add the sugar to the juice mixture. Bring the mixture to a boil. Turn the heat to low. Simmer 15 minutes, stirring often. Store the shrub in the refrigerator. Then when you are ready to serve it, put 3 tablespoonsful in an 8-ounce glass. Add 6 ounces of water. Fill the glass with ice. You can garnish it with a fresh mint leaf.

> — *The Colonial Cookbook* by Lucille Recht Penner

Poems

Bibliography

Boatner, Mark. M., *Encyclopedia of the American Revolution*, New York, David McKay Co., Bicentennial Edition, 1974.

Bumsted, J. M., *The Peoples of Canada*, Toronto, Oxford Univ. Press, 1992.

Earle, Alice Morse, *Colonial Dames and Good Wives*, New York, Houghton Miffin Co., 1895.

Earle, Alice Morse, *Home Life in Colonial Days*, New York, Houghton Miffin Co., 1898.

Earle, Alice Morse, *Two Centuries of Costume In America*, New York, Houghton Miffin Co.,

Fredericton, NB, *Founding Fredericton: The Last 200 Years*, Chapter 2, Centennial Print & Litho Ltd., 1980.

Gilmor, Don & Turgeon, Pierre, *Canada A People's History Volume One*, Toronto, Canada, McClelland & Stewart Ltd., 2001.

Glubok, Shirley, *Home and Child Life in Colonial Days*, New York, ed. by Shirley Glubok, 1969.

Halsted Van Tyne, Claude, *The Loyalists In The American Revolution*, New York, The Macmillan Co., 1902.

Leach, Douglas Edward, *Roots of Conflict*, Chapel Hill, Univ. of North Carolina Press, 1986.

Miles, Clement A., *Christmas In Ritual and Tradition Christian and Pagan*, London, T. Fisher Unwin, 1912.

The Oxford Dictionary of Quotations 2nd ed., rev., London, Oxford University Press, Amen House, 1955.

Penner, Lucille Recht, *The Colonial Cookbook*, New York, Hastings House, Pub., 1976.

Pollan, Michael, *A Place of my Own, London*, Penguin Books Ltd., 1997.

Provincial Archives of New Brunswick

Roberts, Cokie, *Founding Mothers*, New York, Perennial Harper Collins Pub., 2004.

Taylor, Dale, *The Writer's Guide to Everyday Life in Colonial America From 1607-2783* ed. by Jack Jeffron and Roseann S. Viederman, Cincinnati, Oh., Writer's Digest Books, 1997.

Thomas, Jean Karen, Baker, Jerry, *Oddball Ointments, Powerful Lotions and Fabulous Folk Remedies*, Wixom, Mi., American Masters Products, Inc., 2002.

Tunis, Edwin, *Colonial Living*, New York, Thomas Crowell Co., 1957.

Tunis, Edwin, *The Tavern at the Ferry*, New York, Thomas Y. Crowell Co., 1973.

Wernecke, Herbert H., *Christmas Customs Around the World*, Philadelphia, Pa., Westminster Press. 1959.

Whiton, Sherrill, *Elements of Interior Design and Decoration*, Chicago, J. P. Lippincott Co., 1951.

Wilbur, C. Keith, *Pirates & Patriots of the Revolution*, Guilford, Ct., The Glove Pequot Press, 1973.

Wolcott, Imogene, *The Yankee Cookbook*, New York, Ives Washburn, Inc. Pub., 1939.

Wolf, Stephanie Grauman, *As Various As Their Land*, New York, Harper Collins Pub., 1993.

World Book Encyclopedia

Worrell, Estelle Ansley, *Children's Costume in America 1607-1910*, Harrisburg, Pa., T. Fisher Unwin, 1980.

Made in the USA
Charleston, SC
18 February 2013